RED QUEEN, YELLOW KING

THE BOOK OF ALICE #1

JACK FINN

EDGE WEAVER LLC

Red Queen, Yellow King
The Book of Alice

Edge Weaver Realms is an imprint of Edge Weaver LLC

Book Design: Marie Ito

Kindle ISBN: 978-1-968100-22-3

Paperback ISBN: 978-1-968100-23-0

Published in the United States of America

Edge Weaver LLC
19360 Rinaldi #681
Porter Ranch, CA 91326-1607

CONTENTS

PART 1: WONDERLAND

“Let the Looking-Glass creatures, whatever they be, Come and dine with the Red Queen, the White Queen, and me!”

— *Lewis Carroll, Welcome Queen Alice*

So begins The Book of Alice . . .

CHAPTER 1: DOWN THE RABBIT HOLE

Alice opened her eye. She blinked several times to clear the blur of long sleep from her right eye; the muscles inside her scarred left eye socket contracted reflexively, a distant echo to when it held a blue-pupiled orb. Darkness surrounded her, the only illumination coming from a distant light far above as if she lay at the bottom of a deep hole.

As Alice's eye adjusted to the darkness and her senses became more acute, she realized she lay in a bed in a darkened room, a blanket covering her body up to her neck. A single oil lantern hung above her with the shutter opened, illuminating the bed in a small circle. Anger surged within her; the light made her feel like a circus animal on display. A dank odor of damp stone mixed with sweat and human waste assailed her nose.

Wherever this is, it's definitely not my room in the Queen's palace.

Alice's eye scanned the impenetrable darkness. Something pressed into her buttocks, and she realized with mounting horror that someone had placed a bedpan beneath her. She rocked her hips back and forth, relieved to find the bedpan was presently empty. She tried to sit up, but pain radiated through her skull, so sharp she saw a flash of light, before she lifted her head more than a few inches. She laid her head back on the soft pillow and exhaled deeply.

I'll try that again later. The thought fought its way through her pain-strewn mind.

As she slid her hand up her body to attempt to rub away the blinding pain in her temples, Alice suddenly became aware of something else—she was completely naked beneath the blanket.

Now that's interesting.

Alice probed her memory for the last thing she remembered before waking up here. She recalled screams, blood, and chaos. A battle. She was in a battle.

Memories began flooding back to her. Alice had been on a bridge beside the White King, guarding his back as they fought to reach the gate to King Cormoran's castle, the giants' stronghold in Wonderland. She recalled Danavi, the Red Knight, standing beside the gunslinger, Hatter, on the riverbank below them, yelling something indiscernible up to her.

She remembered that moment now with crystal clarity. Blood and gore covered Danavi's helmet and armor—indeed, a red knight. Hatter was there too, though his ridiculous top hat was absent, no doubt lost in the battle's chaos. He clutched his black powder rifle in one hand and cupped his mouth with the other as he yelled to her.

After that, all Alice could recall was an explosion of pain in her right knee, then falling, blackness, and awakening here in this place. She gingerly moved her right leg and felt tightness and pain in the knee. Her memory appeared sound.

Did we lose the battle? Am I a prisoner inside King Cormoran's castle?

The thought terrified her; from what she had heard of their adversary, prisoners found no mercy in their clutches, whether man or woman. Alice imagined the women's fates were far worse than mere death.

"Miss Alice?" a man's hesitant voice called from the darkness. "Miss Alice, are you awake?"

Careful not to repeat the searing pain of her last attempt, Alice slowly raised her head. The voice appeared to be coming from directly in front of her.

"Who's there? Who is that?" Alice refused to let a hint of fear creep into her voice. "Who's the hero that likes to watch a naked woman sleep from the darkness?"

"Oh, no, it's not like that," Alice could hear the man fumbling in his pockets and a sudden flare of light penetrated the dark as he struck a wooden match to life.

Alice took in everything she could in the moments the match bathed the room in a soft, flickering light. Heavy black curtains surrounded three sides of what appeared to be a cell with the curtain at the front of the cell pulled aside. A wall of thick steel bars ran from floor to ceiling with a heavy metal-framed door constructed of the same bars in the center.

A short, pear-shaped man stood before the cell door holding a match as it slowly burned. He wore a double-breasted black vest over a white mandarin collared shirt and high-waisted trousers with off-white and black stripes on a gray field. Wisps of unkempt blonde hair slipped from beneath the man's black derby hat and gave his plump face a cherubim-like quality.

"I'm no hero, ma'am; I'm Clodword."

The man responded in such an awkward manner that Alice wondered if he was unaccustomed to speaking to women or people in general.

"What is a Clodword?" Alice slowly raised herself onto her elbows, causing the blanket to slide down far enough that it barely covered her breasts.

Clodword noticed and Alice saw the embarrassed look on his face as the match winked out and returned him to darkness. Alice heard Clodword strike a second match and, as the light revealed his features once again, she noticed he was making a concerted effort to avert his eyes.

"Clodword is a who, not a what; I am Tinker's son," Clodword said with a pleasant smile, pointing to himself. "Clodword."

Alice's eye narrowed with suspicion. "The White Knight's son is named Gryphon. I know him well. We have fought alongside each other many times and he has never mentioned a brother."

"Half-brother, actually; on our father's side," Clodword gestured to his generally unfit body as the match extinguished. "You can imagine why Gryphon would not bring me up often in conversation."

As Alice heard Clodword fumbling for another match, she reluctantly agreed with his point. While Gryphon had often spent time with Hatter, Danavi, and her, Alice could not remember the man speaking of much beyond his athletic prowess and conquests in combat or the bedroom. She could see how Gryphon's ego could keep an uninspiring half-brother out of the conversation. Clodword; even the man's name sounded awful and embarrassing.

Gryphon always reminded Alice of a picture she had seen in a book depicting the Mongolian warlord, Chinggis Khan, and the White Knight, who Alice thought looked strikingly like Kaiser Wilhelm, often remarked that his son looked far more like his mother than himself. Gryphon was tall, muscular, and broad-shouldered with long black hair and almond-shaped eyes like his mother. He was always clean shaven, except for a ridiculous mustache that he cultivated across the top of his upper lip and then down the corners of his mouth to extend long past his chin. His mother had been deceased for many years by the time of Alice's arrival in Wonderland, however, by all accounts, Gryphon had been very close with her and the White Knight had been entirely devoted to his wife. The thought that he had been unfaithful to the woman and sired a secret child out of wedlock, while clearly not impossible, shocked Alice. She imagined that to Gryphon it would have felt like a cruel betrayal of his mother, and he was not the kind of man to let grievances slide.

Clodword did bear a striking resemblance to what Alice imagined the White Knight may have looked like in his younger days, albeit had the man chosen to master the culinary arts instead of becoming one of the realm's most renowned warriors. Still, something about Clodword's claim rang untrue to Alice.

She had been in the White Queen's service for ten years, nearly the entirety of her time in Wonderland, and to not have come across Gryphon's brother, a second son of the White Knight, seemed highly improbable.

Wonderland, or as it was more commonly known by its denizens, the Land of the Two Queens, was a forested kingdom on the shores of the Great Wide Open, a sea rumored to have no end. The ageless Indira, the White Queen, and her younger sister, Lairen, the Red Queen, ruled jointly as Queens regnant of Wonderland and its surrounding territories.

Although they ruled the kingdom side-by-side, each Queen kept her own court. Their husbands, the White and Red Kings, handled the more mundane administrative aspects of their rule; that is, until the Three Kings War when the Queens dispatched them to lead their armies against the giants that descended upon the kingdom. The forests were the purview of the White Queen and the Great Wide Open that of the Red. From time to time, banditry and piracy issues necessitated the Queens each maintain a Knight Champion to deal with such matters.

The tan, dark-haired, black-eyed Danavi had served as Queen Lairen's Red Knight since before Alice arrived in Wonderland and, she admitted, served even more admirably as Alice's lover for the past five years. In sharp contrast to Danavi's vigor, the aging Tinker had served Queen Indira as her White Knight; however, in recent years, Tinker had spent the majority of his time squirreled away in a lower chamber of the castle inventing all manner of devices for the Queen while Gryphon executed the more martial duties of the title. On numerous occasions, Gryphon had implored the White Queen to retire his father and bestow the title and honors upon him, however, Queen Indira refused even to entertain the idea.

She had found a special place in her court for Alice, handling issues that required a more discreet hand among the nobles and the borderlands. One such matter had lost Alice her left eye and gave her a pale scar from her forehead to her cheek, but it had cost the treacherous Duke Enderton his life in return. The queens' rule was rarely challenged, making such unpleasant tasks were thankfully infrequent.

Enderton was a power hungry sycophant and his death was necessary to keep good order and discipline among the nobility, after all, there would be no rebellions in Wonderland. It turned the usually mild-mannered Duchess Enderton into Alice's enemy within the White Court, a regrettable consequence of the whole affair, but one she could live with. The Duchess' was relatively harmless and her actions never rose above unflattering remarks and gossip about Alice, a trivial and inconsequential cost to pay for the removal of a cancerous presence among the nobles.

More troublesome to Alice was the loss of her eye. Alice was never one to fuss over her looks, and scars and scrapes came with the job. However, it took countless hours of training with Danavi to overcome the loss of depth perception and restore her fighting skill to her normal level of prowess. Though, Danavi did often comment that the scar and eye patch exuded a certain aura of danger that was quite sexy and attractive, and Alice certainly did not mind that sentiment from the Red Knight.

Thus, as well-connected as Alice was within the Red and White Court, it seemed highly unlikely to her that the existence of a second son of the White Knight, even a well-hidden one, would have escaped her notice for long; though perhaps the White Knight was slyer than she had given him credit for all these years.

As the match light extinguished, casting Clodword into darkness, he again rummaged in his pockets for another match. Alice swung her legs off the bed, wincing as the action caused tendrils of pain to blossom in her skull. She intended to run at Clodword, reaching through the bars to grab his throat and demand answers to the flurry of questions swirling in her mind, however Alice seriously underestimated the weakness in her right knee and the joint buckled as she sprung forward from the bed. Naked, Alice stumbled forward and crashed into the cell bars, grasping at the cold steel and barely able to keep herself upright as the bedpan clanged loudly against the floor behind her.

Clodword, having only just managed to light another match, staggered backward in shock, dropping the match and extinguishing the flame. Alice heard him sputtering and stammering in the darkness, apparently surprised by her actions and flustered by her nudity. As her eye grew accustomed to the darkness, Alice could make out the dark outline of the squat man holding up his bowler hat to seemingly block the sight of her naked body as he regained his footing and staggered down the hall.

She smirked. *Gryphon would certainly be disappointed in his brother. He was never phased by the sight of a naked woman. Hell, he worked too hard to get many of them that way in the first place. Quite an endearing trait you've got there, Clodword, and such an easy weakness to exploit.*

"I'm sorry, Miss Alice, I meant no disrespect; I did not see anything, I swear." Clodword's voice faded as he retreated down the darkened hall. "I will retrieve your sister and have her bring your clothes."

A smile crossed Alice's face at the panicked sound in Clodword's voice. Perhaps the White Knight had kept this man locked away somewhere after all.

Alice's eye trailed to the darkened cell across from hers. The only illumination in the cell was a small pillar of light, no more than a foot wide, which shone down from a tiny barred window high in the ceiling. She could make out the hulking shape of two forms sitting silently in the darkness. Two sets of eyes shimmered in the faint lantern light of her cell as they stared at her. Alice suddenly became very aware of her nakedness as she backed away from the cell bars and retrieved the blanket, wrapping it around her as she sat back on the bed.

She pulled her knees up to her chest and wrapped her arms around them, her blonde hair cascading down over her forearms as she dipped her head forward.

What the fuck is going on? Where am I? Where are Danavi and the others? Surely, they know I am a prisoner here, wherever here is.

Closing her eye, Alice listened intently to the sounds around her, trying to pick out individual noises. Alice could hear the two in the cell opposite her breathing: slow, deep, measured breaths. There were other sounds, noises she would expect to hear in prison: whimpering, mumbling, and someone calling out in their sleep, a strangled, pitiful cry. Then something else caught her attention from the cell behind her: a low growl, the sound of footpads on the stone floor, and something else. Alice strained to listen. Nails? Claws? Was there an animal in there with them?

"Alice." The girl's voice was soft and almost cheerful.

Alice's head shot up. She was so preoccupied with discerning the strange sound that she had not heard the girl approach. The girl, no taller than five feet, even with boots on, stood by the cell door, her face enshrouded in the dark hood of a cloak pulled up around her head. She bore a small pile of folded clothes in her hands, topped by a pair of well-worn boots that Alice quickly recognized as her own. Behind her, two guards towered over the girl clad in the livery of Queen Lairen, a black spade emblazoned on a field of red. One of the brutish-looking guards carried a lantern while the other held a large, curved axe. Both men eyed Alice with suspicion and looked like they would welcome the opportunity to do violence.

Despite everything, Alice smiled at the girl; she knew that voice almost as well as her own.

"Ava." Alice grinned, relieved to see her younger sister.

"Good to see you up and around, Alice." The cheerful voice drifted from the hood's darkness.

The guard with the axe nodded for the other to unlock the door and admit the girl. As the man stepped forward with a large key ring, the guard with his axe pointed the curved blade at Alice. The man had an unpleasant, meaty, boar-like face with small, deep-set eyes.

"Move an inch off that bed and I'll take this little kitten's head off and then I'll split you from hair to hooch," sneered the guard, his voice dripping with a bully's menace.

"Look at you, all charm and good looks," Alice retorted, the smile never leaving her face.

He probably has an immensely small dick.

The guard unlocked the door and opened it only far enough to push Ava through before slamming it closed behind her. The lock engaged with a loud click and the guard turned away without giving either of the women another glance. The pig-faced guard peered into the other cell and ran the blade of his axe against the steel bars, each bar clanging loudly against the steel blade.

"Wake up, you shit-eating giants." The guard gave a malicious laugh and ran his thumb along the edge of the axe blade. "Maybe the Red Queen will put your head up on the wall today with the rest of her collection. Stick you on a pike right next to your daddy."

Giants! Alice stared into the cell's darkness, but the two imprisoned giants stayed rooted in the shadows and showed no reaction as the guard walked away, his wicked laugh echoing down the prison corridor.

"Ava, what the fuck is going on?" Alice reached for her sister as Ava placed the pile of clothes on the bed. "Come here, let me see you."

"Alice." Ava hesitated, pulling back from Alice's outstretched hand.

"Ava, what is it?" Alice felt suddenly alarmed as Ava looked away, her face shrouded deep within the recesses of her hood.

Alice leaned quickly forward, sending waves of pain through her skull so severe she felt nauseous, as she grabbed Ava's hood and yanked it back. Ava cried out in surprise as the hood fell away, and Alice gasped in horror. Her younger sister's face was pale in the lantern light and framed in long blonde hair, the same as Alice's and their mother's. However, once as smooth and unblemished as a porcelain doll, the skin of the young girl's face was now covered in dozens of thin, red ragged scars. It looked as if an animal had repeatedly swiped its claws at her sister's face, leaving lines of thin, sharp scratches deep enough to scar. Alice noticed the absence of any gouges from the animal trying to latch onto or subdue Ava. The scratches were surface-level, like a cat toying with its prey.

Ava's eyes, as blue as the waters of the Great Wide Open, welled up with tears at the revelation of her ravaged face. She quickly pulled the hood back up over her head and stepped back, a sob choking in her throat.

Alice's emotions churned as she felt equal parts rage and grief for her sister. "Ava, who did this to you? Tell me what the fuck is going on here, right now!"

"Hooka did this to me," Ava gestured toward her face as her voice cracked with emotion. "He said we were sisters and now we look more like twins."

"Hooka? That fucking caterpillar did that?" Alice now had a target for her rage.

"He's not a caterpillar anymore. The Red Queen changed him into some kind of flying monkey. He did this with his claws as some of the Red Queen's men held me down; that big fucker with the axe was one of them. I could smell the onions on his breath as he laughed."

"What?" Alice could not believe what she was hearing. "Queen Indira would never stand for such a thing! What did she do?"

"Alice, you need to understand; you've been unconscious for a long time, the better part of a year." Ava stepped closer and glanced over her shoulder to see if the guards were returning. Seeing no one, she turned to Alice and lowered her voice, "So much has changed since your injury. You mustn't say her name out loud. It's the law now. By order of the Red Queen, under pain of death."

Alice blinked, stunned. "Ava, what's happened here?"

"Alice, the White Queen is dead. You are Queen Lairen's prisoner," Ava replied in a hushed tone. "I'm sorry. I know Indira meant a lot to you; she meant a great deal to both of us."

Alice recoiled. The words struck her like a physical blow and Ava reached out and grabbed her hand, giving it a reassuring squeeze. The air felt as if it had been sucked from Alice's lungs with such force that she was sure her body must be imploding. She searched her sister's scarred and ravaged face for some sign that this was all some horrible joke, a cruel jest by Hatter and the others. Ava stared back at Alice, the depths revealing how deep a hurt retelling the horrible news caused.

Reflexively, Alice's mind locked tight like a steel trap snapping upon a rat. Now was not the time to grieve. Her Queen was dead and her sister maimed. These were blood debts that must be paid. She needed to know where her people were. Where were Hatter, Gryphon, and especially Danavi?

A hollow feeling opened in her gut. Danavi was her lover and, as Red Knight, a trusted member of Queen Lairen's court. Alice had never confided in anyone about their relationship, not even Ava, and certainly not the Red Queen. Queen Lairen would have no reason to hide Alice's imprisonment from her knight champion and Danavi would never leave her to rot in a prison cell. Unless, of course, Danavi was dead too.

"What happened to me? Tell me everything," Alice's eye was hard and her voice cold. "The last thing I remember is being on the bridge at King Cormoran's castle."

"The White King died on the bridge, crushed by a catapult stone the giants launched over the wall. Our lines almost broke after that but Gryphon, that crazy bastard, rallied the forces and charged the castle. They say he mounted the wall and slew Cormoran single-handedly." Ava gave a faint smile. She had always had a schoolgirl's crush on Gryphon. Alice could picture Gryphon storming the castle, his long dark hair and flowing mustache blowing in the breeze as he roared his war cry and felled the giant king with his broad sword.

"The other giant kings, Thunderdel and Galligantus, fled the castle when Cormoran fell," Ava continued. "They did not make it far. Duke Cheshire filled his cannons with grapeshot and ambushed them on the road. The carnage was so great that you couldn't tell where one giant ended and the other began when he finished. After that, the fight went out of the giants' army. The Red King had all the kudzu vines hacked down and burned so the giants could not return to their land. He hunted the stragglers and took no prisoners. As far as I know, those two are the last giants alive in Wonderland."

Ava gestured over her shoulder to the cell across from Alice's. Alice looked at the two hulking forms in the darkness, "Who are they?"

"Cormoran's sons, Bore and Rebeck," Ava shrugged. "They are the Red Queen's hostages against the day the giants ever try to return."

"But what about me? What happened to me?"

"Alice, you fell from the bridge and injured your head. We did not think you would ever awake,"

"I . . . fell?"

"Well, you were shot and fell from the bridge. Danavi pulled you from the river. You never regained consciousness until now."

Alice studied Ava's face. The girl pursed her lips, a nervous habit when withholding something. "What are you not telling me?"

"Hatter shot you, Alice. He shot you in the leg and you tumbled from the bridge."

"That jackass. What the hell was he aiming at?" Alice shook her head in irritation then noticed the grim look on Ava's face.

"I think he was aiming for you, Alice. I think Hatter shot you intentionally."

"What? Why would he do that?" The notion shocked Alice.

"I don't know." Ava shook her head. "There was a lot of friction between Danavi and Hatter after that, but I don't know if the friction was over Hatter shooting you or Danavi pulling you from the river."

"Ava, what are you saying?"

"Look, let me explain what happened after the battle and then you can decide for yourself," Ava said, holding up a hand to preempt any further questions.

"You were in bad shape; you struck your head in the fall and they brought you back to the palace to recover. The White Queen saw that you received the best medical attention available. Still, you were not getting any better," Ava said in a low, conspiratorial tone. "Queen Lairen thought you might receive more thorough care back in England and suggested someone carry you back through the Looking Glass. Danavi and Gryphon volunteered, but Queen Indira would have none of it. The issue became moot a few weeks later."

"Why's that?"

"Alice, she broke the Looking Glass; shattered it to pieces."

"What?"

"Gryphon told me that the Red Queen had called a special counsel to discuss the incursions into Wonderland by the Pan and Queen Indira just walked in and announced she had destroyed the Looking Glass. The Red Queen was furious; she dismissed everyone from the room and she and Indira argued for hours. After that, neither Queen ever brought it up publicly again."

"That makes no sense. Why would Queen Indira do that?"

"I don't know. But we're here for good now, Alice; there's no going back to England, ever."

"There was nothing back there for us anymore. I am sure grandfather has passed by now." Alice felt a pang of regret at the thought of the kindly old man dying without any family around him, but there was nothing to be done about that now. "You said the Pan was making incursions into Wonderland? How is that possible? I thought the Kraken barred the way to and from Neverland."

"It does." Ava nodded. "The Pan has been sending a black cloud across the water. The people call it The Dark. It steals children."

Alice had never seen Peter the Pan and, as far as she knew, no one in recent memory, except the two deathless Queens who banished him centuries ago, had ever seen him. Most people believed he had died alone in his island exile long ago and existed now as a fairy tale to scare misbehaving children.

"Be good or the Pan will get you" was a common threat by all parents in Wonderland.

However, Alice had learned from the White Queen that the Pan was as unaffected by time as she and her sister were. Like them, Pan was a creature from before Wonderland and thus aged far more slowly than ordinary mortals. Peter had committed some unspoken affront against the Queens, and they had banished him to a remote island, never to return. In time, the island became known as Neverland, which also became a refrain of parents: "You will be sent to Neverland with all the nasty little boys and girls if you are not good."

Alice had used some of those threats herself on misbehaving children in the palace, delighting at their looks of fear. Now none of those threats seemed amusing anymore. The Pan was taking children, whisking them off to Neverland.

"Why is Peter stealing children?" Alice was becoming overwhelmed by the sheer volume of change that occurred during her coma. "And what has happened to the White Queen?"

"I don't know why he is doing it." Ava shook her head, then grew somber. "I am getting to that part . . . about Queen Indira, I mean."

"Ok, I am sorry." Alice put her hand on Ava's leg.

"The Queens called for an expedition to stop the Pan and kill him if necessary. The Red King outfitted a ship. Danavi went as the Red Queen's champion and Gryphon went representing the White Queen since his father was too old to fight."

"They went by ship? Ava, the Kraken would never let them reach the island!"

"The White Knight invented a device. As you know, that's what he is best at these days. It was like a brass hand-cranked siren with a warbling disc inside. He believed the noise would keep the Kraken from the ship."

"Did it?" Alice felt a lump form in her throat at the thought of the Kraken pulling Danavi into the depths.

"They are over six months overdue." Ava's voice cracked, and Alice knew her sister must be thinking the same thoughts about Gryphon. "Whether something befell them at sea or on the island, everyone believes they have been lost or captured. Queen Lairen is convinced that Peter is holding the Red King hostage."

"Why does she think that?"

"I don't know." Ava shook her head. "Grief at the thought of the Red King's death or the torment of not knowing his fate. I think that was the reason for her madness."

"What happened after that?"

"Things got tense between the Queens. They seemed at odds often and disagreed on what to do next. Then, without warning, the Red Queen launched a surprise attack on the White Queen and her followers. Duke Cheshire was ambushed and killed on the road and the Red Queen's ships anchored around his castle, trapping Lady Cheshire and the Duke's men inside, ready to lay siege."

"The fighting in the palace must have been horrific." Alice paled at the thought of hand-to-hand combat and musket fire in the close quarters of the palace halls.

Ava's countenance darkened and she shook her head. "There was no fighting in the palace."

"The White Queen yielded without a fight?" Alice stared in disbelief at her sister.

"No." Ava's face soured as if she had eaten a rotten cherry. "The Red Queen's men crept through the White Court like rats in a barn and slaughtered most of Indira's soldiers in their sleep. Hatter turned on the White Queen. Alice, he beheaded her! She was still dressed in her nightgown. Queen Lairen had her head placed on a spike atop the wall of the palace alongside Duke Cheshire's."

"Hatter sided with the Red Queen over Indira?"

"Yes. That is why I believe him shooting you was no accident. I think they planned this betrayal for a long time."

"I'll kill that fucking traitor." Alice's hands balled into fists.

"I don't understand why Hatter did what he did. I do know that when Queen Lairen's men burst into your room, Hatter prevented them from hurting us. He threatened to shoot anyone who tried to harm us and convinced the Red Queen that you may still be of use if you ever awoke. She agreed to keep you imprisoned down here. I was allowed to remain free in the palace as an assistant in the Royal Library with the understanding that any attempt at betrayal or escape would result in your immediate death."

"Did any other members of the White Court survive?"

"The Red Queen spared the White Knight, but only because she held out hope that he could repair the Looking Glass. Hatter demanded that Clodword stand guard over you, day and night, to prevent any of the Queen's men from coming down to the prison to take liberties with you while you were unconscious."

"From what I saw of Clodword, it would be unlikely he would be able to prevent a bee from stinging me, let alone fend off a guardsman or two."

"Oh, you would be surprised. I have heard only rumors, mind you, but several guards tried just that in the days after the palace coup and received a thorough thrashing from Clodword."

"So the White Knight survived. Any others?"

"Only Lady Cheshire and her daughters. Hatter arrived at Cheshire Castle under the guise of assistance from the White Queen, however once the guards admitted Hatter into the castle, his men, the Red Queen's men, threw off their disguises and seized the castle. They captured the Lady Cheshire and both her daughters."

"Uggh, is there no end to that man's treachery?"

"The Red Queen had Indira's section of the palace closed off." Ava paused. "There is one more thing you should know . . . Queen Lairen is different now."

"Different how? She was always a mean-spirited bitch; I don't expect committing sororicide has lightened her disposition."

"No. She has powers now; she can change living things into animals,"

"Like turning Hooka from a giant caterpillar into a fucking flying monkey?" Alice immediately regretted the words as she saw Ava reflexively touch the scars on her face. Alice hated that she had brought those memories flooding back to her sister and she mentally added Hooka to the list of people she would see pay for what they had done. The Red Queen, Hatter, Hooka, and that guard with the fucking axe. Danavi? Would she add Danavi to that list? If Danavi still lived. The thought of her lover's potential betrayal stung her to her core.

"Yes . . . and worse. Anyone loyal to the White Queen that she did not have put to death, she transformed into rodents—rabbits, rats, door mice. They walk, talk, and dress like before except now they are animals. She changed Lady Cheshire into a black jaguar although she still retains the ability to speak. Her daughters are in the cell on the other side of you," Ava gestured toward one of the dark drapes covering the cell wall. "They were transformed into jaguars like their mother."

"I knew the Queens had powers. Indira had hinted at it several times, but she never revealed anything about them,"

"I'm afraid, Alice. The Red Queen hates us, Alice, you and I. I don't know why, but I can see it in her eyes."

"Well then, your big sister is just going to have to close those fucking eyes forever." Alice grinned and Ava smiled back a truly genuine smile.

CHAPTER 2: STEM TO STERN

Ava lay on the bed watching Alice slip on the leather trousers and cotton shirt she had brought. Alice winced as sliding on the high leather boots jostled her bad knee.

"Does it hurt bad?" Ava asked, hating to see her sister in pain.

"It's really just an ache," Alice admitted, her voice tinged with a hint of resignation. "I suspect it will be some time before I can walk without a limp, if ever."

"Fucking Hatter," Ava spat with distaste.

"Fucking Hatter," Alice agreed as she laid down alongside Ava, facing her.

"Alice, tell me again the name of the place where father died?" Ava's voice sounded small and childlike, as it always did when she spoke about their parents.

"It was called Isandlwana," Alice replied, brushing a few stray strands of hair from Ava's forehead. "He was an officer in the Natal Native Horse under Colonel Durnsford; he was very courageous."

"Isandlwana," Ava repeated the word, trying to remember it this time. She sat quietly for a moment and then her eyes brimmed with tears. "I miss him."

"I miss him too," Alice smiled at her.

"Do you miss mother?" Ava's voice cracked as she asked. Alice bit her lip. She knew this conversation was a wellspring of hurt for Ava and tread lightly with her response.

"Ava, mother loved you so much; so very much. She loved you so much that she gave all of herself to bring you into this world to be my sister."

A thick, watery tear streamed down Ava's cheek, taking a haphazard path down the network of red scars to make a dark, wet circle on the pillowcase. "You don't hate me for taking her from you?"

"Ava, you didn't take her from me; she gave me to you, which was the world's greatest gift." Alice leaned forward and kissed Ava on the forehead.

They laid there quietly as Ava sniffled and wiped away her tears. Alice rolled onto her back and stared at the lantern, the flickering light burning overhead.

"Ava, do you ever regret coming through the Looking Glass? Leaving England and all your friends behind?"

"Sometimes I miss Grandfather." Ava sighed. "I don't particularly miss England, and I cannot say I had many friends back there."

"You don't miss going to school?" Alice glanced sidelong at her sister.

"Going to school?!" Ava laughed loudly. "Who would miss going to school?"

"You know what I mean." Alice shook her head with mock indignation. "Going to school and meeting boys. You would be going out on dates by now."

"Well, there are boys here too," smiled Ava, and Alice wondered if she were imagining Gryphon. "And honestly, until the coup, this was a pretty great place to live."

The sound of a heavy metal door opening in the distance wiped the smiles from their faces as a corridor of light extended down between the cells.

"I think they're coming to take me back," Ava's eyes clouded with apprehension.

"It'll be okay, Ava. I promise we'll see each other soon," Alice squeezed her sister's hands.

"I'll bring you lemon balm and chamomile; it will help with your headaches," Ava promised as heavy footfalls sounded down the corridor.

The girls sat up as the two guards from earlier approached and stopped at the cell.

"The little bitch leaves now," the guard with the axe sneered as his compatriot unlocked and swung open the door.

The sisters embraced. Ava slid off the bed and hurried out the door, pausing to glance at Alice. Moving too slow for the guard, he shoved Ava with the haft of his axe, causing her to cry out and stumble before catching her balance and moving quickly down the corridor and out of sight.

"You know," the guard turned to leer at Alice, licking his tongue across the front of his teeth as the other guard closed and locked the door, "if I had known you two would wind up in bed together, I would have stayed and watched the show."

"What's your name?" Alice flashed the guard an alluring smile.

"Starkey." The guard stared lasciviously at Alice as she slid off the bed, her brown leather pants hugging her hips and conforming to the contours of her body.

"Well, Starkey, what do you say you unlock that door and come join me in here?" Alice purred as she patted a hand on her bed. "And then I'll take that axe and split you from stem to stern."

A look of confusion crossed Starkey's face, quickly replaced by anger as the words sank in. "Fuck you," he spat as he turned and stormed off.

Alice smiled as she watched the humiliated guard stalk off. From the darkness across from her cell she heard the sound of a deep, guttural laugh.

Alice laid on her bed staring at the flickering lantern overhead, her hands folded behind her head. The pain in her skull had diminished to a dull ache, and she could ignore it most of the time if she did not think about it.

Her mind raced. What the fuck had happened to her world? Queen Indira and the White King were dead, Danavi and

Gryphon were lost, Ava was little more than a prisoner, and Hatter was a traitor. The incongruity of the world since she awoke infuriated her. Locked in the cell, Alice felt helpless to do anything to help the ones she loved and avenge those she lost.

When she and Ava stepped through the Looking Glass, Alice left behind a future that offered little more than marriage and family. Even if she had married well, a prospect that had diminished significantly with the death of her parents, her life would have been confined to a small circle of close friends, tea parties, and pursuing such womanly pastimes as reading, embroidery, music, and handicrafts. England's patriarchal society did not grant her the same opportunities as it did men; her place would be in the home, caring for the household, a delicate flower of femininity.

However, Queens ruled the Wonderland she stepped into and they had dominion over all. Alice cared little that the White Queen had destroyed the Looking Glass; she had never intended to return to England or that world. Even as a young girl, Queen Indira had seen Alice's potential; she was intelligent, perceptive, and eager to embrace her new world. The White Queen took the girls in and made a place for them in the White Court where they could excel based on their wits and ability.

Ava had been intrigued by the history and lore of Wonderland and apprenticed in the royal archives where she satiated her thirst for knowledge while Alice, with her desire for adventure, received an education in everything from the art of diplomacy to the ways of war. She became an expert with the flintlock pistol, sword, and longbow, a much stealthier weapon than the cumbersome muskets carried by soldiers in Wonderland.

As the years passed, Alice had enjoyed the status of a trusted and valued member of the White Queen's court, a position earned on the merits of her abilities. Her reputation had grown as she handled the Queen's most sensitive problems with discretion and thoroughness. She had caught the eye of Danavi, the Red Knight, a dalliance Alice first eyed with great suspicion. Although the two Queens ruled side-by-side as equals, much intrigue still occurred between the Red and White Courts as each vied for increased wealth and power. Alice had initially suspected Danavi's ulterior motive was to gain information on the White Court. Alice, in turn, had decided that aside from her physical attraction to Danavi, she would entertain the romance to gather inside information on the plans and machinations of the Red Court, fully confident the Red Knight would be no match for her sexual wiles.

What had started as a tryst, with frequent episodes of wild lovemaking in the dark and secret places of the castle, had grown into a genuine relationship. Each respected the boundaries of the other's loyalty to their Queen and Court, placing what they had above the politics of the palace.

Alice had insisted they keep their love a secret from the Courts. Although Danavi protested at first, the Red Knight conceded that if their relationship became known, it would jeopardize their positions of trust with their respective Queens.

However, as the months grew into years, the dilemma of what to do with their relationship became a source of friction between them with Danavi wanting more than just fleeting nights and moments with Alice.

As Alice stared at the glow of the lantern, she wondered if, in the end, Danavi was more Queen Lairen's Red Knight than Alice's lover. Danavi had not stopped Hatter from shooting her on the bridge, likely to eliminate one of the White Queen's closest allies, but had rescued her from the water.

As Red Knight, Danavi would have known of Queen Lairen's plans to assault the White Court and kill Queen Indira, something Alice would have given her life to prevent and never have forgiven. Queen Indira's murder was a blood debt that Alice would repay; Danavi would have known that. Maybe that was why Danavi had offered to take her through the Looking Glass back to England: to save her from what was to come—a final act of love.

"Hey," a harsh voice called as metal clanged loudly against the bars. "Here's your dinner."

Alice sat up, so lost in her thoughts that she had not heard Starkey approach with her evening meal. The burly guard placed a metal plate containing a grayish hash through an opening on the bottom of the cell door and slid it across the stone floor. Behind him, the other guard rolled a wooden cart piled with similar plates, stopping to slide two into the giants' cell before moving on.

"It's not very good, but don't worry . . . I added some extra flavoring," Starkey laughed as he slid the tip of one gnarled fingertip into a nostril and waggled it around.

"Stem to stern, Starkey," Alice glowered at the guard as he turned away.

"Whatever you say, princess," Starkey laughed, his voice fading as he followed the cart.

Alice heard the metal grating on stone as other plates slid into the cells around her. She stared at the plate for a minute then laid back on the bed, listening to the sound of the prison at mealtime. The daughters of Lady Cheshire, transformed into jaguars according to Ava, noisily ate in their cell. Alice heard the beasts' teeth clinking against the metal plates, their long, feline tongues licking up the last morsels. Moving aside one of the heavy black curtain panels, Alice peered into the Cheshire girls' cell. The two jaguars, coats as black as night, had their long bodies hunched over their plates of food as they ate. One of the animals lifted its head and stared at her with intense yellow eyes.

"Hey, it's Alice. Do you remember me? I was a friend of your mother's," Alice called to the jaguar in a low voice to avoid attracting the guards' attention.

The jaguar flicked its long tail from side to side and the powerful muscles in its shoulders bunched as it turned to regard Alice. The beast gave Alice a deep, guttural growl that reminded her of someone sawing wood and returned to its meal.

"We remember you," the other jaguar replied, looking up from its meal. "We spoke with your sister often when she came to care for you." The jaguar's eyes grew sad. "You are a bird in a cage like us, trapped in this terrible place. Trust me, Alice, you'll wish you never woke up."

Alice was about to speak, but the jaguar turned back to its meal, clearly wishing to talk no more at the moment. She let the curtain fall back into place and swung her legs over the side of the bed.

Alice heard the rattle of metal plates as the guards worked their way back down the line of cells, collecting the empty dinnerware. A stack of two plates slid out of the darkness of the giants' cell to rattle against the guard's booted foot as the cart returned. Starkey's eyes moved lazily from Alice to her untouched food then returned to her as a wicked smile crossed his face.

"Not hungry tonight, princess?" Starkey grinned. "Finish your fucking food and give us the plate."

"Why don't you come in here and get it, Starkey?" Alice's eyes narrowed, letting a hint of malice slip into her tone.

Starkey eyed her as his face broke into a shit-eating grin. "Nah. You can let the rats eat that shit if you want, but you get no more food until we get a clean plate from you. I'll tell you what, though . . . if your food gets cold and you want me to come back and warm up your dish, you be sure to call, princess."

Alice glared back at the man, disgusted at the thought of his hands on her. *Stem to stern, Starkey.* The words repeated in her mind like a mantra.

Alice sat on the cold stone floor, the chill of the wall pressing into her back as she leaned against it. As a child in England, the notion of a prison as a fearful place full of dangerous men willing to do violence at the first available opportunity had terrified Alice. However, as she sat in the perpetual isolation of her cell, Alice began to realize the actual punishment of prison. The boredom, monotony, and craving for outside human connection as the emptiness of the cell closed about her like an ocean consuming her in its depths.

Movement in the giants' cell caught her attention, and she watched as one of the occupants moved into the small pillar of moonlight that shone down into the cell. The giant was easily eight feet tall with skin as dark and richly brown as a roasted coffee bean. The moonlight shone on his face as he tilted his shaved head toward the opening. A tree-limb thick arm, heavily muscled and lined with scars from untold conflicts, extended from the man's leather vest and reached up through the moonlight. Alice could see the giant's eyes, dark and soulful, as they stared upward at the night sky. There was a sadness in the man's countenance. There was a mournfulness in his eyes that inexplicably broke Alice's heart. She wanted to cry as she watched him but did not understand why.

Alice had faced men like this across from her on the battlefield in the Three Kings War when the three giant kings invaded Wonderland with their armies. She had watched giants fall, gurgling with her arrows in their throats or felled like timber from a long shaft embedded in their chest. They were her enemies and a threat to the Queen. The giants had descended into Wonderland from high stalks of twisted kudzu vine that had stretched into the sky as if they had come from a kingdom in the heavens. Ava had known better. She had discovered the truth buried in the palace archives; the ends of the kudzu at the top of the vines emitted an oily vapor that congealed in the air like a slick cloud. These clouds acted akin to the Looking Glass, allowing the giants to pass to and from their world into Wonderland.

Alice shook off the feeling of melancholy. *Fuck this.* The giants were her enemies; they had killed the White King and countless others during their war. She was not going to feel pity for their confinement, nor was she going to sit in this cell and wait for the Red Queen, Starkey, Hatter, or whoever else thought they could take a swipe at her, to come and get her.

Alice leaped to her feet, stumbling slightly as her wounded knee threatened to buckle beneath her. She limped across the cell to where the plate of food sat on the stone floor and dumped the contents into the hole in the floor that served as a toilet.

Out of the corner of her eye, she could see one of the giants turn to study her curiously as she hobbled to the cell door and, with great effort, bent the plate around the bar until it looked like a metal sausage roll. Then, flipping the plate so the spine of the taco was along the bar, Alice pulled the edges to bend the plate in the opposite direction. The strain of the effort caused her head to throb, but Alice fought through the pain.

Alice repeated this process several times, grunting ferociously with the effort as her blonde hair matted against her sweaty forehead until a split formed on each end of the bend.

"Yes." Alice's eye lit with excitement as she repeated the process twice more until the metal plate split in two. She grinned like a feral child as she touched each half's sharp, exposed edge before slipping one into the side of each boot.

Grabbing the closest curtain, Alice dug her fingers deep into the thick fabric and leaned back to leverage her weight as she yanked and pulled at the curtain. A loud tearing noise rended the air as the curtain ripped from its fastenings and cascaded to the ground. The jaguars in the adjacent cell leaped back, snarling in surprise as the curtain fell away. Alice ignored them and quickly ran to each of the remaining curtains. She repeated the process, uncovering the barred walls and leaving the heavy cloth curtains strewn on the cell's floor. Her chest heaved from the exertion and sweat poured down her face as she surveyed her work.

The Cheshire girls paced their cell, their long black tails flicking nervously as their paws padded against the stone floor. They studied her with yellow eyes that almost glowed in the darkness.

Alice looked sidelong at the giants' cell; the second giant had now come to stand alongside the first, equally immense and dark as the first with long black hair that hung down to his shoulders. She heard voices too, farther down the line of cells as information passed from prisoner to prisoner that something was afoot.

Alice pulled the blanket off her bed and knotted one corner several times to give it some weight. She twirled it over her head several times, testing its heft. Unsatisfied, Alice knotted the corner two more times so that the fabric balled from the size of a small apple to that of a grapefruit. Adrenaline was pumping through her veins now, and she wanted to leap up onto the bed in dramatic swashbuckling fashion but instead climbed up, lest her knee give out and she knock herself unconscious again against the bars.

Alice flashed the giants a grin as the one with the long hair cocked his head to watch her with intense curiosity; his companion met her gaze and stared back without any noticeable emotion.

She twirled the knotted edge of the blanket several times and released it to sail upwards. The knot bounced off the stone ceiling with a muffled thud and then fell back to earth.

With brows knitted in concentration, Alice stared at the large oil lamp suspended above her bed by four copper chains that met at the ceiling. The lamp was ovoid-shaped and made from reddish-brown terracotta, with a wick burning brightly at one end of a rounded nozzle. She had seen this manner of an oil lamp in the palace before and knew it had a deeply recessed center with a filling hole.

This is no different than archery; the knot will go where your eyes look.

Twirling the knot to build up speed, Alice released the end of the blanket and watched as it sailed upward then hung as if suspended in the air. The knotted end of the blanket laid over where one of the copper chains connected to the terracotta lamp. Alice tugged on the blanket, careful not to pull hard enough to dislodge it from its perch. The lamp above rocked and swayed on its chain, oil spilling from the refill holes to splash the blanket and rain down on the bed in thick droplets. She continued to pull on the blanket, like a priest ringing a church bell, soaking the bed and blanket in oil.

Whoosh.

Alice's face illuminated in a warm glow as the oil-soaked blanket made contact with the flaming wick and ignited. The lamp rocked violently on its chains as Alice yanked the burning blanket with enough force to dislodge it, flaming oil droplets raining down on the bed. As the bed began to smoke and burn, Alice held the blanket like a fiery snake, dipping it down so its flaming tongues could touch and ignite each crumpled pile of curtains.

The flames hungrily consumed the bed and curtains, billowing smoke from the cell. Alice smiled as she surveyed her handiwork then tossed the burning blanket onto the bed adding more kindling for the fire.

As the Cheshire sisters growled and hissed in fear as they stared at the flames, Alice heard the voices of prisoners begin to shout in alarm as smoke filled the prison block. Only the giants remained stoic and silent.

The cacophony of shouts and cries rose, and Alice could hear the guards working the lock on the door. They would be rushing into the prison at any moment. Alice could feel her face flushing with the heat of the flames surrounding her as she tied her blonde hair back into a ponytail and drew the jagged halves of the plate from her boots.

She tested her knee. It felt weak, but there was no helping that now as she faced her cell door and crouched into a fighting stance.

The sound of the prison door swinging echoed above the prisoners' shouts and Alice could hear the heavy footfalls of booted feet running down the passageway to the cells. It would not be long now.

Across from her, the giants stared dispassionately into her burning cell, their dark faces unreadable in the firelight. The thrill of impending battle coursed through her veins, and she licked her lips and smiled wickedly at the thought of the carnage that was to come. Alice blew the giants a kiss and thought she noticed the barely perceptible hint of movement at the corners of the bald one's mouth.

"What the fuck?" Starkey cursed as he stormed up to Alice's cell with two guards trailing behind him. His eyes flared angrily in the firelight of the burning cell as he surveyed the damage before they fell upon Alice, grinning madly at him.

Starkey shifted his axe in his hands and Alice thought he was readying himself to charge into the cell, but he just turned to look down the row of prison cells and bellowed, "Shut the fuck up! I will personally knock every fucking tooth out of the next person's mouth that makes a sound."

The shouting prisoners immediately ceased as if someone had thrown a switch; none doubted that Starkey would be true to his word.

In the cell beside her, the Cheshire sisters continued their pacing, albeit now quietly. The two guards, each holding polished wooden clubs, dented and scratched from frequent use, stared expectantly at Starkey.

"You two, get in there and bring me that crazy one-eyed bitch. I don't care if you have to cave in her skull to do it." Starkey handed one of the men the cell key and then shouted toward the prison door, "I need more guards in here, now!"

Alice shifted her feet, balancing her weight off her weakened knee, and studied the two guards as they unlocked the cell door and cautiously approached. The guard to her left looked like a grizzled veteran, his club held in position to strike a blow or parry a thrust from Alice's makeshift weapons. The man had an eagerness in his dark eyes, an excitement at the prospect of violence and the chance to inflict pain. However, the man on the right was younger and had nervous, uncertain eyes. He held his club up high like he was ready to swat a fly, an awkward, inexperienced stance. He would hesitate when the battle came.

Left it is then.

That was good; she could push off with her strong leg, giving her more burst and speed than if she struck first to the right. She turned her eye toward the younger man, staring at him with a predatory gaze; Alice saw the man's eyebrows raise slightly in surprise.

Good. The man's nervousness just ratcheted up an octave or two; his guts are probably knotting enough to blow a stream of liquid shit out of his ass.

Alice's eye stayed on the younger man who advanced on her uncertainly, yet her attention remained focused on the veteran she watched in her periphery. The man would think she was distracted and try to press his advantage. Alice just had to wait.

"C'mon, take her," Starkey goaded the men from the safety of the corridor.

From the corner of her eye, Alice saw the veteran make his move, surging forward with his club swinging in an arc toward her head. Alice lunged to her left, sliding under the man's blow and pivoting on her good leg. She spun her right hand, slashing the jagged edge of one plate across the man's neck, severing his jugular. Arterial blood sprayed from the man's neck in a wide arc as he dropped his club and collapsed to the floor, gurgling and clutching at the wound as his lifeblood rushed between his fingers. Alice's dance of death continued as she pirouetted, her left hand opening the younger guard's throat with a back slice before the man had time to process what had happened. The man's eyes looked utterly shocked as his head lolled backward, his neck opening like a second mouth as he collapsed backward. His club struck the stone floor with a loud clang that reverberated over the sound of his companion's choking death throes.

Billowing smoke stung Alice's eye as she turned to look at Starkey. The man's mouth hung slightly open, and shock was evident in his deep-set eyes at how easily Alice had dispatched the two guards. As their eyes met, Alice let a slight smile curl the edges of her mouth.

Starkey sneered in contempt and reared back his axe to deliver a killing blow as Alice charged him, her makeshift blades slicked red with blood and held wide. She felt like a bird of prey swooping in to strike her quarry with razor-sharp talons and unleashed a primal scream of fury as she rushed toward the guard—one of the men responsible for holding down her sister as a monstrosity clawed her face.

Then Alice's right knee wobbled and she staggered, nearly losing her footing.

Oh no, not this way.

A feeling of cold dread ran through Alice's mind as she tried to regain her balance. Before her Starkey roared as he lunged forward to cleave Alice's head from her shoulders. A searing pain radiated up her leg as her injured knee refused to cooperate and she dropped to one knee.

She readied her blades, hoping to land a fatal thrust between Starkey's ribs as he decapitated her. She would take this bastard to the grave with her.

Starkey gave a surprised grunt. A large, muscular arm had snaked out of the giants' cell and closed around his neck, pulling him back against the cell bars. He struck the cell hard, the sound of bone striking the metal bars echoed through the prison. The other giant grabbed the guard's arm, the one holding the axe, and held it fast as Starkey frantically beat against their hold with his free hand. Smoke from her small inferno rolled along the ceiling, obscuring the prison door in a dark gray haze.

"Alice, there are more coming," one of the Cheshire jaguars shouted a warning. Her sister let out a ferocious roar to deter any guards daring to enter the smoke-filled fray.

Out of the corner of her eye, Alice saw a guard armed with a flintlock pistol and a hand axe charge through the smoke with Clodword running close behind him, his bowler hat threatening to tumble free from his unruly blonde hair.

Alice put all her weight onto her good leg and propelled herself forward in a desperate leap, slamming both blades into Starkey's chest and burying them deep into his rib cage. The man's eyes grew wide with shock and pain, the axe slipping from his fingers. Alice released her grip on the blades and spun, grabbing the axe as it fell and turning to thrust the sharpened tip of the axe into his groin. Starkey screamed in pain and Alice matched his scream with one of fury as she used all her strength to force the axe upward, ripping and tearing through the guard's flesh until it lodged just above his stomach. Blood and gore splashed upon the floor as Starkey's innards pushed through the gaping wound.

"From stem to stern, Starkey," Alice sneered into the man's face as his body trembled and eyes dimmed. Behind him, she could see the eyes of the bald giant, cold and emotionless, watching her. The giant released his grip, arm sliding back into the cell like a giant snake as Starkey slid lifelessly down the steel bars.

Click.

Alice heard the approaching guard pull back the hammer of his pistol as he slowed and aimed the barrel at her head. The deep, dark hole at the end of the pistol's barrel reminded Alice of staring into a rabbit hole as the guard readied his shot. Behind him, the oncoming Clodword lowered his shoulder and barreled into the guard with all the force of a charging bull.

The guard's pistol roared and bellowed a cloud of black smoke as it fired, the musket ball sailing so close to Alice's face that she heard it whiz by and felt the passing rush of air on her cheek. She had no doubt that had Clodword not struck the man, the shot would have punched a fist-sized hole in her skull.

The guard gave a startled cry as the blow from Clodword propelled him forward, the axe and pistol falling from his hands as he sought to brace himself before striking the hard stone floor. As the man hurtled toward the floor, the second giant thrust his knee upwards through the bars and caught the man under the chin. The guard's head snapped back, seeming to go back farther than a neck would allow. He crashed face-first into the floor, skidding along until there was a loud bang as his skull made contact with the metal bars of the cell, stopping his forward progress. Lying motionless on the floor, the giant brought the heel of his foot down hard on the back of the guard's neck. The man's feet jerked up behind him as a stomach-turning crunch sounded from beneath the giant's foot.

Bang. Bang.

Two loud reports echoed in the narrow prison corridor as Clodword, who had somehow managed to stay on his feet, slid a small two-shot Derringer pistol from his vest and fired toward the prison door. Alice saw two guards with muskets topple down the stairs as they emerged through the smoke shrouding the prison door, but a half-dozen more guards rushed through the smoke and took up firing positions. Three guards knelt and aimed their muskets toward them while three others stood on the stairs above them and did the same.

The two giants receded into the darkness of their cell, getting clear of the barrage of musket balls that would cut down Alice and Clodword. The gunshots had already renewed the shouts and cries of the prisoners to a fever pitch.

"Alice, get behind me," Clodword glanced over his shoulder at her and shouted above the uproar of the prisoners as he spread his arms wide to shield her to the greatest degree possible. It was almost impossible to hear him over the din surrounding them, and she spied the Cheshire sisters, their yellow eyes wide and fearful, crouched low against the ground.

"Everybody stay your hands," a man's voice called through the smoke atop the stairs. "I will shoot the first person to put his finger near the trigger."

Alice's eye narrowed and she felt herself unconsciously bare her teeth in a primal growl as the man slowly walked down the stairs. Before her, Clodword's shoulders visibly sagged; whether in relief or defeat, Alice could not tell.

The man dressed like an outlaw, the kind Alice had seen in the penny dreadfuls in England depicting the Wild West in America. He wore black cotton trousers tucked into leather riding boots with a gray shirt visible beneath a long black rifle coat. There was a repeating rifle strapped to his back, the lever action kind that cowboys used, and around his waist he wore a black leather holster belt with a pistol on each hip, though the right holster was empty; the six-shooter revolver was in his left hand, the long barrel pointed directly at the head of the small blonde girl by his side—Ava. The young girl blinked the smoke from her eyes and looked from the bodies crumpled at the bottom of the stairs to Alice, her expression a mix of fear and desperation.

He stared at Alice, his dark eyes peering at her from beneath the brim of a black Western-style gambler's hat that looked more appropriate for a riverboat gambling house than a Wonderland prison. Dark stubble along his cheeks and chin gave Alice the impression that he had not shaved in a day or two.

"How about we all just relax so these fine gentlemen don't have to fill you both full of musket balls and I don't have to splatter this young lady's brains all over the walls, eh?" The cowboy flashed a roguish smirk. "What do you say, Alice? Can we all calm down?"

Clodword stepped aside and turned to give Alice a questioning look.

"Hatter." Alice breathed the word like a curse.

CHAPTER 3: HATTER

"There, now we're all friends again." Hatter smiled as two guards locked manacles and chains around Alice's wrists and ankles, glancing around at the bodies littering the cell and corridor. "Though I have to say, you're losing you're touch; six dead and only three are your handiwork."

Alice looked down at the chain connecting her manacled ankles then hefted the one connecting her wrists as she glared at Hatter and gave him a sardonic smile. "Friends huh? How about I give you a friendly hug around the neck."

Ignoring Alice's comment, Hatter rolled over one of the guards with the toe of his boot. The man's death mask was one of pure shock with his eyes opened wide and his mouth agape. Hatter knelt to inspect the bloody hole in the guard's tunic, a perfectly placed shot that would have ruptured the man's heart. "Well, Clockwork, I guess we can tell your father the new Derringer prototype works according to specification."

"I assure you Sir, it was a complete necessity." Clodword shifted his feet uncomfortably.

"I am sure the Red Queen has more guards where this one came from." Hatter stood up, the roguish smile returning to his face. "She couldn't have turned them all into rabbits after all."

"Pity you had to settle for being turned into a rat, Hatter; long ears and a bushy tail would have suited you," quipped Alice.

"Ah, ever the quick wit aren't you, Alice." The smile slipped from Hatter's face as he caught sight of the Cheshire sisters pacing in their cage. He watched them for a moment and Alice thought his eyes looked contemplative, maybe even a little sad.

Alice narrowed her eyes and studied the subtle movements of his face: the slight downturn at the corners of his mouth, the furrowing of his brow, the deepening of the creases about his eyes . . . *What are you up to, Hatter?* Alice wondered as her eyes roamed his face. His carefree brown eyes were now intense as they tracked the movements of the two black jaguars.

There was a time when she thought he looked dashing, maybe even handsome, and that irked Danavi to no end. Alice, Gryphon, and Hatter had been like Alexander Dumas' three musketeers, though the reference was lost on everyone but Ava. They presented a formidable force for any who threatened the White Queen or her court.

Although Gryphon and Hatter were close and constant companions, and they had faced significant perils side-by-side, Alice never felt romantic feelings toward either and viewed them as brothers; though that did little to staunch Danavi's jealousy of either man or the time Alice spent with them. Alice sighed; those had been simpler, happier times.

The devil-may-care expression, the ever-present façade that Hatter showed the world, snapped back into place as two guards approached with Ava walking quietly between them. The two sisters made eye contact and exchanged faint smiles; a lot had been lost in the time Alice was unconscious, but she still had Ava, and Alice would protect her like a lioness.

"What do we do with this one?" a gruff-voiced guard asked, gesturing toward Ava.

"Leave her here, she'll be no trouble," Hatter responded with an air of indifference.

"Clodword, thank you for saving my sister." Ava smiled and dipped her head in gratitude.

The man returned an awkward, embarrassed smile. "My father wished for me to protect Miss Alice. I would never let him down."

"And Hatter," Ava's eyes grew cold as she turned to the gunslinger, "thank you for not shooting me in the head. It's good to see you're still such a chivalrous bastard."

"Oh, please," Hatter waved a dismissive hand at Ava, "I was never going to shoot you. I just needed Alice here to listen to reason for a moment before she took on the whole of the Red Queen's guard. What did you think you were going to do?"

"I was going to kill everyone in this fucking palace. You . . . especially you . . . your traitorous bitch of a queen . . . and then I was going to slice the wings off Hooka and make him a worm again for what he did to my sister."

"There's that spunk. I missed that! There hasn't been enough spirit around here while you were asleep." Hatter grinned and pointed at Alice. "Technically, I believe Hooka was a caterpillar before, not a worm."

"I want to see the Red Queen," Alice felt her jaw muscles tighten with irritation at Hatter's flippant attitude. He was so much like the Hatter of old; Alice had to keep reminding herself that he had shot her and betrayed the White Queen.

"No, Alice, you don't." The smile slipped from Hatter's face.

"Sure as hell I do." Alice filled her gaze with steely resolve.

"No." Hatter shook his head, his carefree expression replaced by a grim look. "Alice, trust me on this."

"Trust you?" Alice raised one eyebrow. "Trust the man that shot his friend and betrayed his Queen? Trust the man that sent his friends to their death in Neverland while he stood safely on the parapets and waved goodbye? Trust the man who deceived the Cheshire guards so the Red Queen could turn those two girls over there into giant cats?"

"Miss Alice," Clodword beseeched her, a pained look upon his face.

Alice detected a wincing twitch of Hatter's eyes, as if her words caused physical pain before his face hardened and his eyes grew cold.

"You want to see the Queen, Alice." Hatter's words were laced with acid and he nodded. "Ok. I will take you to see the Queen."

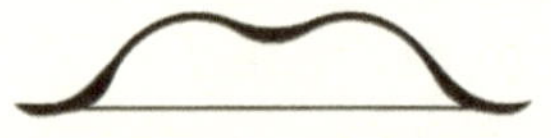

Alice gritted her teeth as the short length of chain connecting her manacled ankles restricted her to a shuffling walk that sent tendrils of pain spidering through her right knee. The pain made droplets of sweat form on her forehead and the awkward gait made her limp more pronounced. She caught Hatter glancing sidelong at her as they walked down the stone hallways of the palace to the Red Queen's court, his eyes trailing down to her bad knee. Behind her she could hear Clodword and Ava talking in hushed conversation as they walked. From the few words she caught between them it sounded as if they were talking about gardening and Alice almost laughed. Her sister could find any topic deeply interesting.

Aside from the numerous guards clad in the Queen's red-trimmed black livery and carrying long muskets, there was little of the hustle and bustle of palace staff and visitors that Alice had remembered. As they passed by an open window Alice stopped and breathed in deeply of the crisp sea air. She watched as guards on each tower held a telescope to their eye and ceaselessly scanned the seaward horizon.

"The Queen is very concerned about an attack by the Dark upon the castle," Hatter said, following her gaze.

"So it seems." Alice turned to look at Hatter. "What is the Dark exactly?"

"I don't know. I don't think anyone does except maybe the Red Queen." Hatter shook his head then stared out the window at the waves rolling across the Great Wide Open. "The abductions began shortly after the Three Kings War concluded and the Red King felt certain it had something to do with the Pan. The attacks have increased significantly since Lairen seized power."

"Like some kind of weapon?"

"No." Hatter shook his head again. "The Dark seems to be sentient, some kind of living smoke. It's capable of crossing the Great Wide Open and taking things back to wherever it came from. So far only children, but I think the Queen fears it will try and take her. And Alice, anything that can make the Red Queen afraid absolutely terrifies me."

"Can it be killed?"

"I honestly don't know. We shot it. Bullets, even cannonballs, pass right through it. We've tried fire, but that had no effect."

Alice looked back to where Clodword and Ava had stopped, huddled in conversation, "I didn't know Gryphon had a brother, did you?"

Hatter glanced over at Clodword and smiled. "No, that was as much a surprise to me as anyone else. He showed up a little while after Gryphon disappeared with the others. Alice, I am sorry about Danavi. I know you two were . . . close."

Alice did not want to discuss Danavi, and certainly not with Hatter, so she quickly redirected the conversation. "Why do you call Clodword, Clockwork?"

The familiar roguish grin returned to Hatter's face. "Because Clodword is a stupid name."

Alice laughed. It was a very Hatter response. It felt good to laugh for the first time since awakening in this nightmarish new reality and, for the briefest moment, things felt like they did before.

"What happened to you, Hatter?"

"What do you mean?" There was something in Hatter's tone that Alice knew meant he understood exactly what she was asking.

"The White Queen didn't die; she was murdered. She was dragged from her bed and slaughtered with less dignity than we show the worst criminals in Wonderland; and you fucking did that! Of all of us, you were the closest to her. Indira would have died before she allowed anyone to do that to you. Yet you forsook her, undoubtedly to save your own skin. I cannot fathom the depth of betrayal she must have felt at your treachery in those final moments. How could you be so heartless, Hatter?" Alice felt the rage within her burning away the feeling of reminiscent friendship she had felt for Hatter moments before.

Hatter sighed as he took off his cowboy hat and leaned his head back against the stone wall. "It's complicated, Alice."

"Well then, try and explain it. You owe me that." His nonchalance only served to fuel her fury.

"You're right, I do." Hatter nodded and ran a hand through his brown hair before turning to look at her. "The Queens are not like us, Alice; you know this. They are something older and more powerful. Their relationship, their alliance, was based upon something ancient. I think the Dark figures into it somehow. But Indira knew that one day either she or Lairen would break that truce. The White Queen erred in thinking that day was far off. The appearance of the Dark and the loss of the Red King unbalanced Lairen far more than anyone realized, and by the time she made her move it was already too late. It was checkmate. The White Queen had lost. I did what I did to save what I could and who I could. Ava's alive because of the choices I made, and so are you."

"You want me to thank you?" Alice felt incredulous that Hatter tried to paint himself as some kind of hero or martyr. "You shot me."

Anger flared in Hatter's eyes. "It was an errant shot and, if it wasn't for that bullet in your leg, you'd be as dead as the White King and everyone else on the bridge. So yes, maybe you should thank me. From where we stood, only Danavi and I saw the catapult shot clear the castle wall. We shouted a warning, but with all the fighting on the bridge, no one heard us. You're only alive because you tumbled off the bridge before it struck."

"An errant shot?"

"That's what I said," Hatter responded as he slipped the hat back onto his head.

"What were you shooting at?"

"It was a fucking battle, Alice. I was shooting at the enemy," Hatter snapped back.

Alice eyes narrowed with suspicion, "A moon-sized rock is about to kill everyone on that godforsaken bridge and, you what . . . decide to put one of the giants out of his misery a few seconds early?"

Hatter sighed. "Look, Danavi spotted one of the giants charging the White King. I tried to take him out on the chance the catapult shot didn't kill you all, and I missed. I hit you."

Alice gave a joyless laugh. “Well isn’t it convenient that Danavi is not here to dispute that. And in all honesty, Hatter, it wouldn’t matter. I know you. I see what you’ve done. You look out for you; you always have. Danavi always warned me not to trust you, that one day you would have to choose between yourself and one of us, and that you would always choose yourself.”

Hatter opened his mouth to speak then closed it. He looked stunned by her words, maybe even a little hurt, and that made Alice feel good.

Fuck him. Traitor. Queen killer.

Alice suddenly became aware that Ava and Clodword were staring at them. Her sister glared balefully at Hatter, however, Clodword’s face was etched with concern.

A procession of three of the Queen’s household servants moved up the corridor toward them flanked by four guards, their heavy-booted feet moving in step in a steady *thud-thud* cadence. The man in front with dark slicked back hair, beady eyes, and sharp angular eyebrows that pushed the brow down in the middle, scowled at them as he approached. He wore the long black sack coat with red trousers and tie that signified he was a butler to the Queen. His thin lips turned up into a sneer as his eyes fell on Alice and the others standing in the way.

“That’s Gaetz, the Red Queen’s Dining Butler. He’s quite the self-important prick,” Hatter said, clearly relieved to have Alice’s focus elsewhere for the moment.

"Well, it takes one to know one," Alice replied without taking her eyes from the oncoming procession. "I remember a Gaetz from the kitchens, a baker if I recall."

"One and the same. He informed on most of the kitchen staff that their sympathies lay with Queen Indira. Those that were not executed were transformed into rabbits. Gaetz went from baker to butler overnight. I think you'll find the present Red Court is full of opportunists."

"Clearly." Alice let the insinuation hang in the air.

"Make way for the Queen's business," Gaetz droned nasally as he gestured for one of the guards to clear a path through.

One of the guards stepped from the procession, leather gauntleted fists clenching as he moved toward Ava.

"That won't be necessary." Clodword spoke as politely as a man turning down a cup of tea as he raised his hand to stay the guard and gently ushered Ava toward the wall.

"Bringing the Queen some fresh baked buns, Gaetz?" Hatter quipped as the procession continued on their way.

Gaetz glanced sidelong at Hatter, a sour look upon his face, "It would be a terrible shame if you had to ruin your pretty hat to make room for some bunny ears, Hatter."

Hatter just smiled and tipped his hat as the man passed. Alice looked past the burly guards to the two women who trailed behind Gaetz: one carried a large gold serving platter with a matching dome-shaped cloche covering it and the other a similarly covered gold soup bowl. As they passed, Alice noticed that both women looked deathly afraid of spilling their precious cargo as they struggled to keep up with Gaetz's brisk pace.

"That's the Queen's breakfast?" Alice looked back at Hatter and he nodded. "And they're taking it to her right now?"

When he nodded a second time in acknowledgment, Alice stepped away from the wall, cursing as her knee protested. The manacles and chains would make it impossible for her catch up to the quick-moving procession but Alice felt certain she could manage to follow close behind.

"Miss Alice, I don't think that's a very good idea," Clodword called to her, concern evident in his voice.

"Its fine, Clockwork, I'll go with her. You stay and wait here with little Miss Sunshine." Hatter adjusted his hat.

"Fuck you, Hatter," Ava shot back, and the gunslinger raised his middle finger in response as he stepped away from the wall.

"You shouldn't speak to her like that." Alice glared at Hatter as he easily caught up to walk beside her.

"Afraid I'll hurt her feelings?"

"No." Alice shot him a withering look. "I'm afraid she'll kill you before I do."

"You two make such a charming little family."

"What would you know about family, Hatter?" Ava's voice shot from behind them, far closer than Alice had expected. "To have a family you have to love something more than yourself."

Hatter turned at the sound of her voice and gave an exasperated roll of his eyes when he saw the girl following close behind them. He turned his ire on Clodword, "Really Clockwork? You couldn't control a nineteen year old girl half your size?"

Clodword shrugged. "She was very insistent."

"Sisters stick together." Ava glared at the gunslinger.

"Apparently so." Hatter sighed and continued walking. "Don't say I didn't warn you."

"Clodword's not coming?" Alice asked as she struggled to keep from tripping over the between her feet.

"No, the Queen does not care for Clodword, and that is not good for his health."

Up ahead of them, two guards dressed in the red and black of the Queen's guard stood on either side of the throne room's black, wooden French doors holding long, bayoneted muskets. The guards reached over and opened the doors to admit Gaetz and the two servants as they approached. One of the guards, a large, red-bearded man with piercing grey eyes and a face that looked permanently etched into a scowl, nodded slightly to Hatter then eyed Alice and Ava with open suspicion. Alice could see his eyes moving from her manacled ankles and wrists to Ava's scarred face.

"Hatter, are these two going to be any trouble?" The guard addressed Hatter and dipped his head toward Alice.

"Just look at them. These two are always fucking trouble, my good man," Hatter quipped, but the man seemed unamused, and the other guard shifted his feet and adjusted the musket in his hands. Alice suspected he was better positioning the musket for a deadly thrust of the long steel bayonet if the situation suddenly warranted.

"We'll be no trouble," Alice reassured the guard. "We have business with the Queen."

The guard glanced sidelong at Hatter, who shrugged. "If you can't trust a woman in chains who can you trust?"

The guard looked to his companion who appeared to give a slight nod of approval.

"Go on in." The guard nodded toward the open doors. "It'll be your head up on a pike, Hatter, with the crows pecking at your eyes if there is any trouble."

Hatter gave the guard his best roguish smile and led the sisters into the Red Queen's throne room. As the doors closed behind them the smile slipped from Hatter's lips and his expression grew grim.

"Alice, I'm serious. Tread lightly here. The Red Queen is dangerous."

"I find your concern for my wellbeing touching, Hatter. Pity such concern did not extend to Queen Indira." Alice glanced sidelong at Hatter before casting her gaze about the Queen's throne room.

The briny scent of an ocean breeze blew in from the Great Wide Open through the six wide arched doors along the throne room's western wall that led onto a stone balcony. The doors were all opened wide and the curtains drawn back to offer an impressive view of the rolling waters of the Great Wide Open that stretched to the horizon. Guards in the full red and black helmet and armor of the Queen's House Guard stood on each side of the open doors and lined the eastern stone wall of the room. Each held a bayonetted musket against their right shoulder with black gloved hands and wore a long scabbarded sword on one hip and a holstered flintlock pistol on the other. The men stood as rigid as statues, though Alice had little doubt they were capable of springing into action at a moment's notice.

Two rows of six thick, black marble pillars rose from a floor of crimson-hued marble slabs to line the way to the Queen's dais. Centered upon the raised dais was an obsidian throne, black as night, carved into the shape of crashing waves that gave the Queen the appearance of emerging from a darkened sea when she sat upon it. A smaller throne, similarly carved, sat on a lower platform to the right of the Queen's throne—the Red King's throne. A single red rose lay upon the obsidian seat, so fresh it looked as if it was just cut, marking the absence of the missing royal. A lower platform to the left of the Queen's throne sat unadorned and empty—the place where the Red Knight would have stood when the Queen was in attendance. Alice felt a lump form in her throat at the sight of the vacant space, the place where Danavi would have stood. She felt her anger rise that no rose marked the absence of the Red Knight.

The procession of servants had stopped beside two cherrywood doors at the rear of the throne room, the entrance to the Red Queen's Tower. Alice knew the doors led to a winding stairway that ascended the tower to the Queen's private chambers. She glimpsed the torchlit corridor beyond as the doors opened and Gaetz led the small procession through, the red doors closing behind them like an unholy womb.

A flicker of movement caught Alice's eye and she spied a large black jaguar sitting atop a cushioned bench along the wall. The powerful looking beast was studying her with intense yellow eyes as its tail flicked off the edge of the bench, the only movement emanating from the stoic cat. Lady Cheshire, Alice presumed; though it seemed possible the Red Queen may have turned others into similar creatures.

"Is that Alice?" a nasally voice droned mockingly.

Alice looked up and felt a wave of repulsion as a creature descended from the high vaulted ceiling of the throne room. It looked like a taxidermist's insane experiment. The creature closely resembled a pot-bellied capuchin monkey covered in black fur, with blonde fur on its neck, throat, chest, shoulders, and upper arms. However, two leathery black wings extended from its back, stretching from the creature's shoulders down to the black nub of a tail. Its hands looked more raccoon-like than primate, with curved black claws, and its pink face appeared like the horrific amalgamation of an old man and a baby, equally plump and wrinkled, with a piggish nose and dark beady eyes. As it descended from the ceiling, it licked its tongue over thick, red lips, allowing Alice a glimpse of a mouthful of narrow, needlelike teeth.

"Hooka," Ava gasped, taking a step back. The creature's eyes lit with excitement at the reaction.

"Hmmm, my artistry seems a bit off." Hooka slowed his descent, flapping his wings to allow him to hover before them as he glanced from Alice to Ava.

Alice bit her lip to suppress a growl at the grotesque creature and wondered if Hooka was close enough to swat from the air and stomp flat against the red marble floor. She almost smiled at the thought of the crunching of his bones beneath her heel as she brought her foot down onto that old man baby face.

"I think I need to add more scars to this one," Hooka pointed a hooked claw at Alice and then at Ava, "and pluck an eye from this one."

Ava stifled a cry and shrank back against the wall. Alice felt her eyeball burn hot with rage as she brought her hands together, balled into fists.

"Fuck off, Hooka, or I'll put a musket ball through one of those bat wings," Hatter warned, his voice laced with menace.

Hooka turned toward Hatter, a mocking retort on his plump lips, and in the creature's moment of distraction Alice lunged forward and swung her hands at the creature. Although Hooka hovered just beyond her reach, the thick metal extended over a foot of slack when she held her hands close together. The heavy link sailed through the air and would have landed a devastating blow to Hooka's monkey skull had the creature not felt the rush of air from the oncoming blow. He squealed in terror, a thin line of urine escaping from between his legs spraying across Hatter's chest as he furiously flapped his leathery wings to dodge the attack.

The chain failed to connect with the flying monstrosity by a hair's breadth and the momentum of the swing threw Alice off balance causing her knee to waiver and buckle. Alice winced as she sank to one knee, refusing to give Hooka the satisfaction of crying out in pain. In her periphery, Alice saw Lady Cheshire's feline eyes watching the exchange with keen interest.

"She tried to kill me," Hooka's voice was high-pitched and panicked. "The Red Queen will hear of this!"

"I said fuck off, Hooka." Hatter grabbed Hooka by the scruff of his neck and flung him toward the ceiling. The creature tumbled through the air before righting himself and hurled a string of curses down at them as he landed on a perch atop one of the black marble pillars. Hatter looked down at his urine-stained duster with disgust. "Isn't this just wonderful."

The doors opened behind them and a young, doe-eyed woman, elegantly attired in a pale blue dress with a bejeweled red butterfly pin in her dark hair strode into the throne room. The woman was staring straight ahead and seemed oblivious to the presence of Alice and the others until she caught the aroma of Hooka's urine on Hatter's coat. Her hand flew up to cover her nose with a startled gasp and she threw Hatter a shocked and distasteful look before nearly tripping over the kneeling Alice. The woman's arms flailed to keep her balance as she teetered on feet apparently unaccustomed to sudden movements. Hatter reached for the woman to steady her; however, she contorted away from his grip in disgust and would have tumbled to the ground had not Alice stood and grabbed her.

"Oh, thank y—" the woman's gratitude died on her lips as she looked into Alice's face.

"It is good to see you well, Duchess Enderton," replied Alice with a tentative smile.

The Duchess glanced down at Alice's manacled hands, her face going impassive. "It is good to see you have been imprisoned for your crimes. Is that wretched smell the stench of the prison upon you?"

Alice opened her mouth to reply and then closed it and sighed.

"I'm afraid that smell is courtesy of Hooka, Duchess," Hatter replied, dipping his head in respect.

"Foul creature." The Duchess' eyes flitted to where the leering Hooka sat perched atop the pillar then back to Hatter, ignoring Alice's presence altogether. "Where is the Queen?"

"I believe she is having her morning meal," Hatter responded with all due politeness.

"Yes, the Queen does like to start her day with her longfish and sanguis, does she not?" The Duchess smiled politely at Hatter and sidestepped Alice as she continued into the throne room.

"Indeed she does, Duchess," Hatter bowed slightly as the Duchess passed.

"Apparently the Duchess still holds a grudge." Alice watched as the woman walked over to where Lady Cheshire lounged on the bench.

"Yes, well, such things happen when you slide a knife between someone's husband's ribs," Hatter quipped.

"She should be thanking Alice," Ava returned from sheltering against the wall. "Duke Enderton was a pig and nearly three times her age. One would think she would be thrilled to not have his big belly rutting atop her every night."

"Well, apparently the Duchess sees it differently," Hatter withdrew a handkerchief from his coat pocket and tried to wipe Hooka's urine from his coat.

"Duke Enderton was a traitor to the White Queen, and he died a traitor's death. Whether the Duchess is happy about that or not is of no consequence to me." Alice glanced at Hatter. The man momentarily stopped dabbing at the wetness on his coat but made no response, though Alice was certain he caught the meaning of her words.

Alice watched as the Duchess appeared very animated in her hushed conversation with Lady Cheshire. From the way those yellow feline eyes tracked over to her, Alice had little doubt as to the topic. To Alice's surprise, Lady Cheshire easily conversed with the Duchess, the lips of her black muzzle clearly forming words as she spoke.

Alice glanced at Hatter, who had disgustedly shoved the handkerchief into his coat pocket, resigned that the garment was ruined. He too, now watched the conversation between Lady Cheshire and the Duchess with great interest. Hatter's face was an unreadable mask, the emotions behind his dark eyes undiscernible. Alice thought she detected a tension in his jaw and around his eyes, though what that could mean was unclear. This man that had been her friend and comrade in arms for the better part of a decade was now completely alien to her.

Alice mulled the Duchess' words. "Longfish and sanguis. What is that?"

"I have seen reference to longfish in the archives. It is some kind of fish that lives in the deep waters of the Great Wide Open. There is some association to the Mother of Sea, the deity sailors and fishermen worship, but the connection is only vaguely alluded to in a few passages. Its meat was a delicacy until it was jointly outlawed by the Queens over a century ago. I have not found any record as to why" Ava replied.

"Yeah, well, it's not outlawed any longer," Hatter said with a hint of sourness. "It is all the Queen eats now, and she has a fleet of black ships dedicated to the catch."

"And sanguis?"

Ava shrugged, unfamiliar with the term; however, Hatter gave a mirthless laugh.

"Sanguis is an old Wonderland word. It probably has not been used since they ceased hunting longfish way back when my great grandfather was a child." Hatter glanced over at the sisters. "It means the fish's blood."

CHAPTER 4: THE RED QUEEN

As the doors from the Red Queen's private tower opened, Alice steeled herself to meet the woman responsible for the White Queen's execution. There had never been any warmth between Alice and Queen Lairen. She had always found the Red Queen to be cold and aloof. Her mother would have said that the Red Queen had a "certain Frenchness about her." It was one of the woman's many polite insults regarding other women. However, Queen Indira chided Alice not to mistake her sister's assured and resolute countenance for indifference. The Red Queen was an acute observer and consummate tactician.

"*My sister sees the world as a constant chess match,*" Alice recalled the White Queen saying. "*She is forever moving pieces on the board in search of victory.*"

Alice felt a heaviness in her heart. If only the White Queen had minded that chessboard as well, maybe her head would not be withering upon a pike on the castle wall. She glanced at Ava; the girl was biting her lip apprehensively, eyes riveted to the opening doors. It was incomprehensible that the Red Queen could so heartlessly murder her own sibling. Though,

Alice had to admit, it was difficult to comprehend that the two women were sisters.

Queen Indira was a lithe woman with dark hair that flowed down about her shoulders and large, kind, brown eyes. She was naturally beautiful with skin as tan as a roasted chestnut and Ava had remarked that she looked like the Egyptian Queen Nefertiti reincarnated. In contrast, the Red Queen was tall, pale, and slim, with angular features that gave her a feral, lupine appearance. Her pale gray eyes were intense without a shred of warmth in her gaze, and she wore her black hair pulled back tight against her head, adding to the harshness of her appearance.

The two ageless Queens reigned amicably together, for centuries by all accounts, with their contrasting personalities serving to complement their rule. Indira's warmth and kindness softened the hard edge of her sister in dealing with the denizens of Wonderland while Lairen's shrewd, tactical mind and decisiveness proved invaluable in times of crisis or strife.

The sisters had seemed to recognize the strength of their sibling counterbalancing a weakness in themselves. They had sought the counsel of the other before rendering decisions. Although the Red Queen maintained primacy over all matters concerning the Great Wide Open and she delivered swift justice to pirates, it was not uncommon for her to openly ask the White Queen's thoughts before passing judgment on an errant fisherman. Likewise, Indira deftly handled land disputes with fairness and understanding but closely consulted with her sister on acts of banditry and other serious offenses.

The Red Queen had disapproved of the White Queen granting Alice and Ava a place in the palace, one of the few open disagreements between the two. However, Indira had remained resolute in her decision and the matter was laid to rest, though relations had remained tense between Alice and Queen Lairen thereafter. Alice presumed her presence was a constant reminder to the Red Queen of Indira's public defiance in the face of her insistence. That did not bode well for this meeting.

Gaetz led the two servants through the doors and lined up along the eastern wall as Hooka glided down from his perch to rest upon the top of one of the open cherrywood doors. He folded his leathery wings against his back and craned his neck to peer through the doorway. By the way the two serving girls held the golden platters and cloches before them, Alice could tell their contents had already been consumed.

"Queen Lairen, the Red Queen of Wonderland, Lady of the Great Wide Open, Protector of the Cursed Isles," Hooka announced in a shrill, high-pitched tone as a shadow filled the doorway.

Immediately, Gaetz and the guards bowed their heads as the Duchess and the serving girls curtsied, placing one leg behind the other and slightly bending their knees as they bowed their heads. Out of the corner of her eye, Alice saw Ava perform a similar curtsy. Alice glanced curiously toward Lady Cheshire, as she could not imagine a jaguar performing a curtsy, and saw the great cat standing on all fours beside the Duchess with her head bowed respectfully.

"Alice," Hatter hissed, glancing sidelong at her as he bowed his head.

Part of Alice's mind screamed for her to stand tall, yell "long live the White Queen," and show the Red Queen she would not bow to a usurper. However, that would most definitely get her head up on that wall alongside Queen Indira, and likely Ava's as well. She did not trust her weakened knee enough to try a curtsy, and Alice had no intention of falling flat on her face in front of the Queen, so she dipped her head. Beside her, Hatter let out a sigh, though whether it was from exasperation or relief Alice could not tell.

Alice turned her body slightly so that with her head bowed she could keep a view of the throne in her periphery. She watched as a figure emerged from the open doorway and was surprised to see the Queen eschewed her normally ornately stitched and bejeweled dresses for a pleated dress of midnight black with a thin, blood red hem along the bottom and around the loose-fitting sleeves. A long black hooded cape, hemmed with the same fine, red stitching sat upon her shoulders and brushed lightly against the floor as she ascended the dais and sat upon the throne. The pale skin of the Queen's face and hands were accentuated by the black obsidian of the throne.

Alice could feel the woman's intense gray eyes glaring at her. As she raised her head, she saw the Duchess tentatively approach the throne to speak then halt as the Queen raised a hand. The Duchess froze mid-step, as if terrified to defy the Queen with even the slightest gesture.

"Hatter." The Queen's voice was laced with menace. "What have you brought me?"

"Your Majesty." Hatter bowed his head. "Alice has awakened."

"Thank you for stating the obvious. Bring her forward, and the little one."

Alice shrugged off Hatter's hand as he reached for her elbow to lead her to the Queen and took a shambling step forward. Hatter sighed, shaking his head, and followed alongside her as Ava slipped in behind them. Alice's chains clinked loudly on the floor with every step, a constant reminder that she was a prisoner. However, she held her chin up, a silent act of defiance before the woman who had killed her Queen.

The Duchess stared tight-lipped as Alice passed, her large, brown eyes unsympathetic to the woman who had killed her husband. Beside her, Lady Cheshire sat studying Alice with her yellow feline eyes. Alice dipped her head almost imperceptibly in greeting toward the woman who, in happier times, she had counted as a friend. The jaguar sat stoically as she passed, but Alice she did see one of the intense yellow eyes wink. Along the side wall, Gaetz began to usher the servants out of the room.

"Stay," the Red Queen commanded Gaetz without taking her eyes from Alice.

Hooka swooped down from his perch above the door, flying so close to Alice's head that she had to duck to avoid his foot talons. The beast cackled with delight at her reaction as he glided to land on a stone outcropping above Gaetz and the servants who stood quietly before the wall. Two black clad guards stepped away from the wall and took up positions on either side of the throne. They held their muskets across their chest in a non-threatening manner, though Alice noticed they had repositioned their hands to easily swing the rifles down to fire upon them or run them through with the long, slender bayonets. Hatter took this as their cue to halt and sucked air between clenched teeth as Alice took an additional step forward before stopping.

"Chains?" The Red Queen raised an eyebrow.

"She caused a bit of a stir down in the prison."

"Of course she did." The Red Queen smiled a tight smile that did not reach her eyes and faded quickly from her face. "Why is she here?"

"She requested an audience with Your Majesty and—" Hatter shifted his feet uncomfortably as the Queen cut him off mid-sentence.

"And you thought, 'why not bring Indira's favorite assassin to see the Queen?'" the Red Queen's pale gray eyes flared with outrage. "Hatter, tell me, is it that you are that much of a fool, or are you just another traitor in my palace?"

The guards on either side of the throne turned their heads in unison to look at the gunslinger. Hatter opened his mouth to speak and then closed it, his shoulders sagging slightly in resignation. Alice wondered if Hatter was picturing what he would look like as a rabbit or whether he was imagining the crows sitting high on the castle wall feasting upon his eyes.

Hatter appeared to steel his resolve and met the Queen's gaze, "Alice is a weapon, and one we may need if there is to be conflict with the Pan."

"And why would this *weapon*," the Red Queen spat the word as if it was distasteful, "not turn against me?"

The two guards' heads turned in unison once again, this time to look at Alice.

"Because I will rescue the Red King. The King and any other survivors held by the Pan," Alice replied, her voice low and dangerous.

"Alice." Hatter shot her an angry glance.

"You know me. You know what I am capable of. Provide me a ship. I will reach the Cursed Isles. I will retrieve the king. There is no one else in Wonderland that can do it but me."

The Red Queen sat back in her throne, her eyes appraising Alice as she tapped bone-white fingers against the obsidian throne. The rolling waves carved into the black obsidian appeared to course and surge around the Queen and Alice could not tell if this was a trick of the light or a manifestation of the Red Queen's powers. Alice met the Queen's gaze, her blue eye locked with the cold, steel gray eyes of the monarch.

"Why would you do this?" the Queen asked, her eyes studying Alice's face for any hint of deception.

"I do this, I return with the Red King, and my sister and I go free."

"Go where?" the Queen gave a mirthless laugh. "The Looking Glass is shattered; you cannot return to your England."

"Where I go and what I do will be no concern of yours," Alice replied, ignoring Hatter's warning glance. "You get the Red King and we get our freedom."

The Queen, her face inscrutable, turned to gaze out over the Great Wide Open. Alice knew that behind those gray eyes a brilliant tactical mind was at work, calculating risks and weighing possibilities. She was envisioning the chessboard before her, assessing the players and the outcome of moves.

"Ava, child, come to me," the Red Queen said without turning her gaze from the ocean.

Ava paled at the Red Queen's words and looked to Alice with wide, terrified eyes. Alice gave her a little smile and reassuring nod that things would be okay. Hesitantly, she stepped from behind Alice and walked slowly toward the throne, the guards' helmeted heads following her approach. As Ava approached the throne, the Red Queen turned to look at the young girl and gestured for her to come closer. A knot of apprehension twisted in Alice's gut, and she looked sidelong at Hatter, his face bearing an expression of similar unease.

"I will grant this request." The Queen nodded to Alice as she placed a hand on Ava's shoulder. "Hatter has a ship at his disposal in the harbor. He will accompany you. I am sure you two have much to discuss on the journey."

"Yes, Your Majesty." Hatter bowed his head, though he could not hide the displeasure in his voice.

"The Duchess will accompany you as my emissary to the Pan. If diplomacy fails, then Alice, you are to do all in your power to return the Red King. Regardless of the means he is returned to me, you and your sister will have your freedom."

Alice nodded, feeling some of the tension in her body ease.

"My Queen," the Duchess approached, wringing her hands nervously. "I could never make such a journey. My health; I have certain dietary requirements."

"Then your cook will accompany you as well," the Queen replied, her tone making it clear there would be no further discussion as she returned her gaze to Alice.

"There are two giants held in the royal prison, I would like to bring them as well." Alice met the Queen's gaze.

"No," replied the Queen.

"If freeing the Red King becomes a matter of force, the giants could prove invaluable," Alice argued.

"Damn it, Alice, quit while you're ahead," Hatter cautioned her in a harsh whisper.

"No." The Queen's cold gray eyes narrowed.

"Very well, My Queen," Hatter interjected. "I will prepare the *Eaglet* for the journey. We will get underway within the fortnight."

"You will set sail tomorrow." The Queen turned to Alice, her hand tightening on Ava's shoulder. "Your sister will remain here with me as my Dining Butler."

"Yes, My Queen. We will set sail on the morn." Hatter bowed his head in acknowledgment, throwing Alice a look of irritation. His clear displeasure brought a fleeting moment of satisfaction.

Ava's bottom lip trembled as she looked at Alice, her face etched with fear and despair. She must have registered the sudden concern on Alice's face, because Ava stiffened her back and appeared to steel herself, pushing down her emotions. Alice knew her sister was thinking of the dangers she would have to face in Cursed Isles and was steeling herself to be strong for Alice despite her own fears. Ava was strong. She had survived the massacre of the White Court and life in the Red Queen's palace, and she would survive this too. Alice knew it. Ava knew it.

"My Queen?" Gaetz stepped forward. "But I am your Dining Butler."

The Queen slowly turned to look at the man, extending her arm in his direction.

"No," Gaetz shook his head. "No, My Queen, please."

Gaetz turned to run, however, before he could take a step the Queen spoke in a language Alice had never heard before. The words were harsh and guttural, and the Queen's voice turned from eloquent to gravelly. The air in the room shimmered with power and Gaetz screamed, a terrified, pain-filled sound. He crumpled to the ground, writhing as he curled into a fetal position, his skin darkening as coarse black hairs ruptured through his skin.

The Duchess gasped, bringing her hand to her mouth to muffle the sound, and Alice looked to where Lady Cheshire sat. The jaguar turned from the twisting form on the ground and caught Alice's gaze before looking away. However, in that moment, Alice read in those yellow eyes the Lady Cheshire's pain of remembering her own transformation from woman into beast. Alice realized the woman would have watched her own daughters go through the agony of such a transformation, an experience that would have left an indelible mark on a mother's heart.

When Alice returned her gaze to Gaetz, the man had shrunken to nearly a fifth of his size with his body transformed into a hairy, black, bulbous shape with four long, spindly legs extending on each side and finger-like spinnerets protruding from the end of his round abdomen.

A loud clang filled the throne room as one of the serving girls dropped her platter upon the marble floor and began screaming hysterically. Hooka swept down from his perch to land on the girl's shoulders, his man-baby face contorted into a maniacal look of pure joy as he raked his clawed hands across her throat. The girl's scream transformed into a hoarse gurgle as she collapsed, her lifeblood pouring forth from her mortally wounded neck in crimson waves as Hooka leaped clear before she crashed to the ground. He gently flapped his wings to hover directly in front of the remaining serving girl, who shook so badly that the platter and dome in her hands faintly clinked. She stood with eyes forward and tears streaming down her cheeks but kept her mouth tightly shut. She must have bit down on her lip so hard to keep from crying out that a slim trickle of blood ran down from the corner of her mouth to her chin. Alice shivered with revulsion as Hooka glided closer to the girl and ran his pink tongue over the bloody streak. The girl muffled the cry that rose in her throat as Hooka stared expectantly into her face, ready to silence her screams if the opportunity arose.

Alice glanced back to Gaetz, whose head had transformed into a shell-like black carapace with two large fangs pointing downwards on either side of his maw. Gaetz had been nearly a head taller than Alice when he passed her in the hallway; now his spider body was barely more than a foot in circumference. He righted his body onto its eight spiky legs and glanced about with two rows of four glistening black, pearly eyes then skittered up one of the pillars and across the ceiling, halting above the Queen's throne like a blackened stain upon the red marble tiles.

A rending sound drew Alice's attention back to where the serving girl lay. She watched with revulsion as Hooka sat on her shoulders, his teeth sunk deep into the dead girl's face, rocking back and forth as he jerked his head to tear free a strip of flesh from her cheek. The girl's head lifted and thudded against the floor, splashing in the pool of red blood, as each attempt separated more meat from her face with a sickening tearing sound.

"Oh, come now, is that really necessary?" Hatter looked at the creature with unfettered disgust, but Hooka just smiled back at him, showing a mouth full of jagged teeth stained red with blood as he noisily chewed a chunk of flesh.

Hooka appeared ready to dig into the girl's face for another bite when Lady Cheshire landed alongside him, closing the eight feet between them in a single leap. The jaguar's paws landed deftly on the marble floor without the slightest sound and Alice was certain she could have swallowed Hooka whole before he knew she was there. Lady Cheshire emitted a low rumbling growl and bared her teeth, wicked-looking things thicker than a man's thumb. Hooka squealed in terror and took flight as the jaguar snapped at the air inches from his body, a clear warning that his behavior would not be tolerated by the great cat any longer. Alice saw Lady Cheshire's yellow eyes meet Hatter's, and she held his gaze for several heartbeats as Hatter nodded his head in gratitude. The great cat, her fur coal-black, appraised him for a moment longer, and then returned to stand beside the Duchess without further acknowledgement of the gunslinger.

Hatter, you haven't a friend in the world.

Alice glanced at the gunslinger, who seemed lost in thought.

The Red Queen barked a phrase in that harsh guttural tongue and then a scream, Ava's scream, tore through the throne room. Alice turned, instinctively rushing toward her sister; only Hatter's restraining grip on her arm prevented her from rushing into certain death on the tips of one of the guards' wicked looking bayonets now firmly pointed in her direction. The Red Queen's right arm was outstretched, a length of green vine extending from the inner folds of her sleeve to wrap around Ava's neck. Small, sharp thorns dotted the vine and pierced the soft flesh of the girl's shoulder. Ava fell to her knees, one hand breaking her fall, the other clutching at her wounded shoulder as the vine released its hold on her and retracted into the Queen's sleeve. A trickle of blood ran between her fingers as she crawled down the steps toward Alice.

The Red Queen sat back on her obsidian throne and wiped a droplet of Ava's blood from the hem of her sleeve with one finger, then looked curiously at the blood smearing the digit before laying her hand palm upwards on the throne. Hooka immediately fluttered across the room to land on the arm of the throne and looked expectantly at the Queen, who nodded slightly. He hunched his monkey-like body over and licked her finger clean, his wrinkled cherubim face taking on a look of ecstasy.

Alice pulled her arm free of Hatter's grip and knelt down to hug Ava as her sister collapsed against her chest sobbing. Brushing aside Ava's hair, Alice looked at the puncture wounds on her neck. She could see the clear indentation of where the vine had pressed tight against Ava's skin and a series of puncture wounds ringed her neck like a macabre necklace. The holes pulsed thin streams of blood and the skin around them looked red and swollen. Hatter bent to look at them and shook his head unknowingly at Alice's questioning gaze.

"Alice, it burns," Ava managed between strangled sobs.

"What have you done?" Alice turned to the Queen, fury in her eyes.

The Red Queen smiled, a smug self-satisfied look upon her face. "I have provided myself assurances."

"Assurances? What are you talking about?" Alice held Ava close as the girl rocked in her arms.

"Maybe you'll break our deal. Maybe you'll take your sister and flee. Or perhaps you have thoughts of avenging my sister," the Queen replied. "Or maybe little Ava there gets the idea to poison my food. I have provided myself assurances that those things will not happen."

"I would not have broken our deal."

"Now you most assuredly won't. Hatter, you can take those chains off of her. Alice is no longer a threat to me."

"Tell me what you've done to her." Alice felt hot tears forming in her eyes but refused to cry in front of the Queen.

"The vine is nightshade. Ava is quite the student of botany. I am sure she can tell you a great deal about it, though this species is one of my own creations. The plant has introduced a poison into your sister's body. It is quite lethal I assure you." the Queen's voice was as dispassionate as if she was commenting on the weather. "However, so long as you adhere to our bargain, I will have an antidote administered to her each morning. Though I am afraid it will not be pleasant."

Ava looked up at Alice, blinking back her tears. "What does she mean?"

The Queen rubbed her hands along the curved ends of the throne's arms as if savoring the touch of the cool obsidian. "To counteract the poison, your sister will have to submit each morning to a bite from her predecessor. The spider's toxins will neutralize the poison for a day; without it she will die a very prolonged and agonizing death. If I were to die, so would Gaetz, and so would your sister. Assurances."

"No," Ava shook her head, renewed sobs wracking her body at the thought of submitting to the spider's bite. "No, Alice, no."

Alice's eye was fixed on the ceiling, her blue eye staring into the black orbs of the spider as they glistened with menace.

CHAPTER 5: THE WHITE KNIGHT

Alice saw the alarmed look on Clodword's face as they rushed toward him, Ava cradled in Hatter's arms as they left the throne room.

"What's happened?"

"The fucking Queen poisoned her with some kind of nightshade plant." Alice's voice was a mix of rage and despair.

"She's going to be okay," Hatter interjected as he passed Ava into Clodword's arms. "Clockwork, get her to her room; she needs to rest."

"Yes, Hatter." Clodword nodded then smiled down at Ava as he effortlessly held the girl. She wrapped her arms around his neck and pressed the side of her face against his shoulder. "We'll get you taken care of young miss, don't you worry."

"Thank you, Clodword." Ava sniffled back the last of her tears.

"Alice, give me your hands," Hatter said as he slipped a small key from his pocket. Alice raised her manacled hands, and Hatter twisted the key in the lock, popping the heavy iron cuffs open. He knelt and did the same with the manacles around her ankles then slid the manacles and chains across the floor. The sound of metal scrapping on stone echoed down the corridor ending in a loud clang as they struck the wall. Alice rubbed at her wrists, massaging the tender skin where the heavy iron had begun to chafe.

Alice jumped as the throne room doors swung open again and she chided herself for having such raw nerves. The serving girl, still grasping her serving platter and dome-shaped cloche, walked briskly from the room; lines of tears stained her cheeks. As the door closed behind her, a sob escaped her lips as she broke into a run, the platter and cloche clanging loudly with every step. She ran past without even glancing in their direction.

"That's one lucky girl," Hatter commented as he watched her run by.

"I'm going to get Ava to her bed and let her rest." Clodword's brow creased with concern.

"Ok, Ava can fill you in on what's happened." Hatter nodded.

"I'm going with her." Alice lightly brushed some of the hair from Ava's face.

"No, you're coming with me," replied Hatter.

"The fuck I am." Alice rounded on Hatter, her hand slamming into his chest causing him to stumble back a step.

"Listen, Alice, you just signed a lot of people up for a voyage that no one has ever returned from, and we leave tomorrow. I am sorry about what happened to Ava, I really am. She's a pain in my ass at times but she's a good kid. However, everyone, including your sister, is counting on the success of this mission. If that's going to happen, I need your help and I need it now."

"Alice, he's right. I'll be okay. The thorn cuts barely even hurt anymore. Go with Hatter." Ava reached her hand out and Alice took a hold of it. Alice's eye searched the scarred face of her little sister and saw the strength in her blue eyes. She suspected they would both face unspeakable horrors in the days to come but they had a path to freedom from this nightmare. Everyone had a role to play now, and Alice had to play hers.

"Ok." Alice nodded then looked at Clodword. "You'll take good care of her?"

"The best, Miss Alice." Clodword nodded and smiled. "Once I get her settled, I will see what I can learn about nightshade poisons in the archives."

"Thank you, Clodword."

"Will you come see me before you leave?" Ava asked.

"Of course, I will. I'll come sleep next to you just like I used to on stormy nights," Alice squeezed her hand and smiled.

"Alice used to be very afraid of thunder. I had to be very brave for her," Ava looked up at Clodword with as earnest an expression as she could muster.

"Is that so? I should very much like to hear all about it," Clodword remarked as he turned to carry Ava to her room. Alice watched the pear-shaped outline of Clodword, with the Bowler hat seated slightly askew upon his head and Ava's legs dangling from his cradled arms, recede down the hall until they turned and disappeared from sight. She could still hear the faint sound of Ava's voice speaking to him until that too was gone.

"Afraid of thunder?" Hatter gave Alice a roguish grin as she turned to face him.

Alice sighed, "Hatter, get this straight. We are not partners and we are not friends. Not anymore. Not after what you've done. Nothing will change that. We're in this together because that's what the Red Queen ordered. But no part of my bargain with her concerned you coming back alive. Do you understand?"

Hatter gave a joyless laugh and smiled, "Perfectly."

"Where do we need to go now?"

"We have to see the White Knight and then I need to introduce you to Suarez."

"Who is Suarez?" Alice searched her memory, but the name drew a blank.

"He's the captain of our ship, the *Eaglet*," Hatter smiled, more genuinely this time. "And trust me, he's going to love you."

The White Knight always fancied himself an inventor and Alice had to admit that he had become quite accomplished over the years. When Alice first crossed through the Looking Glass, while Gryphon questioned her incessantly about the English way of war, especially after learning her father was a soldier, Tinker was intensely interested in learning all he could about the machines that were reshaping nineteenth century Europe. He had spent endless hours talking to Alice about locomotives, steam engines, batteries, and motors. With his years of fighting prowess behind him, the White Knight had immersed himself in a world of gears, wires, and pistons. The White Queen had indulged his interests and had seen that he received all the necessary materials to build his inventions.

As Alice watched Tinker now, seated at his workbench, he appeared to be worrying over a large jigsaw puzzle made entirely of black pieces. The man was so intently studying the various shapes and sizes that he paid no attention to Hatter's knuckles rapping on the open wooden door of his work area. With an exasperated roll of his eyes, Hatter gestured for Alice to follow him in.

The room was filled with wooden boxes overflowing with wires, pipes, glass vacuum tubes, and gears of all sizes. The boxes of mechanical parts, adhesives, and lubricants were stacked along the floor and filled several floor to ceiling shelves. The air in the small workspace was saturated with smell of oils that left a metallic taste in Alice's mouth. She glanced in one corner and was saddened to see a small unmade bed with rumpled sheets; the one-time champion of the White Queen now slept in accommodations better suited for the palace stable hands.

As they approached the hunched over form, Alice got a better look at the jigsaw puzzle that so commanded Tinker's attention. The puzzle was bordered by a six foot by three foot wooden frame constructed of three ornately carved and intertwined wooden vines. She knew that because she had once ran her fingers along the polished wood, tracing the path of each vine, with every twist and cut back, to their origin at the bottom of the frame. It was the frame to the Looking Glass, the portal she passed through to enter Wonderland. Its twin resided in her grandfather's study back in England. Ava's information had been correct; the Looking Glass was shattered into hundreds of jagged pieces. The glass had blackened to an opaqueness so dense it appeared to absorb light; not even the gaslight hanging directly above the shards cast so much as a glimmer of a reflection.

"So it is really destroyed." Alice said it more to herself, but Hatter took it as a question.

"Yes, Indira was quite thorough." Hatter nodded as he looked at the remnants of the Looking Glass. He missed the sidelong glance Alice threw him; it rankled her every time he used the White Queen's name.

Tinker turned, startled by the unexpected voices in his workshop. His face was a mix of surprise and elation as his eyes fell on Alice.

"Child you are awake," Tinker stood from his stool, his pale blue eyes searching her face. "And well?"

"I am as well as can be expected," Alice could not help but smile. The White Knight had always been kind and grandfatherly to her and, aside from Ava, was the first person she was genuinely happy to see. He had aged in the past year, his once muscular frame now thinned to the point of gauntness. The few remaining blonde strands that had remained in his unruly hair and flowing mustache had surrendered to match the snow white of their kindred. Beneath bushy, white eyebrows, the skin around his eyes looked tired and wrinkled, but the pale blue orbs themselves looked as sharp and alert as ever.

"Are you trying to repair the Looking Glass?" Alice looked over the hundreds of blackened shards scattered about the table.

"As far as the Red Queen is concerned, it is my highest priority," Tinker tried to look very serious but he could not hide the mischievous twinkle in his eye.

"And is it?"

"If Queen Indira wanted it destroyed, destroyed it will stay," Tinker gave an authoritative nod. "It shall never be repaired; at least not by my hands."

"The Red Queen is not known for her infinite patience, Tinker," Hatter warned.

"No, she is not. Our good Queen has made that abundantly clear."

"What will you do?" Alice's heart swelled with pride at the White Knight's defiance of the Red Queen, though it was filled with fear for his safety.

"I suppose I will have to develop a fondness for carrots," Tinker held two fingers behind his head like rabbit ears and bit at his bottom lip with his front two teeth.

"That's not funny, Tinker. You should come with us. We could use you on this trip," Alice insisted.

"Oh? Where are you going?" Tinker's eyes bounced from Alice to Hatter.

"That's what we're here about, old friend. I need those items I requested. We're making a run for the Cursed Isles," Hatter's voice took on a serious tone.

"They are ready," Tinker folded his arms across his chest and leaned back against his workbench. "I have tested the tracking device and it works. However, I have not discovered what its maximum range is. As for the siren, it will sound, of that I am certain. Though what the Kraken will do when it hears it, I just don't know."

"Do you think it failed the Red King?" Alice asked. "That the Kraken destroyed his ship?"

"I don't know," Tinker shook his head and looked troubled. "I tested the Dodo's siren on local squid and octopus and it repelled them, so in theory it should do the same to the Kraken. I made modifications to the new version that should make the sound more distressing to the Kraken, but I don't know. It's all just theory, you see."

"And my watch?" Hatter asked.

The White Knight bit his lip and nodded, "Yes, that is ready too."

An uneasy silence descended upon the three as Alice looked at the matching grim expressions on the two men's faces. Tinker sighed heavily then walked over to one of the shelves and removed a milk carton-sized wooden box and carried it over to an old oaken wardrobe in the corner where he set it on the floor. They watched as the White Knight stood on his tiptoes and pawed one hand searchingly atop the wardrobe, sending up little plumes of gray dust. Alice glanced questioningly at Hatter and the gunslinger shrugged his shoulders.

"Ahh, there you are," Tinker muttered to himself as he withdrew a small leather packet tied closed with thin rope.

Tinker placed the leather packet on the box and carried them over to his workbench setting them down atop his stool.

"There is nothing like this in all of Wonderland," Tinker ran his hand over the leather packet. "Maybe not anywhere."

Hatter reached for it and the White Knight held it a moment longer, staring at it as if a serpent was about to spring forth from the beneath the leather folds.

"Tinker, my watch please," Hatter stood with his hand outstretched.

"Oh yes, of course," Tinker smiled weakly and placed the packet into Hatter's hand.

The gunslinger tucked the packet into the inside breast pocket of his vest and gestured toward the box. "Is everything else in there?"

"It's all there. Do you need me to explain how it all works?"

"No, I should be able to manage just fine," Hatter replied as he slid the box from the stool. "Alice, say your goodbyes. We still have a ship captain's day to ruin."

"It was good to see you, Alice," Tinker grinned so widely his eyes wrinkled.

"It was good to see you too Tinker. When I get back we need to discuss this secret you've been keeping from me, Tinker," Alice feigned anger and pointed her finger at the White Knight.

"I have?" Tinker looked surprised but his eyes darted to Hatter for the briefest of moments.

"I met Clodword. He saved my life earlier, down in the prison this morning."

"Did he now?" Tinker's face visibly brightened and a smile creased his weathered face.

"Was that only just this morning?" Hatter sounded exasperated. "It feels like you have been awake for so much longer, Alice."

"He's a good man," Alice ignored Hatter's sarcastic quip. "I am sorry you felt the need to hide him from me all of these years."

Again Tinker's eyes darted quickly to Hatter and then back to Alice.

Why does he keep doing that? Alice wondered. *Has Hatter known about the man all along*?

"I am sorry, Alice. Please forgive me," Tinker looked genuinely contrite then his eyes grew wide and excited. "Take him with you. On your trip. Take him with you."

"Tinker, I don't know if that's a good idea," Hatter shook his head.

"Please, Hatter, he can be very useful to you," the White Knight's voice was tinged with desperation.

"Tinker, it's just that this journey is going to be very dangerous and with Gryphon still missing . . ." Alice's voice trailed off when she saw the anguish on the White Knight's face.

"You said it yourself," Tinker beseeched Hatter, "the Red Queen does not have much patience and what little she does have has grown quite thin waiting for me to repair the Looking Glass. When that day comes it will be far better for Clodword to be far away from here."

"Tinker, there is a good chance we may not return," Alice placed her hand on the White Knight's arm.

"Even a slim chance is better than what awaits him here," his pale blue eyes moved from Alice to Hatter. "Please Hatter, do not make an old man beg. Let me keep what little pride is left to me."

"Okay," Hatter relented, nodding slightly. "He can travel with us."

"Thank you, Hatter. Thank you for this."

"After all, what harm is one more fool on a ship of fools?"

CHAPTER 6: THE EAGLET

Alice's knee ached as she followed Hatter through the palace gates and onto the road leading down to the port. Merchant's Way was paved with well-worn granite cobblestones and each step sent a wave of renewed pain through her damaged limb. Hatter, the White Knight's wooden crate tucked under his right arm, kept a brisk pace as the palace quickly receded behind them and Alice suspected the gunslinger was intentionally moving quickly because of her wounded knee. She caught him discreetly glancing down at her limp several times when he thought she was not looking.

Not today, Hatter. You don't get to appear the chivalrous knight and offer to slow down for the sake of the damsel in distress.

"How is your knee feeling?" Hatter asked, infusing his voice with concern.

Right on time, Hatter.

"Like someone put a fucking bullet through it." Alice refused to even glance in his direction.

Alice gritted her teeth against the pain and continued forward as Hatter noticeably slowed his steps. Her knee protested with each stride, the pain exploding like a blacksmith striking an anvil every time her foot made contact with the cobblestones. She began to quickly outpace him and Alice heard Hatter give an exasperated sigh then quickly catch up to her.

"So Hatter, what's with the cowboy hat?" Alice had little interest in conversation with Hatter, however, she would suffer through his self-important prattling if it kept her mind off the pain. "I was rather fond of the old top hat."

"It got lost at Cormoran's castle. Probably flattened by some giant, I suppose," Hatter flicked his finger against the underside of the hat's wide brim. "Danavi brought this one back for me from London. It's rather fitting don't you think?"

"What?" Alice stopped walking and stared at him thunderstruck. The gunslinger stopped alongside her, a roguish smile on his lips. "When was Danavi in London?"

"The Red Queen sent Danavi through the Looking Glass, I don't know, maybe a half-dozen times."

"Why?"

"To bring back information, sometimes blueprints. Tinker made these guns from schematics that Danavi returned with." Hatter gestured to his pistols. "They're just prototypes; the same with Clockwork's Derringer. These are based off of something called a Colt Army Model 1860. The rifle is a Henry Model 1860. Incredible weapons. Tinker has only made a limited supply of ammunition though."

"The Queens sent Danavi to my world for weapons?"

Hatter shook his head, "Only the Red Queen; Indira knew nothing of these trips. As a matter of fact, she was furious when she found out."

"You used these weapons, guns from my world, to overthrow the White Queen?" Alice felt her rage beginning to surge again.

"No, Tinker made these prototypes after that," Hatter grew serious, the muscles of his face tightening. "The Red Queen sent Danavi through the Looking Glass seeking weapons to use against The Dark. Alice, you have to understand, after the giants were defeated, the Queens were preoccupied with whatever Peter was planning out on the Cursed Isles. They were constantly at odds over what to do. After the Red King failed to return, they became desperate. It was the first time I ever saw either of the Queens exhibit anything close to fear. That is when Indira destroyed the Looking Glass. I believe she did it to prevent Peter from capturing it and using it to escape Wonderland."

Alice nodded. Indira always placed the well-being of others first, a quality that made her a compassionate ruler. It tracked that she would destroy the Looking Glass rather than risk it falling into The Pan's hands, to prevent him for using it for whatever malign purpose he had planned. If the Red Queen was using the Looking Glass to seek weapons to stop Peter, she would have been furious that Indira unilaterally decided to destroy it.

"So the Red Queen killed Indira to punish her for destroying the Looking Glass?" Alice asked.

"The Red Queen was furious with her sister, that was abundantly clear," Hatter shook his head, his expression darkening, "but no, Alice. Queen Lairen did not kill the White Queen in a fit of rage. She is too much the tactician to do that."

"If not in anger, why kill her?" Then the realization struck Alice, as jarring as if she was struck by a bolt of electricity. Her eye grew wide and she opened her mouth to speak but could not find the words. The gravity of the implication was too heavy on her heart. Hatter's eyes softened as he looked at her. He understood that the pieces had fallen into place for Alice and he nodded in confirmation.

"After Queen Indira destroyed the Looking Glass, the Red Queen saw her as a wild card, a liability. The White Queen had grown unpredictable in the face of the threat from The Pan. I believe the Red Queen was convinced she needed control of all the pieces on the chessboard to defeat Peter. Total control." Hatter explained.

"But why kill Indira? Why not just imprison her?"

"I don't know, Alice."

"This all seems so pointless. Do we even know if Peter is responsible for The Dark? For that matter, how do we know The Pan still lives? There has been no sighting of him for hundreds of years, over a thousand by some accounts."

"The Queens certainly believed Peter was still alive and if anyone would know about living for a thousand years it would be them, would it not?" Hatter gave a harsh, joyless laugh. "To beings like the Queens and The Pan, we live our short lives and then we die, vanish from existence leaving behind our bodies like so many flies on a window sill. There are always more flies Alice. It's a wonder they even bother to tell us apart."

"Hatter, you were always an asshole but this depressing asshole look is a new one for you."

"My point is this, Alice, things don't change for creatures like them. But when the White Queen died . . ."

"Was killed. When the White Queen was killed," Alice corrected him.

"When the White Queen was killed," Hatter gave her an exasperated look, "everything changed. The world became . . . wrong. The Dark grew stronger and the Red Queen changed. She's still Lairen, but I mean, changing people into animals? And whatever the fuck that was she did to Ava?"

"So you're saying it's up to us flies to save the world?" Alice could not resist a wry smile.

"No, Alice, I am saying it's up to us to save as many flies as we can because no one else will."

They had reached an accord. Alice would carry Tinker's box and Hatter would walk at a pace that no longer resembled a man desperate to reach a bathroom before shitting himself. A quiet had settled between the two as they walked and that suited Alice perfectly.

Talking with Hatter made it too easy to feel like old times. Alice was beginning to have a better understanding of what had transpired during her period of unconsciousness and she would never forgive Hatter for his role in the White Queen's murder.

Alice inhaled deeply as a warm breeze blew in from the Great Wide Open. The sea air always felt restorative to her, imbued with a freshness and energy that she experienced nowhere else. Her eyes scanned the horizon, taking in the endless waves, watching the seagulls swoop down to the cool waters as they filled the air with their clarion cries. Despite the prospect of near insurmountable dangers, Alice felt the thrill of an adventure out across the watery expanse.

The road wound down into the city and Alice's senses were instantly assailed with the sights, sounds, and smells of a marketplace that had likely existed for as long as there was a castle. Merchants hawked sweet meats, produce, crockery, and clothing from tables and booths built from roughhewed timber with thatched rooves. Little had changed since Alice had last walked these streets, despite the seismic changes in the royal palace, and she thought the affairs of Queens likely had no effect on the everyday lives of the denizens of Wonderland.

Then she saw him.

He was a boy of teenage years, dressed in the loose-fitting white linen shirt, red neck handkerchief and dark blue breeches common to Wonderland's sailors except, he was not a boy, he was a rabbit. Light brown fur covered the boy from the tips of his long ears down to his feet. Alice felt certain that, had he not been wearing pants, a fluffy white tail would be evident for all the world to see. His hands were human-like, fur aside, and Alice wondered if his feet were as well or if they were large paws tucked into his black leather boots.

"It takes some getting used to," Hatter looked from the boy to Alice and smiled at her shock.

"Lady Cheshire and her daughters are all feline. He appears so human."

"Well, the Red Queen is pragmatic if nothing else. She made it abundantly clear the punishment for supporting Indira, but she was not about to lose half the workforce in Wonderland. The Queen's Guard rounded up everyone in town and herded them into the palace courtyard. Those who bent the knee and swore allegiance to the Red Queen were fine, but everyone who was still standing wound up like that," Hatter nodded his head toward the rabbit.

"How many people did she do that to?"

"Half the city, maybe a little more. Once word spread, dissenters became few and far between. That lad is actually one of ours."

"One of ours?"

"Part of Captain Suarez's crew on The Eaglet," Hatter called toward the boy and waved. "Casey."

The rabbit turned and a smile crossed his face, revealing two large, square incisor teeth on the top and bottom of his mouth.

"Hatter," Casey exclaimed and trotted over to greet the gunslinger. Alice was relieved the boy did not hop like a bunny.

As Casey approached, his brown eyes trailed over to Alice noticing her for the first time. His ears went rigid, a reaction Alice took for shock or surprise, and then his grin widened.

"You're Alice! You're *the Alice*!" Casey completely bypassed Hatter to stare moon-eyed at Alice.

"Ah, yes. Glad to meet you, Casey," Alice shifted the box to under her left arm and extended her hand in greeting. Casey shook it enthusiastically, his palms warm and furry.

"I know all the stories about you," Casey's eyes were alit with excitement. "How you fought the bandits Hind and Turpin to make the Queens' Road safe, your battles with the giant king, and even that nasty business with the traitor Enderton."

Alice felt herself flush with embarrassment and was at a complete loss for words.

"You're quite the legend around here, Alice, especially among Indira's people," Hatter smiled.

"They make all the sailors wear these red neckerchiefs to show our allegiance to the Red Queen," Casey lowered his voice in a conspiratorial tone. He leaned in close to Alice, glanced around to ensure no one was watching, then flipped his neckerchief over and pointed to a thumbnail sized swatch of white cloth sewn underneath, "but we all still wear the white. Well, all except our first mate Mister Cooper; he still believes the Red Queen will change him back into a man if he behaves."

Alice glanced uncertainly at Hatter who shrugged and patted Casey on the shoulder, "Casey is the lookout on The Eaglet. Of all the ships in the harbor, only Captain Suarez and his crew refused to bend the knee to the Red Queen."

"So they're all . . ." Alice hesitated.

"Yes, ma'am. We're all rabbits. Every one of us," Casey nodded with a look of pride. Alice could see he viewed his rabbit form as a mark of defiance and wondered if that was common among the transformed people of Wonderland.

"The Red Queen is sending us on a ship crewed by men whose loyalty she questions?" Alice asked.

"We're sailing?" Casey looked excitedly from Hatter to Alice. "Alice is sailing with us?"

"We're on our way to see Captain Suarez now. It' s best we discuss these things on The Eaglet," Hatter lowered his voice and touched his index finger to his lips to signal discretion and Casey nodded in understanding. Hatter turned to Alice, "The Eaglet is under my employ. The Red Queen is likely unaware of a matter as trivial as crew composition."

Casey stumbled forward as a swarthy, thick-necked man dressed in similar sailor attire shouldered him roughly in the back. The man turned to a tall, blonde sailor walking beside him and uttered something. Alice could not make out the words but by the tone of his voice and the mocking laughter that followed she knew the man's actions were deliberate.

"Hey!" Alice shouted at the man's back. "You bumped into my friend."

"Alice," Hatter warned under his breath. "We don't have time for this."

The man turned, a bemused look on his face, as Alice handed Tinker's box to Casey who stared at her wide-eyed. Alice could see that the confrontation had caught the attention of several merchants and visitors in the market, including a number of rabbits who watched apprehensively.

"You say something, lassie?" the man glared at her, folding thick, muscular arms across his chest. The blonde sailor, a weak chinned man with nervous blue eyes, stood alongside him grinning wickedly with a mouthful of yellowing teeth.

"I said you banged into my friend. I think you owe him an apology."

"Is that so?" the man looked passed Alice and then spit on the ground. "All I see is a fucking rabbit."

"It's okay, Alice. Grech was just walking by. Let's just go to the ship," Casey nodded toward the port.

"You got girls fighting your battles now, Casey?" the blonde man taunted. Alice's eye narrowed as she glared at the man.

"Good thing my friend here is kind enough to be willing to forgive your insult to keep the peace," Alice sneered at the two men, "but I am not so kind." Alice took a step toward the men, "I am not so forgiving." She took another step closer, "And I am most certainly not so peaceful."

Alice ran through the sequence of events in her mind. She would launch a palm strike up into Grech's nose with her right hand, shattering the cartilage and snapping his head back. As his head came back forward, she would follow through, bending her left arm tightly and rotating her hips and shoulder to forcefully thrust the point of her elbow into his throat. As he crumpled to the ground, she would pivot on her left leg and bring the heel of her right foot down on the side of the blonde man's knee. If her injured knee held up, she would have both men incapacitated on the ground in seconds.

"That boy is a rabbit," Grech jutted his chin toward Casey. "He made his choice. I am a Queen's man. I could skin him, eat him for dinner, and use his fur as a pillow to rest my head on and no one would say shit—because he's a fucking rabbit."

A loud *click* sounded as Hatter stepped between Alice and the men, a black steel pistol in his hand, the hammer cocked back with his thumb as he pointed it at Grech.

"Alice has already killed three of the Queen's men today and, frankly, I don't have the time for her to kill two more," Hatter pointed the pistol directly at Grech's face. "So for the sake of time, if there's killing to be done, how about I just do it quickly and get on with my day?"

Grech chuckled, a malicious rumbling sound, and held his hands up.

"There'll be no trouble from us, Hatter. We'll just be on our way," Grech smiled and winked at Alice as he backed away, the blonde man alongside him.

Hatter turned to Alice and gave her an exasperated shake of his head as he holstered the pistol, "Let's go."

The Eaglet, at no more than sixty feet in length, was easily less than half the size of the other vessels flying the Red Queen's royal standard. It reminded Alice of a small child standing amongst its much older siblings. Unlike the three-masted, square-sailed ships in the Queen's Navy, the Eaglet boasted a single mast.

A rabbit of pure white fur stood atop the rounded roof of the stern cabin, a vantage point that gave him an excellent view of the ship and the surrounding harbor. He wore a long red coat that covered his black trousers to the thigh with decorative metal buttons along both front sides. Long, white ears poked out along the sides of his Tricorne leather hat. The rabbit held his hands clasped behind his back as he glared at the small group boarding the vessel. Even at this distance, Alice could clearly make out a scowl on the rabbit's face.

"She's the fastest ship in the harbor," Casey beamed as he led them up the wooden walkway to the ship.

"She's going to have to be with those pea shooters," Alice glanced at the three cannons lining each side of the main deck, small three or four-pounders, and she doubted they would do much good against a beast like the Kraken.

Hatter followed her gaze and groaned.

"Hatter, where are the nine-pounders you promised me?" the white rabbit barked, clearly annoyed. "A shipment of nine-pound cannonballs arrived, but no guns. Do you expect me to blow them out my ass?"

"That is our esteemed Captain Suarez," Hatter glanced at Alice and grimaced.

"So I gathered," Alice did not try to hide the smile at his discomfort, not even a little.

"Hatter says we're to set sail, Captain," Casey called to Suarez as he stepped onto The Eaglet's main deck.

"Is that so?" Suarez cocked his head. "Is that what Hatter says?"

"We need to talk, Suarez; in private," Hatter replied as he boarded the ship and Casey handed him the box.

"What you need to say you can say in front of my crew. We have no secrets on the Eaglet."

Hatter looked around and several rabbits of various hues and colors, all dressed in sailors' attire, stopped their work on the deck to look at him. He ran his tongue over his teeth.

"We sail on the morrow," Hatter met the gaze of each of the rabbits in turn before looking last to Suarez. "We sail for the Cursed Isles."

Murmurs and curses spread through the assembled crew but Captain Suarez just stared, unmoving.

Alice halted before boarding the ship and turned to face Suarez. The white rabbit narrowed his eyes, studying her.

"You coming?" Hatter asked.

"Captain Suarez," Alice called, ignoring Hatter, "requesting permission to come aboard."

Suarez studied her for a moment longer then slowly nodded his head, "Permission granted."

As Alice stepped onto the wooden deck of the Eaglet, she caught sight of the approving gazes of several of the sailors. She was not sure where she had heard that it was proper etiquette to request permission before boarding a ship, but her decision to do so clearly had been the right one.

Beneath their new leporine exteriors, Alice could see these were experienced seamen—sailors used to the harsh realities of life at sea. Her grandfather would have called them 'salty' and their respect would be hard won. The Eaglet was their home and Alice had treated it with due deference. They were about to sail into great peril and this crew would be asked to risk their lives alongside her. It was a good start.

She spotted Casey watching her and nodded to him, causing a wide grin to spread across his face that showed all four of his incisors. He stood clustered among a group of sailors and Alice was certain word would spread through the crew of her confrontation in the marketplace, adding to her reputation. That had not been her intention but *Alice does Alice things*. She remembered when Hatter first said that, shaking his head as he listened to Gryphon's story of Alice charging into a band of brigands on the Queens' Road.

"Mister Cooper, Mister Jakers, please join us in my cabin," Captain Suarez called to a black rabbit and a tan rabbit with a black muzzle, both similarly attired to the Captain in officers' uniforms.

"Aye, Captain," Jakers, his black woolen watch cap pulled low over his ears, nodded.

Suarez's gaze fell upon Hatter, his expression none too pleased, "Hatter is going to enlighten us with our sailing orders."

Mister Jakers lit several oil lanterns, basking the room in a warm glow, then folded his arms and leaned against the wall. The corners of his mouth turned down in what Alice supposed passed for a scowl on a rabbit.

The Captain's cabin was smaller than Alice had expected, not much larger than the cell she had inhabited in the Queen's dungeon. The room was dominated by a large wooden table in the center with a small pyramid of a half-dozen rolled maps stacked on one end alongside four palm-sized, square stones. Several brass instruments were scattered across the table, of which Alice only recognized a compass, a circular astrolabe, and a pie-shaped instrument she believed was a sextant. The other instruments looked likely to be torture devices or children's toys as they were to be navigation aids.

A small bed, fastidiously made, sat against one wall with a locked wooden chest at the foot. Aside from a wardrobe and a narrow bookcase filled with volumes of maritime histories and nautical surveys, Captain Suarez displayed no personal effects or mementos from his travels.

"I am Captain Esteban Suarez." The white rabbit pointed to the black rabbit, unrolling one of the maps, placing one of the square stones on each corner to hold it in place, "This is Mister Cooper, my First Mate and second-in-command. The other officer is Mister Jakers, the Eaglet's Chief Navigator and helmsman."

Mister Cooper made a slight bow of acknowledgement while the helmsman nodded curtly to Alice.

"It is a pleasure to meet you, Captain. I am—" Alice began.

"I know who you are," Suarez held up a hand, cutting her off. "Hatter, what is this nonsense about sailing tomorrow?"

"The Queen's orders. We're to sail at once for the Cursed Isles to retrieve the Red King," Hatter placed the wooden crate on the table. "I have everything we requested from the White Knight."

"Does it work?" Suarez eyed the crate as intently as if he could see through its wooden sides.

"He's tested the tracker and believes it will work as long as the distance is not too great. The siren," Hatter shrugged, "it's anybody's guess if that will work. How prepared is the ship to sail?"

"The men are ready but we'll need enough supplies to last one month, maybe two." Suarez placed his hands on the table studying the nautical chart before him. "If we overshoot the Cursed Isles or get blown off course, I want to have enough food on hand to sustain us for several weeks at sea."

"I can arrange that," Hatter nodded.

"Like you arranged for the nine-pounders?" Suarez's dark eyes glared up at Hatter.

"There's nothing to be done about that now. We'll just have to sail with the three-pounders."

As Alice listened to the exchange, a dawning realization came over her. Despite no known vessel ever reaching the Cursed Isles and returning, Captain Suarez did not appear surprised at their intended destination. "Were you already planning an expedition to the Cursed Isles?"

"We've been planning this since The Dodo failed to return," admitted Hatter. "Your outburst in court this morning, accelerated our time table a bit."

"So you've been planning to rescue the Red King all along?"

"Of course. The Red King is our sovereign," Cooper replied.

"Fuck the Red King," Jakers growled. "The Dodo is our sister ship. The captain and crew were our shipmates once, even if they did bend the knee to the Red Queen. They may not matter to *Her Majesty*," Jakers spoke the last words as if they were a curse, "but they matter to us and we'll not leave them to their fate. If they survived the Kraken and reached the Cursed Isles, we'll bring them home."

"And we put a stop to The Dark," Suarez shot Hatter a baleful gaze. "That is the deal Hatter, is it not? We get you to the Cursed Isles and you destroy that fucking thing."

"That is the deal," Hatter nodded.

"And how do you intend to do that?" asked Jakers, not bothering to hide the skepticism in his voice.

"Your job is to get us to the Cursed Islands, mine is to destroy The Dark. I'll leave the sailing to you and you leave the killing to us," Hatter shot back, uncharacteristically shedding his devil-may-care nonchalance.

"You keep saying 'us'. Who else is coming on this little journey of ours?" Suarez eyed Hatter and Alice, suspecting more unpleasant news to come.

"Aside from Alice and myself, Clockwork and the Duchess will be coming with us. And her cook... I think," Hatter replied, his cool demeanor restored.

"A Duchess," Suarez rubbed a thumb in a circular motion in the space between his eyes, attempting to ward off a headache. "Where am I supposed to put a Duchess on the Eaglet?"

"She's bringing her own cook?" Jakers snorted, "Is our food not good enough for her?"

"She has certain . . . dietary concerns," Hatter fumbled, trying to find the right words.

"Dietary concerns?" Cooper shot Hatter a quizzical look.

"Most food makes her shit herself," Alice added with a wink.

Jakers barked a harsh laugh and Suarez's mouth opened slightly in surprise before giving way to a smile, "Oh, I like her Hatter. She's not a prissy little shit like you."

Alice smiled and gave him a nod of acknowledgement, "Captain, you don't know how right you are."

"I have one question," Cooper walked over to the table and looked down at the map then glanced at Alice and Hatter. "How do we know the Dodo found these unfindable Cursed Islands and passed this unpassable Kraken guardian?"

"Because of the pigeon," replied Hatter, the corners of his mouth twitching into what Alice thought looked like an uncomfortable smile.

The unflappable Hatter is certainly looking very flapped these days.

"Come again?" Jakers looked confused. "Did you just say a pigeon?"

"That's right," Hatter nodded, "If the Dodo reached the Pan's island, the crew was to release a carrier pigeon to get word back to the palace."

"And *that* pigeon came back?" Cooper looked skeptical.

"Cooper means, are you sure it's the right pigeon? After all, there are a thousand of the flying shitboxes in the port alone," Jakers interjected pointing skyward.

"It bore a note saying 'we have reached the island.'"

"Captain, I want to bring our mates home as much as anyone," Jakers looked to Suarez, "but if legends are true, there are over a hundred islands in the Cursed Islands. How do we find the right one? And we're going to take on the Kraken with three-pound guns? They say that octopus is large enough to break a ship in two."

"Mister Jakers, that box there holds the key," Suarez nodded to Tinker's crate sitting on the edge of the table. "The tracking device should get us to the island and, Mother be watching, the siren in there will scare off the Kraken long enough to let us pass."

Jakers looked from the Captain to Alice and Hatter then, with a sigh and a resigned sagging of his shoulders, he nodded and fell silent.

"Now speaking of dietary concerns," Suarez straightened up and rolled his shoulder, "it is time for the crew to take our midday meal. Would you two like to join us in the ship's galley?"

"Sorry," Hatter waved dismissively, "I'm really more of a meat and potatoes kind of guy. Besides, we need to arrange those supplies for tomorrow morning."

"Hatter, I think you can manage without me. I would like to take the Captain up on his offer and dine with our new crew."

Captain Suarez and the two officers looked both surprised and pleased that she would be joining them. Hatter gave her a bemused smile, "Sure. Fill your belly with lettuce and carrots and oh, maybe they'll throw in a radish for their special guest."

"I'm sure the meal will be just fine. After all Hatter, like the Captain said, I'm not a prissy little shit like you."

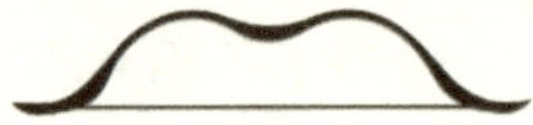

The galley, where the Eaglet's crew took their meals, was a narrow space in the center of the ship with a long table and thirty tightly packed chairs. Captain Suarez sat at the head of the table adorned, as Hatter had predicted, with bowls of fresh greens and vegetables. One of the crew had retrieved a chair for Alice from elsewhere in the ship and Casey eagerly made room for her to sit beside him.

A gray-haired rabbit with small round spectacles on the bridge of his nose, held in place by a leather strap that attached around the back of his head from one arm of the frame to the other, was seated on the other side of Alice and nodded in greeting as she took her seat. He appeared to notice her interest in the spectacles and smiled warmly.

"I had to figure a way to keep them from slipping off my face once my ears traveled northward," he tapped one finger against one of his long ears.

Alice felt her face flush warm with uncharacteristic embarrassment. "I am sorry I did not mean to stare, I guess I never thought how someone's", she fumbled mentally for the right word. ". . . change . . . would effect such everyday things."

"Oh, it's quite alright," he smiled and extended his hand. "My name is Alistair, you must be the new crew member young Casey here has been chattering on about."

"Alistair is the ship's doctor," Casey leaned over to interject.

Alice shook Alistair's hand, the fur was warm and soft but the man's grip otherwise felt very human. She smelled a slight but unmistakable whiff of alcoholic spirits about the man. Not a strong odor like what wafts off a drunkard, but a slight aroma, like when her father used to add a nip of brandy to his tea in the wintertime.

"Oh, well doctor is a bit of an exaggeration. I run the ship's apothecary," Alistair waived off Casey's comment then winked good-naturedly at Alice, "but if you find yourself feeling a bit sea sick during our journey I can fix you right up with a tried and true tincture."

"Thank you, I will remember that."

The bowls were passed clockwise around the table and each crew member took turns piling wilted looking leafy greens, soft carrots and cucumbers, and badly bruised blueberries onto their plate. Alice made a mental note to ensure Hatter was securing the crew fresh vegetables packed well enough to keep for the journey. She filled her plate, as did the others, and was conscious of the eyes of the crew that were watching to see if she would turn her nose at the aged vegetables. One pleasant surprise was that the bread was warm and fresh, likely baked in the ship's kitchen.

The crew, all rabbits, ate their meal in relative silence with the exception of a quiet conversation between Captain Suarez and Jakers at the end of the table. Alice noticed that Cooper ate quietly, largely ignored by the crew. A few of the crew cast glances in her direction, clearly attempting to not be obvious or rude. Beside her, Casey chomped noisily on his wilted vegetables but smiled appreciably every time she glanced in his direction.

"Casey here," a large gray rabbit seated across from Alice pointed toward the younger rabbit with a freshly torn piece of bread, "tells us you killed three of the Queen's men this morning. Is that true?"

"And nearly two more in the market," Casey chimed in.

"Mister Begley, let's not harry our guest," Suarez scowled from the end of the table.

"No, Captain, it's quite alright," Alice smiled at Suarez then turned to the gray rabbit and nodded. "I killed three of the prison guards. I found their accommodations no longer to my liking."

Cooper frowned noticeably but Begley and several of the other crew members chuckled quietly. Then the gray rabbit grew serious, "How is it that you do a thing like that and now you're here sitting with us? Why's your head not on a spike up on the wall?"

"Because she's Alice," Casey threw the older rabbit a dark look.

Alice does Alice things.

"That was when the White Queen was alive and she ain't alive no more." Begley narrowed his eyes as he looked at Alice, "Your head is still on your shoulders and your ears aren't long and thin. Why is that?"

"Mister Begley, that is enough," Suarez's scowl deepened.

"Yes, Captain," the rabbit dipped his gray head to look down at his plate of greens.

"Alice, forgive my Gunner's Mate, he forgets himself," Suarez's expression softened.

"No, Captain, Mister Begley has a right to ask," Alice addressed the Captain, who nodded appreciatively as she spoke and Begley looked up at her surprised. She looked up and down the table, speaking to all the assembled crew, "The Red Queen is holding my younger sister hostage until I return with the Red King. If I fail, she dies. If I return with the Red King, that bitch will probably put my head on the wall anyway. But I have to try, for my sister."

Solemn head nods and murmurs of agreement rippled through the crew. Casey cursed the Red Queen under his breath then met Alice's eye and nodded, "We'll help you get your sister back, Alice."

Begley stared at her, a contrite expression on his face as their eyes locked. The gray rabbit reached up and untied the red neckerchief from around his neck and reached across the table to hand it to Alice, "Every member of the crew on the Eaglet, wears one of these."

"Thank you, Mister Begley," Alice replied as she took the neckerchief. She turned it over in her hands, searching.

"Alice is there something wrong?" Captain Suarez asked.

Finding what she was searching for, Alice smiled and looked up at Begley, "No, Captain, everything is perfect. I was just making sure there was a white cloth sewn into it."

Begley's face broke into a wide grin that showed all four of his incisor teeth. The crew around her whooped and cheered approvingly, some pounding their fists on the table, as Alice tied the neckerchief around her neck.

Cooper unceremoniously tossed his napkin onto his plate and stood so abruptly that the room quickly fell silent. The First Mate's face looked tense and strained as he turned to Suarez.

"Captain, with your permission I would like to take my leave to continue my inspection of the ship's upper rigging."

"Oh, come now Coop, the lads were just having a bit of fun," Jakers cajoled his fellow officer. "Sit back down and finish your meal."

"I see nothing funny about these silly patches the men have sewn into their neckerchiefs," Cooper rounded on the navigator, his eyes flashing with anger. "It is nothing more than a provocation and will bring down the Red Queen's ire on the whole crew."

"I remember when you acted like you were part of this crew," Begley grumbled under his breath, though loud enough for all to hear.

"And I remember when the Master of Guns showed respect to his officers," Cooper snapped back.

Begley looked ready to continue the fiery exchange, but Suarez slapped his hand down hard on the table, immediately silencing the conversation. All eyes turned toward him as he glowered at the warring factions.

"Permission granted, Mister Cooper, continue your inspections and take Casey to assist you. He's the most familiar with the rigging up there."

Casey looked with incredulity from his plate of half-eaten food to the Captain. "But I have not finished eating," he began to protest, then at the sight of the Captain's angry stare put his fork down with resignation, "Yes, Captain."

"And Mister Begley, you can continue with your inspections of the canons," Suarez turned his baleful glare to the Master of Guns.

Apparently knowing than better to argue, Begley nodded and abandoned his own half-eaten plate of food, "Yes, Captain."

As the three sailors left the table, the meal resumed in silence. The only sound in the room was the scraping of silverware against plates and the muffled crunching of vegetables as the sailors chewed their meals. Alice watched Casey as he exited the room behind Cooper and found herself wondering what Casey had looked like before the Red Queen transformed him. Although his fur was chestnut brown, she pictured him as a sandy-haired youth and could picture him as a teenage boy running along the wooden deck of the Eaglet. He seemed close in age to Ava and under other circumstances, Alice thought the two may have become very fond of each other.

She caught Alistair watching her when she turned back to her meal, as the other sailors resumed their mealtime conversations, albeit in quieter tones than before.

"He's a good lad," the doctor inclined his head toward the door.

"Yes, he is," she agreed before skewering a large green lettuce leaf with her fork and slipping it into her mouth.

"I was surprised at how well he's taken to the sea life," added Alistair crunching noisily on a piece of carrot.

"Why's that?"

"Do you not know how Casey came to join us?"

Alice shook her head as she swallowed another mouthful of lettuce.

"Well, he was a farmer's son, probably never even saw the Great Wide Open growing up. He lost his whole family during the first of the giants' incursions into Wonderland at the start of the war."

Alice swallowed hard, Casey was an orphan, just like her and Ava, "How did he wind up here?"

"He made it to city with other refugees. Captain Suarez spotted the boy one afternoon, gaunt and half starved, stealing bread from a merchant's booth in the city market. If that boy didn't have bad luck he'd have no luck at all, you see, the merchant also spotted Casey and was beating the boy severely when Captain Suarez intervened. The way I heard the story, it had cost the Captain tenfold the cost of the loaf, but the merchant finally agreed to release the boy to him. Suarez made

Casey an offer, join the Eaglet's crew and work to repay him or take his chances on the streets."

"That doesn't seem like much of a choice."

"No, it's not," Alistair shook his head, "Casey knew it too, it took him no time to agree and though he had never been on a ship, quickly took to the life of a sailor. He's a quick learner and hard worker, which earned him the respect of the crew. The boy never shirked from a task no matter how unpleasant or arduous. The Mother might not have given him much luck in life, but she gifted him with keen eyes and a total fearlessness when it comes to heights, a trait I admittedly do not share. He earned a spot as one of the ship's two lookouts, seated high upon the mast, you wouldn't catch me up there, not even if the Mother rose up out of the ocean and commanded it."

"Alice, don't let our good doctor regale you with his feats of medical prowess, he spends half his day sleeping and the other half pretending to be awake." Jakers jabbed from down the table, eliciting chuckles from Alistair and the other sailors at the table.

"My good navigator, if you could steer this ship without so much rocking and swaying, I would not need to imbibe such a volume of medicinal tonic for my sea sickness!" Alistair joked back with mock indignation to an even louder chorus of chuckles among the sailors.

"Bah, who gets seasick when they are anchored in port?" Jakers shot back with a mouthful of half-chewed greens.

"Mother save me, it *is* the worst affliction of seasickness I have seen!" Alistair responded with a sly grin, placing both hands over his heart.

"You shouldn't say the Mother's name in vain, Mister Alistair" one of the younger sailors, Rhys, a chocolate-brown rabbit with large expressive eyes piped up from down the table to a round of groans at the killjoy. The boys head swiveled back and forth as he looked for support from his fellow seamen. "What? He shouldn't."

"Shut your blowhole, Rhys!" One of the sailors teased.

Someone tossed an exceptionally large and soggy piece of lettuce that thwacked the young sailor on the side of the head with a loud thwack. He quickly wiped it away as the sailors laughed uproariously, the men on either side of him giving him good-natured jostles and pokes until he was grinning and laughing with the rest of them.

Alice laughed too, a good warm feeling. The feeling of camaraderie was something she missed to her core. How many meals had she spent with Danavi, Gryphon, and Hatter laughing and joking just like this?

Hatter would have been hit with a lettuce leaf. Definitely, Hatter. The bittersweet thought made her smile.

His story finished and his defense laid, Alistair returned to his meal, as Alice scanned the faces of the sailors at the table. Many of them likely had similar stories of hardship and deprivation, compounded only by the Red Queen's punishment for their loyalty to a dead queen. These were good people, tough and loyal, worthy companions for the trials that undoubtedly lay before them.

Alice's hand drifted up to the neckerchief at her throat, her fingers brushing over the thick fabric until they found the white square sewn into the underside. It was a symbol of defiance and unswerving loyalty to the White Queen. Her thumb traced the outline of the square and then she froze as she caught sight of Suarez's hard gaze upon her. She met his gaze, and she read the unspoken message in the Captain's eyes.

This was his ship and these were his men. Their lives mattered to him, Alice suspected more than his own. There was also a warning in his eyes. They were sailing into danger, he would not abide these interlopers on his ship throwing away the lives of his men for a fools errand.

Alice nodded slightly to him, a gesture he returned without breaking their gaze. A silent pact had passed between the two, unspoken but understood. Her reputation preceded her, *Alice doing Alice things*, but not here.

His ship. His men. His rules.

CHAPTER 7: REVELATIONS

The sun was beginning to set as Alice finally made her way to Ava's room. She leaned against the wall across from the wooden door and rested her head back against the cool stone. Her afternoon with the crew of the Eaglet was time well spent and Casey was more than eager to provide an in-depth tour of the vessel and a crash course in maritime terminology. Alice was no seaman, not by a far cry, but the young sailor had well-prepared her for the coming journey. Casey wanted to take her up the mast and show her the harbor from his towering vantage point, however, she had declined, knowing that she already pushed her ailing knee too far that afternoon to risk the climb.

Fucking Hatter. Alice cursed the man as she leaned against the wall and rubbed her sore knee.

Alice was thankful Ava's room was located in a section of the castle that saw little traffic from servants or guards. She had stopped several times to rest her knee when the pain grew too great and had no desire for word of her impairment to spread through the castle's rumor mill. It was later in the day than Alice had hoped to return and she chided herself for not coming to check on Ava sooner. How many times had Danavi complained that Alice became overcome with single-minded purpose when a mission lay before her?

Ava had cared for her, fed her, and bathed her while she lay unconscious for a year. Now that Alice was awake and Ava was in need, where was Alice? Not even awake for twenty-four hours and she is off preparing for her next adventure, dining with sailors, and brawling in the marketplace.

Alice does Alice things.

Alice felt ashamed of herself. Ava was poisoned because of her, forced to serve the Red Queen and submit to that hideous spider's bite every day while she sailed for adventure. If Alice failed, the Red Queen would likely have Ava's head up on the wall. And if Alice succeeded, the Red Queen would probably put them both to death anyways.

The door to Ava's room opened halfway, bathing the dim corridor in the soft glow of lantern light, and Clodword awkwardly squeezed his body out the opening. He turned and jumped slightly, startled to see Alice standing there.

"What were you doing in my sister's room?" Alice eyes narrowed with suspicion.

"I brought her some tea from the kitchens," Clodword gently closed the door behind him. "Ava was rather shaken from her first engagement with the Queen. I brought her some green tea to help calm her nerves so she could sleep."

"Isn't that gallant of you, Clodword?" Alice approached him, limping on her sore knee. The guilt she felt at leaving Ava alone all day was quickly being channeled into anger for the one person who had not abandoned her sister.

He cocked his head. Alice could see the kind, pale eyes, so like Tinker's, reading the scorn on her face as his mind tried to discern the source of her displeasure. "Miss Alice?"

"My pretty little sister, half your age, and all alone and in need of comfort, eh?" Alice stepped close to Clodword. "Maybe there is more of Gryphon in you than you let on."

His brows shot up as his soft face registered surprise at the implication of Alice words, "If you're implying—"

Alice cut him off mid-sentence, "I'm not implying, Clodword, I'm warning you. Stay away from my sister."

"No," there was no anger in Clodword's reply, just firm resolve.

"No?" Alice had expected indignation and outrage at her words, at the besmirching of his honor, as she rebuked him for his lascivious intent, but not stubborn refusal.

"No," Clodword repeated as calmly as if he was rejecting an offer of jam on his morning toast. "My father charged me with watching over you and your sister and that is what I am going to do. I love my father, he has sacrificed greatly for me, and I will not let him down. I will not let you or Ava down either. I am no great warrior like Gryphon. We both know that's readily apparent. However, I did not let anything happen to you, or Ava, while you recovered from your injuries. Ava is a good and valued friend, nothing more . . . despite your insinuations."

Alice felt her anger cool replaced by a sudden rush of shame. She averted her eyes from his gaze, "How is she doing?"

"She's resting. Go see," Clodword nodded toward the door.

Alice pushed the door open and peered in. Through the shifting shadows created by the flickering lantern light she could see the still form of Ava curled in her bed, covers pulled up around her shoulders. She lay silent and still—that's how Alice knew she was awake.

Ever since they were children in England, Ava was a restless sleeper. She tossed, turned, shifted her feet, and mumbled in her sleep. The only thing she did not do was lay still and quiet. Of course, Ava did not know that, so every time she feigned sleep, Alice could always tell by how peaceful her sister pretended to appear.

Alice gently closed the door, playing along with the ruse. Ava would have heard them talking in the hall; if she was pretending to sleep, as Alice was certain she was, it was because she did not want to speak to Alice, at least not at the moment, and Alice would respect her wishes.

"I'm sorry, Clodword," Alice flashed a conciliatory smile. "Thank you for taking care of her."

"No apologies necessary, Miss Alice," Clodword gave her a broad, genuine smile. "Would you like to accompany me to the palace library? Ava requested I retrieve certain texts for her and I would like to gather some materials for our journey."

"Ava and her books," Alice shook her head and laughed as she fell in beside Clodword. "I see someone told you that you'll be coming with us."

"Yes, my father," Clodword nodded. "He explained that I would do greater good accompanying you than remaining here. There are still a few trustworthy servants in the palace. I will ensure they provide any assistance your sister requires."

"I appreciate that, Clodword, thank you."

"These rooms are further from the main palace functionaries so they are quieter. And closer to the library. That's why Ava chose to live here." He looked down at her knee and frowned, "Is your leg up for more walking?"

"Right now my knee is at war with my body," she flashed him a quick wink, "and I don't intend to let it win."

He laughed, a hearty, earnest laugh that reminded Alice of her father. She felt a pang of sadness in her heart at his memory but quickly brushed the feeling aside as they walked through the palace corridors.

"Clodword, tell me about your mother,"

"My mother?" Clodword bit his lip as in deep concentration. "I don't really know much about my mother. I had a very unusual beginning, as you can imagine."

"Did you see Tinker often growing up?"

"My earliest memories are of my father," Clodword smiled.

"You two seem very close."

"We are," Clodword nodded and Alice thought he positively beamed whenever he spoke of the White Knight. "He is my best friend. I know that is a strange thing to say about one's father, but it's true.

"I don't think it's strange. I think it's rather nice actually. I was very close with my father," Alice gave him a tight-lipped smile, fighting back the emotions that came with the memories of her father.

"Is he back in England?"

"He was a soldier and died on campaign." The hurt was still very real for Alice, even after all these years. "My mother died giving birth to Ava, so our father raised us when he was not away."

"Oh, I'm sorry," Clodword's brow furrowed and he appeared ready to ask further about her father.

Alice moved to quickly change the conversation. "Were you close with Gryphon? I imagine things may have been rather awkward between you two."

"I have never met Gryphon, though I hold out hope that he still lives and we will rescue him," Clodword replied, stopping before two large wooden doors. "Ah, here we are."

Alice knew that Ava had spent a great deal of her time in the palace's library reading through the great tomes of knowledge on Wonderland's history, science, flora and fauna. However, in the decade since they traversed the Looking Glass into this strange new world, Alice had never set foot in the library. Not once. In fact, she had thought the ornate wooden doors with the intricate carvings of twisting vines and trees had led to an unused banquet hall until this moment.

It was clear, however, that Clodword was well-acquainted with the library. While Alice gaped at the rows of ceiling-high shelves piled with leather-bound volumes and meticulously rolled scrolls and ancient maps, Clodword adeptly navigated the stacks selecting choice books and documents. Alice wandered down the long rows of shelves marveling at the works that must have taken countless scribes lifetimes to write and accumulate.

"Alice, can I ask you a question?" Clodword asked as he piled another book on top of his growing stack.

"If you are going to ask me if my missing eye itches . . . only when I sneeze," she gave him a sly grin as she glanced over the rows of books, incredulous that there were just so many.

Whoever could have so much time to write all of these?

"What made you come through the Looking Glass?"

Alice glanced sidelong at him, caught off guard by the question, "I thought you would have talked to Ava about this."

"Well, she told me that your grandfather kept the Looking Glass locked in an upstairs room of his home and you and Ava were forbidden to go inside."

"Clodword, you may not have noticed yet, but I don't do well when I am told not to do something."

Alice doing Alice things.

He chuckled, "I think all of Wonderland is aware of that."

Alice remembered back to that rainy afternoon in England, her grandfather snoring loudly on the sofa as she slipped the key from its hiding place in the cupboard. He had stashed it at the bottom of a tin of chamomile tea, a drink Alice despised, and placed it on a high shelf. But little escapes the prying eyes of two inquisitive young girls. Alice slipped the key into her pocket and stole upstairs to join Ava before the forbidden door.

They had expected the room to be filled with all kinds of wonders or fragile collectibles, Ava suspected it would be treasures stolen from her grandfather's time in India. Both girls were shocked to find the room completely barren except for a solitary elongated oval cheval mirror. Its dark wooden frame, decorated with foliate carvings following the form of the mirror, sat seated between two tapering uprights, and finished with a pair of intricately carved finials. Its curved bracketed feet, fashioned to resemble lion paws sat sturdily on the wooden floor The girls observed that the mirror was held in place by a smooth, tarnished brass knob on the side of each upright, which allowed it to be adjusted to tilt for a full-body reflection—except this mirror did not reflect the image of the two girls. The mirror contained swirling smoke that writhed and churned like a stormy sea. Alice hesitantly touched it, the surface was cool to the touch and reminded her of pressing her nose to the window pane in winter. There was something else, the mirror felt more gelatinous that solid. She pressed her hand firmly against the glass and it slid easily through, a warm breeze blowing against her fingers on the other side.

"But what made you go through the Looking Glass?" Clodword's question snapped her out of her reverie.

Alice smiled at him, embarrassed to have been so lost in thought, and sighed, "Back in England they said I was a troublesome girl and an unfortunate orphan bereft of parental guidance and left rudderless in the world. A bad influence on my sweet, younger sister," Alice thought in hindsight the last part may not have been far off. "They said I needed a good husband to settle me down and set me straight, but that was *never* going to be me. My grandfather was a good and kind man, but too old to deal with two young girls. I was bored and my future prospects looked bleak, the Looking Glass, whatever was on the other side was going to be an adventure. I could have stepped through the Looking Glass and fell straight off the face of the earth for all I knew, but I was willing to see what happened."

"You are a very interesting woman, Alice," Clodword smiled, a warm, genuine smile. "And I would not place a wager on anyone who tried to settle you down and set you straight."

She laughed, and then a thought crossed her mind, "What did Ava tell you about that day? About following me through the Looking Glass?"

"Ava told me she had read all the books in your grandfather's library, so what was a girl to do except go in search of more to read," He smiled and turned back to his perusal of the shelves of books.

That certainly sounds like Ava.

A door at the opposite end of the library caught Alice's attention. It was an exact match for the one they had entered with the exception of wooden plank that had been nailed across the two doors, sealing them.

"Clodword, where does that lead?" Alice called out, pointing toward the door.

"The library was accessible from both the Red and White Courts. The Red Queen had all access to the White Court sealed," he replied emerging from one of the rows with a stack of books under one arm and two long, rolled scrolls under the other.

"So this leads into the White Queen's wing of the palace?" Alice approached the door, noticing that only six nails held the plank in place, two on each side of the door frame and two directly into the door.

"Yes, that is correct," Clodword nodded as he walked up beside her.

Beyond that door lay the last remnants of her life before waking to this nightmare. The rooms and hallways that she had called home, once teaming with friends and acquaintances before the Red Queen and her minions laid waste to it, turning it into a charnel house. Part of her feared what she would find behind that door, things she would never be able to unsee; but another part had to see, needed to see, She wanted to find the place where Indira was torn from this world. However, more than just the physical place, Alice knew she was yearning to feel any remnant of Indira's presence that remained, embedded in the walls and stones that witnessed her passing. A sudden sob formed in her throat, and Alice had to fight back against the emotions that threatened to overwhelm her. Now was not a time for mourning, it was time for action. There was work that needed to be done.

Alice studied the plank. The door sat receded in the frame causing the wood to bow slightly in the middle where it was nailed to the door. The space was wide enough for Alice to slide her hands partly into the gap to grip the wood with her fingertips. She gave the plank a firm tug. The nails creaked but held firm. Undeterred, she leaned all her weight back on her heels, grunting and pulling until her arms shook to no avail.

In frustration, Alice swung her right leg back to give what she hoped would be a jarring blow to the plank.

"I don't think that's a good idea," Clodword stepped in front of her. "Let's not push that knee too far."

Clodword carefully set his armful of books and scrolls down on the floor then turned to appraise the door. His fingers were quite a bit thicker than Alice's and it took no small effort to squeeze them into the gap far enough for him to sufficiently grip the board. Alice stepped to the side, giving Clodword some room. She eyed his thick, but decidedly unmuscular, arms and the jiggle of his double chin above the collar of his white linen shirt with no small skepticism. Though she supposed the sizeable rump that so defined his pear-shaped body would add some weight into his effort.

He stared down at the plank and clenched his teeth, straining with the effort. To Alice's surprise the plank began to slowly ease backward as the nails surrendered their purchase. Clodword exhaled deeply as he redoubled his effort and the plank groaned as it slid backward. Then all at once, the nails gave way, tearing free of the wooden door and frame and causing Clodword to stumble backward and nearly fall. Alice had to quickly jump back to avoid the plank popping her in the chin as he flailed, attempting to regain his balance. Clodword released the board and it banged loudly against the stone floor of the otherwise silent library.

"I guess that wasn't so secure after all," he smiled and shrugged as he wiped his hands on his trousers.

Alice pulled open the door; the air that seeped from the corridor beyond felt dry and stale, as if they had unsealed an ancient crypt. The library's lantern light cast a subtle glow a few feet into the hallway but beyond looked dark and cavernous. Clodword unhooked a lantern from the wall and handed it to Alice.

"I don't suppose I can persuade you not to venture into there?" he asked with a grim smile.

"I won't be long. Will you be here when I return?"

"I'll be here. There are a few more books I would like to locate. I will place a lantern outside the library door to help you find your way back."

"Thank you, Clodword," Alice extended her hand and he gripped it. His hand shake was firm and his skin felt cool to the touch. "Thank you for everything. I have not been very fair to you and for that, I am sorry."

"Just hurry back. It's unlikely anyone will come to the library this late but we should not push our luck."

Alice nodded to him and then stepped into the darkened hallway. She heard the scurrying of rats fleeing the encroaching light as she walked slowly forward. Light flared behind her as Clodword placed the promised lantern in the hallway and they exchanged a last glance and nod of the head as he closed the door.

Alice's feet tread lightly upon the stone floor, her childhood fears of awakening monsters in the dark momentarily resurfaced. These halls had seen the death of Queen Indira and her loyalists and she wondered if their unavenged spirits roamed these halls despising the living as the ghosts of her nightmares were wont to do.

The White Queen's court was my home and those murdered souls were my friends and comrades. I have nothing to fear within these walls.

Still, the dark felt oppressive.

The hallways closest to the library were unfamiliar to Alice; however, she quickly reached landmarks she recognized. Paintings still hung on the walls, untouched by the marauding soldiers that had slaughtered the men and women of Indira's court.

The attack was controlled. The Red Queen's men did not pillage and destroy like a conquering army. By all accounts, they killed all they found within, then sealed the hallways like a tomb.

A dark stain marred the stone floor, as if someone had upended a bottle of wine and left its contents to dry. Alice knew it was blood, the final stand of one of the White Queen's soldiers or servants. They had removed the body. Streaks indicated the body was dragged and likely placed upon a cart. Dark footprints marked the footfalls of the Red Queen's men. They must have trod through the crimson pool of spent lifeblood as undaunted as if they strode through a puddle of rain. The thought that one of the White Queen's people, perhaps someone Alice had talked or laughed with in happy times, had spent their final breaths in this cold stone corridor, surrounded by foes, hurt her heart.

As Alice moved further into the White Queen's court, approaching the bedrooms, the bloodstains became more numerous, further evidence that the Red Queen's soldiers had come upon them at night when most were turned in for the evening. The White Court slept unaware that death was coming for them all.

Bastards.

The corridor leading to the White Queen's throne room was so darkened with bloodstains that the stone beneath was indiscernible. The walls were awash in dried droplets and streaks of blood, telltale signs of the arterial spray that occurred when sharp steel sliced into the soft skin of the neck and severed the arteries. The last stand of the Queen's guard against the intruders. Alice hoped that more than a little of the bloodshed in this spot belonged to the Red Queen's men. She stepped carefully across the crimson battleground as if traversing a sacred place she was loathe to profane with her boots.

As she pushed open the doors to the throne room, the lantern light charged into the darkened space and glinted off the opalescent throne of the White Queen. Crafted of pure adularia, the thin crystalline layers of the stone created an optical phenomenon when light struck it, giving the stone a unique sheen that reminded Alice of the reflection of the moon on the waters of the Great Wide Open when the seas were calm. As a little girl, Ava was awed by the adularescent effect and believed the White Queen sat upon a throne constructed of frozen moonlight beams. The soft angles of the throne contributed to that image.

Alice exhaled deeply, only then becoming aware that she had been holding her breath. She had feared that the Red Queen's men would have hacked at the throne with their axes and swords, destroying the enduring symbol of the White Queen's power. However, her fears proved unfounded; the throne sat unmarred by the violence that took place before it. The Red Queen's strike into the heart of Queen Indira's domain had been executed surgically, without emotion—without malice or contempt. The White Queen and her loyalists were eliminated and the evidence of their lives sealed away and left untouched. It reminded Alice of Pompei, the moment the city's life ended preserved within the ash of the sudden violent eruption of Mount Vesuvius.

The solitude of the great throne, sitting abandoned by Wonderland as life moved about as normal outside of this tomb, crushed Alice's soul almost as much as if it had been destroyed. She felt the loss of the White Queen so strongly in this place, this room that had once thrummed with Indira's life and grandeur. Alice could bear it no longer and lowered her arm, pulling back the lantern's glow from the glimmering throne. As the light receded, Alice gasped as the soft beams of light illuminated the solitary dark stain upon the marble stone floor.

She staggered forward, tears flowing unbidden down her cheeks, and fell to her knees before the dark hued stain. At first glance, it looked as if some had crudely painted a leafless tree upon the floor in crimson paint—a thick trunk branching out into spindly branches reaching for the sky. Alice reached out a trembling hand, a sob escaping her lips as she touched the cold stone upon which the White Queen's blood had dried.

"I failed you," Alice choked the words out through a throat tight with emotion. "I should have been here. I should have died beside you."

Alone, in this place of death, Alice finally let herself grieve. She crawled to where the White Queen's body had lay and curled into a fetal position, sobs wracking her body. Not since the loss of her father had she felt so torn asunder, as if her heart was wrenched from her body and shredded. Her body felt turned inside out as she rolled onto her back and stared at the shadows dancing on the ceiling.

The stone felt cool against her neck. Alice fought to regain control, wiping the tears from her eye as she let her grief turn to fury. After several deep, heaving breaths, the tightness in her chest subsided.

No, it was good that she was not here when they came for the White Queen. She would have died defending Indira. Alice would have taken a score of the Red Queen's men with her, but it was an undeniable truth that her blood would have stained the floor beside Indira's in the end. However, alive Alice would see the White Queen and her court avenged.

I will cleave the Red Queen's head from her shoulders and cast her black throne into the sea.

Alice slowly stood and walked to stand before the empty throne. Enshrouded in shadows, away from the lantern's light, the throne radiated none of its adularescent luminescence. It looked cold and abandoned, an ancient monolith yearning to be born back into the world.

Alice bowed her head, bent her knee, and knelt before the throne, "You will be avenged."

Alice's room was much as she left it when she left the palace with the White King's army to fight the giants. A smile crept across her face as the lantern light illuminated her bed. There laid across the down mattress and soft sheets, lay her bow and two quivers of arrows, a score of arrows in each. The bow did not have the range of Wonderland's muskets, but it was a far more nimble weapon and Alice could fire three or four arrows in the time it took a soldier to fire his musket and reload. Beside the bow, someone had placed her sword belt with her shortsword in its battered leather sheath.

"Thank you, Ava," Alice whispered as she ran her fingers over the worn leather then belted it around her waist. It felt good to have a weapon on her hip again. Alice felt comforted as she closed her fingers around the leather-bound hilt, like a reunion with an old friend.

She opened the wardrobe beside the bed and retrieved her boots—her campaign boots. Alice loved these boots. They were the ones she wore when she went off to fight or on a mission for the White Queen. It was partly superstition, since she always returned safely when she wore them, and partly that after all these years they fit her like a glove. Alice had had the cobbler re-sole them a half-dozen times over the years, extending their life. She was thankful someone did not toss them away, mistaken for worn out, when they returned her to the palace to tend to her wounds. They had been placed back in her wardrobe with as much loving care as the weapons on her bed.

Alice sat on the bed and kicked off the boots she was wearing and slid on her campaign boots. It felt like the boots were made to be on her feet and she nearly purred with delight as her feet nestled into the familiar leather. In England, she had seen a woman smoking on the train once and never forgot the look of pure ecstasy on the woman's face as she had exhaled the smoke. Alice imagined her own face somewhat resembled the woman's at this moment.

She rummaged through the bottom of the wardrobe and retrieved an old leather backpack, shoving three tunics and two leather trousers into the satchel. Alice grabbed a handful of undergarments from her dresser that she added to the pack and took the knife she kept hidden beneath her mattress and tucked it into her boot. Opening her bedside table drawer, she retrieved a spare eye patch and slid it into her pocket, then her eye caught sight of a glint of silver and her breath caught in her chest. Her eyes filled with tears as she plucked the trinket from the drawer and rolled it in the palm of her hand.

It was just a silver thimble, unremarkable in every way, except for one—Queen Indira had given it to her as a gift. There was no special occasion, no holiday or birthday. The White Queen was sewing by the window, a hobby she claimed calmed her spirit, and Alice had joked that her aim in life was to keep sharp, pointy objects away from her skin. The Queen had laughed and given her the thimble to "keep the sharp, pointy needle away from her skin" if she ever decided to take up the hobby herself. Alice had deposited the thimble in her night table drawer and never given it another thought. Now there would be no more keepsakes from the Queen, no treasured gifts, no afternoons sewing by the window. Alice slipped the thimble into her pocket.

Maybe it will still keep the sharp, pointy objects away.

Alice closed the door to Ava's room and gently placed the stack of leather-bound tomes on a writing table by the window. She had given Clodword a curious look when he handed her the requested volumes of botanical and herbal studies of Wonderland for her sister. He had gathered a series of nautical maps and journals for himself that he was eager to peruse despite the late hour.

The curtains on the room's large window were thrown open, bathing the room in soft light from the waxing gibbous moon. Alice placed the bow, arrows, and other items she retrieved from her room in a sitting chair beside the window then slipped off her clothes and donned a flannel nightgown. Her sister lay just as she had when Alice last looked in on her, curled unmoving beneath the blankets. Ava was a smart girl, accustomed to thinking her way out of difficulties. In hindsight, Alice realized she should not have been surprised at Ava's requested reading selection. The girl was likely trying to find her own cure for the poison running through her veins.

Alice slipped off her eye patch and placed it on the bedside table. She felt self-conscious about the puckered knot of scar tissue that filled her left eye socket but she liked to air it out when she slept and she knew Ava never judged her.

Lifting back the down blankets, Alice got into bed beside her sister. Ava slept on the left side of the bed, leaving the right side for Alice so that she could lay her head on the soft pillow and easily see Ava with her good eye. As Alice pulled the covers up and turned to face her sister, she could see by the moonlight that Ava's eyes were open.

"Hey," Alice slid her hand across the bed and Ava wrapped her slender fingers around it. Alice gave a gentle, reassuring squeeze and she thought she caught the hint of a smile on her sister's face in dim light. "Can't sleep?"

"No," Ava's voice was soft, almost childlike. "Alice, I brought the Queen her dinner tonight. It . . . it . . . was horrible."

"Did she do something to you? Hurt you?" Alice sat up in bed, suddenly awake.

"No, she didn't touch me. She barely acknowledged me. But Alice, what she ate and how she ate . . ." Ava's voice trailed off as the memories rushed back to her.

"What do you mean?"

"I serve her longfish. She requests it for every meal. The kitchen prepares it in thick slices like steak but, Alice it's raw. The Queen tears off chunks of it and swallows it down. She barely chews it. It's like watching them feed the crocodiles in the London Zoo."

Alice was speechless. She just shook her head incredulously.

"Alice, that's not the worst of it," Ava sat up, her eyes wide enough that Alice could see the white surrounding her irises. "The sanguis . . . the blood of the longfish . . . she drinks it chilled. She fucking drinks the fish's blood, Alice. What the fuck is going on?"

"I don't know," Alice brain struggled to comprehend Ava's revelation.

"She does this every day, twice a day. She had a fleet of ships, those bastards with the black sails, outfitted just to hunt longfish out in the Great Wide Open."

"Tomorrow, I'm coming with you. I'll be there beside you when . . . when the antidote is administered," Alice reassured her.

"No," Ava's voice was firm as she shook her head. "When we wake up tomorrow, we'll say our goodbyes, then you'll go to the ship and I'll go to the Queen. We both have jobs to do and we won't be there to hold each other's hand, so let's do it right from the start."

"Ava," Alice felt her heart swell with pride for her sister. "You are the bravest girl I know."

"And you're the craziest one I know. It's time to get Alice doing Alice things."

They both laughed, an easy silence settling between the two sisters as they laid back down on the bed.

"Clodword brought the books you wanted," Alice finally broke the silence.

"Did he find the *Annalen Der Chemie Und Pharmacie*?"

Alice almost laughed at the excitement in her sister's tone. "Uh . . . yes?" Alice shrugged and the two girls laughed again.

"I'm going to miss you," Ava squeezed Alice's hand tightly. "I feel like I just got you back."

"I'm going to miss you, too."

Thud. Thud. Thud.

A fist pounding heavily on the door caused both girls to jump at the unexpected sound. Alice looked to her sister but Ava shook her head, not knowing who could be at the door. She gestured for Ava to get under the bed and hide.

Thud. Thud. Thud.

The knock came again and Alice could hear the murmured voices of two men talking on the other side of the door. Ava slipped quietly off the bed and crawled beneath it as Alice retrieved her knife and shortsword. She approached the door in a low crouch, weapons ready should the men try and force entry into the room.

Thud. Thud. Thud.

"The Red Queen has summoned Alice to the throne room," one of the men called out.

Has she discovered I was in the White Queen's court tonight?

Alice looked to Ava who peered out from beneath the bed, "It's the middle of the night."

"The Red Queen has summoned you. It was not a request," the man replied his voice gruff and harsh. "If you choose not to come voluntarily, then I'll fucking drag you there by your hair. Personally, I prefer we do it the hard way. You killed one of my friends this morning."

If this turned into a fight, Ava would be right in the middle of it and there was no telling how many soldiers the Red Queen had sent to retrieve her. Alice sighed, "I'll get dressed and be out in a minute."

"You'll come as you are. You have wasted enough time already," the man replied.

Alice mouthed "Don't worry, I'll be fine," to Ava and pointed for her to stay hidden. Ava nodded and slid further back into the darkness beneath the bed and out of sight. After tossing the shortsword onto the bed, Alice slid the knife into the left sleeve of her nightgown.

Hidden, but easily accessible. I like it.

She slid back the bolt on the door and opened it to find two guards in the Queen's black and red livery standing in the doorway. The guard who spoke to her, an older large, blonde man with bushy eyebrows, scowled menacingly. A second guard, younger and ginger-haired, stepped back a pace as she opened the door, his green eyes nervous and apprehensive.

"About fucking time," the blonde man growled.

"You're the one standing here talking." Alice nodded down the hall, "Let's not keep Her Majesty waiting. I would hate for her to give you a little bunny tail for all your trouble."

"She's going like that?" The other guard looked from her bare feet to her nightgown.

"That's her business. Let's get moving," the blonde man shot back. Alice smiled inwardly, seeing that her rabbit comment had sapped his bluster.

Alice had briefly contemplated getting dressed, or at least putting on boots; the stone floor of the passageways was cold upon her bare feet. However, showing up in the throne room in only a nightgown appeared more impromptu and made it unlikely the guards would search her for a weapon. Secreted in her sleeve, the cold steel of her knife felt reassuring.

Maybe the Red Queen's reign ends tonight. Even if it meant her death.

Alice doing Alice things.

She caught the younger guard steeling glances at her when he thought Alice was not looking. The cold night air of the palace had a noticeable effect upon her body, a fact her flannel nightgown failed to hide.

Good, let them look at my chest. Distraction is a girl's best friend.

Her knee ached from the day's walking and, to Alice's chagrin, she limped noticeably. The blonde guard glanced down at her limp and smiled wickedly as he increased their pace. She gritted her teeth and kept pace with him, step for step.

Were the Red Queen's soldiers always such sadistic pricks?

Alice contemplated this as she walked. She had fought alongside soldiers of the Red and White Courts and generally thought well of most of them. However, Starkey, Grech, and now this man, seemed to be more than a coincidence. It was as if the Red Queen's overt cruelty normalized brutish behavior, allowing her followers to revel in their worst selves without consequence. This new ugliness, this erosion of the norms of civility and decency, incensed Alice for reasons she could not explain. She wanted to lash out, punish these ignorant brutes.

"Which one?" Alice asked the blonde guard as they approached the throne room.

"Eh?"

"Your friend, was he the older one or the younger one I killed?" Alice glanced sidelong at the man and saw his spine stiffen and his face grow hard.

"His name was Starkey," the guard's voice was cold.

"Ah, the one I split from stem to stern." Alice smiled and nodded as if reliving a fond memory.

The man stopped, warring emotions on his face as his hand moved toward the hilt of his sword. Alice turned to look at him, her body tensing, ready for confrontation. However, the other guard placed a restraining hand on the man's arm and shook his head.

"The Red Queen wants to see her, Sergeant Vance."

The tension seemed to drain from the blonde man's shoulders and he nodded, moving his hand away from the sword. He turned to Alice, a sneer curling his lip, "Another time then."

"Sure," Alice nodded, her eyes flashing with menace. "I'll make sure you tell Starkey you made my acquaintance."

Alice turned on her heels and strode, as much as her sore knee would allow her, toward the throne room doors. To her surprise, the two guards opened the doors as she approached, allowing her to enter unhindered. She stepped into the throne room and slowed as the guards closed the doors behind. The lanterns were extinguished; the moonlight streaming in the windows casting narrow bands of illumination that left the throne room largely in shadow. The room was silent and as far as Alice could see empty.

A voice spoke in a guttural language that Alice did not comprehend; a short, harsh sounding pair of words. Instantly, an orange glow grew from behind the obsidian throne. The light was constant and lacked the flickering nature of the flame of lantern light. Alice could see a robed figure sitting upon the obsidian throne, unmoving, a golden wine goblet at the end of one hand resting upon the throne's armrest.

Alice scanned the room as the glow chased away the shadows.

No guards. Just the Queen and I alone?

She slowly moved toward the throne, the blood rushing through her veins pulsing against the cold steel of the blade secreted in her sleeve. Just a flick of her wrist and it would be in her hand.

And opening the Queen's throat.

As Alice approached the throne she could see the Queen's head, enshrouded within the folds of a black hooded robe, tracking her movements.

"You wanted to see me?"

The Red Queen spoke another word in that alien language and Alice felt an immense pressure upon her jaw. She almost gasped at the sudden sensation but found she could not move her mouth; it was if her jaw was fused shut. Breaths came out her nostrils in short bursts as she struggled to keep a rising panic from taking hold of her. Her mouth was sealed close as completely as if a metal strap was wrapped around her head.

This is the Queen's doing; more of her dark magic.

A mirthless laugh emanated from within the hood as the Queen brought the goblet up to take a drink. Alice inched closer to the throne, letting the Queen believe she was focused on her immovable jaw as she moved her body in position to strike.

"A smart girl like you has a weapon my guards missed," the Red Queen said, her voice not holding a hint of apprehension. The black form of the spider, Gaetz, scurried up the side of the throne to sit upon one armrest. Backlit by the orange glow, his bulbous body and spindly legs cast long, monstrous shadows upon the ceiling. The Queen placed one slender finger upon his back, as if she was about to press a button. "However, know this, if you move your body a hair's breadth closer or so much as twitch a muscle in a way that displeases me, I will destroy this wretched creature and your sister will die with the coming dawn. Do we have an understanding?"

Alice felt her body go slack with defeat and she nodded.

"Good. Very good," the Red Queen took another deep sip of wine, and Alice wondered if perhaps she was drunk, or on her way there. The Queen's words lacked the crispness they had had in the morning, however, if she was intoxicated, she possessed enough of her faculties to keep her finger poised on Gaetz's back.

"It has occurred to me that maybe I treated you unfairly this morning, that I should have been more . . . magnanimous."

The Queen nodded as if pleased with her choice of words. "I am granting your request for the giants to accompany you on your journey. The guards will deliver them to your ship in the morning."

Alice nodded in acknowledgment if not gratitude as the Queen sat stoically on the throne, saying no more. She could feel the Queen's eyes peering out from the darkness of the hood, staring at her. The silence in the room felt oppressive and Alice wondered if that was why the Queen had called her here. Should she turn and leave?

"You must think me a monster," the Red Queen said at last.

Alice just gazed silently into the darkened hood unblinking and the Red Queen gave a joyless laugh, "Of course, you do. You think that I killed Indira with malice and without regret.

The Queen fell silent and still for several interminably long moments, "her loss wounds me more than you will ever understand. Though Indira was not blameless. It was her actions so long ago, old but not forgotten, that brought us to this. If you show kindness in this wretched world, or worse yet, mercy, it will be repaid with sorrow and blood. Mark my words, Alice, there is no greater truth."

Alice's eye narrowed and she stared cold and hard at the Red Queen. *Is she really seeking pity?*

"My sisters and I are ageless in this world. We watch your short lives come and go by the thousands. Everyone we know withers and dies," the Queen took another long sip of her wine. "Indira was my constant. Her loss to me is more profound than you will ever comprehend, but her death was a necessity—the only way to combat what will come."

Sisters?

Gaetz, oblivious to the Queen's finger pressed against his back and ready to administer death, began to pass the ends of his legs through his jaws, grooming himself.

"I have had scores of Red Kings through the ages. Most for mere pleasure; a few for their bureaucratic skills. Their names and faces elude me, blurred by time; like meeting someone in the market and then never again. Men have such short lives. However, Indira loved all her White Kings and she loved all her lovers, men and women. She cared for them when they aged and mourned them all when they died. For her, it was always about love. I thought she was a fool, wasting tears on lives that burn out as quickly as a candle." The Red Queen sighed, exhaling deeply. "It was Indira that urged me to soften my heart when I took Jack Spriggins as Red King, to love this man that so clearly loved and worshipped me. And I did come to love him. What my sister did not tell me, is of the pain, the rage, and madness that consumes you when that love is taken from you."

She is blaming Indira. If Alice could have opened her mouth she would have laughed in the Red Queen's face.

"Bring him back to me, Alice, and I will cure your sister and let you depart this place if you still wish."

Alice nodded curtly, acknowledging their bargain. The Red Queen went to take another drink and, realizing her goblet was empty, set her arm back down on the armrest. The golden goblet clinked as it touched the obsidian, drawing the gaze of Gaetz's eyes.

"Have you ever wondered why I opposed Indira allowing you to stay?"

The question caught Alice by surprise. It was widely known that Indira and Lairen argued over allowing her and Ava to stay in Wonderland, but Alice had never asked why.

"Did you know that we came from your world?" The Red Queen leaned forward to study Alice closely, the pale moonlight touching her pale skin. She laughed at the shock evident on Alice's face, "No, I can see you did not. It is why we do not age here. My sisters, even that insane Pan, do not age here; though Peter is obsessed with the notion that he is aging, making that slow inevitable march toward death—the fool. We fled your world when the followers of the nailed god made it impossible to remain. Witches, druids, cunning women, and all manner of beast now relegated to myth in the Otherworld, all either died, hid in the shadows, or fled to Wonderland. The Looking Glasses were portals created by beings in this world so that they could pass into our world and become ageless—become gods. We followed them back here in the dark days, when all our kind were hunted and slaughtered. Yet when the creatures of this world returned here, they began to age once again and we became ageless."

'Sisters.' She said it again. Were there more Queens?

The Pan fled from my world. Did The Dark too? What other ageless creatures have sought refuge here?

Then something clicked in Alice's mind and the Queen's words rang false. Her eye narrowed with suspicion and to Alice's surprise a cruel smile crossed the Red Queen's face.

"You're a smart girl. I knew you would see it," the Red Queen nodded her head. "If Indira and I did not age because we fled to this world, how is it that you and your sister age here? How is it that you laid unmoving for nearly a year, yet you could wake up and move as if you had laid down for a nap? Why did your muscles not shrivel and atrophy? Now, you see why I objected to your presence. You and Ava continued to age regardless of whether you were there or here. The only explanation is that one of your parents was from our world and one was from Wonderland."

Had Alice had the ability to open her mouth, it would have hung agape. The implication of what the Red Queen was saying was too impossible to contemplate. Yet, the Looking Glass *was* in her grandfather's study. She had seen pictures of her grandfather as a young man and her mother as a young girl . . .

Father.

Her father had no living family; they were wiped out in one of the cholera epidemics that swept through London. He was an orphan, raised in the Foundling Hospital until he was admitted to the Royal Military Academy Sandhurst on the day he turned seventeen years and nine months old. However, even pictures of him from those days were supposedly destroyed in a house fire. Was all of it a lie? Alice's head reeled and she felt as if she could swoon and tumble to the ground.

"I see I have given you much to think about," the Red Queen leaned back in her chair, sinking back into the shadows. "You are a remarkable girl, Alice; of that there is no doubt. However, you are a mystery to me and I do not like mysteries. Retrieve the Red King and we shall part ways forever. You may leave now."

Alice turned and walked for the door. Her mind running through everything it could recall of her father.

Was it all a lie? Did he really perish at the Battle of Isandlwana or was that another fabrication?

"Alice, one more thing," the Red Queen called to her and Alice stopped in her tracks, not turning around. "I will leave you with this. I did not kill Indira. When my men breached her throne room she was already dead. I took her head and placed it upon the wall so all could see that she had undeniably perished; so The Dark could see who truly ruled in Wonderland. But it was Hatter's hand that slew her."

The imagery of the blood-stained stones in the White Queen's throne room and Indira's cruel end came surging back to her in a wave of emotion and tapped a wellspring of grief and guilt. She had to seal her mouth like a steel trap to prevent a cry from escaping her lips. Alice should have been there in the White Queen's final moments. The knowledge that Indira died alone, amongst enemies, filled with fear and betrayal tore Alice's soul and broke her.

Alice pushed through the throne room doors and as she crossed the threshold she heard the Red Queen utter a phrase in that guttural sounding tongue. Her lips parted and a rush of air escaped her mouth as if she had been holding her breath. The force of it staggered her and nearly brought her to her knees. She gasped in a lungful of air and felt hot tears sting her cheeks.

Despite her bad knee threatening to buckle, Alice began to run as the throne room doors closed behind her.

PART II: THE GREAT WIDE OPEN

CHAPTER 8: INTO THE GREAT WIDE OPEN

"I see you have wasted no time in learning the finer points of the ship's arsenal," Hatter strolled across the deck toward them. Then he pointed to her red neckerchief, "And look at that, you're even dressing like a sailor too."

"That's because she's crew," Begley growled. "You're just cargo."

"Thank you for the lesson, Mister Begley," Alice touched the gray rabbit on the shoulder and smiled. He dipped his head in acknowledgement, a hint of a smile upon his face as he turned to check on the crew's preparations for departure.

Alice felt the blood in her veins go cold as she turned to face Hatter. The Red Queen's words echoed through her mind.

Hatter killed the White Queen. Betrayed her. Slaughtered her.

Hatter rubbed a hand across the dark stubble on his chin and cheeks, giving her a lopsided smile, his eyes sparkling mischievously from beneath the brim of his black cowboy hat. He wore two of the Colt Army Model 1860 revolvers Tinker had crafted for him holstered at his hips, just below the hem of his black vest. She could see the wooden stock of the lever-action repeater rifle rising above his right shoulder, secured for easy access in a sleeve he wore slung across his back. When she failed to return his smile, the grin slipped from his lips and he cocked his head to the side studying her, trying to discern her thoughts. Then he shrugged. Turning to face the port, he placed his hands on the ship's wooden railing and stared out at the barrels and crates of supplies being loaded onto the Eaglet.

Take a last look at Wonderland, Hatter. You'll never see it again. I promise you that.

Among the crowd of rabbits and men carrying boxes up the wooden walkway to the ship, Clodword appeared wearing a brown tweed suit and vest with a suitcase in one hand and yard-long rolls of paper in the other. He was trying to navigate the jostling crowd without damaging or crushing the rolls or losing the black bowler hat seated precariously on his head.

"What the hell have you got there, Clockwork?" Hatter yelled to the man as he stepped onto the walkway.

Clodword searched the deck of the ship, his face alighting in a smile when he located them peering down at him.

"They're blank map papers." Clodword lifted the roll in the air, "I plan to chart our trip to the Cursed Isles."

"Of course you do," Hatter replied shaking his head.

Alice could see Hatter glancing sideways at her, gauging her mood.

"How is Ava doing this morning?" he asked as he stared down the pier.

"She's fine," Alice let the chill seep into her words. "Casey, can you show me to my quarters?"

"Of course!" Casey could not hide the broad grin spreading across his face and he quickly grabbed Alice's leather satchel bag and slung it over his shoulder. "I'll take this for you."

"Thank you, Casey," Alice replied as she retrieved her bow and the two quivers of arrows.

"It's just this way, follow me," Casey pointed toward stairs that led down from the quarterdeck to the Eaglet's main deck.

"I do believe you have yourself an admirer," Hatter gave her a sly grin.

"Go fuck yourself, Hatter," Alice shot him a sour look, "and do it with a nice splintery piece of wood."

"Such a lady," Hatter winked at her, unperturbed by her scorn.

She turned and followed after Casey before Hatter could say another word. Clodword, having finally boarded, was heading in her direction and nearly collided with Casey, who kept looking back at her and smiling. Alice was certain that with Clodword's meaty frame, the slight rabbit would have tumbled overboard.

"Hello, Alice," Clodword stopped to dip his head in greeting. Alice was surprised that despite his apparent lack of physical conditioning, Clodword was not out of breath from the walk from the palace. His cheeks were not even a touch rosy. She was certain she had seen him frantically dashing through the crowd to reach the ship.

"I am happy you made it." Alice flicked Clodword's long roll of papers with her finger, "Now someone can mark the spot on the map when I throw Hatter into the ocean."

"Oh," Clodword frowned and looked toward Hatter as Alice passed by.

Alice followed Casey down the stairs, turning left into an alcove toward the rear of the ship.

"That's the helm." Casey pointed to the door at the end of the hall. "The ship's wheel is right above us on the quarter-deck. When Mister Jakers steers the Eaglet, the mechanism in that room moves the rudder and turns the ship."

Alice gestured to a door to the left of the helm, "That's Captain Suarez's cabin. I met with him there yesterday."

"Correct," Casey nodded, visibly pleased that she was familiar with the ship he called home. Then he pointed to the door to the right of the helm, "That's the head."

Alice must have looked confused because Casey laughed, a pleasant sound closely resembling the laugh of a teenage boy, even coming from a rabbit, "It's what we call the privy on a ship."

"Ah," Alice laughed. "Well, that is certainly good to know!"

"That room is for your cowboy friend and his companions," Casey indicated the room directly to their left.

"He's not my friend."

"Good," Casey said it under his breath but Alice still heard it and smiled. He pointed to the room across from Hatter's. "This one is yours."

Casey opened the door and led her inside. The room was dark and he struck a match and lit a lantern that hung beside the door. The flame leaped to life as the lantern's wick caught fire, the light dancing in Casey's dark eyes.

He turned to her, a very serious look on his face, "Fire is a ship's worst enemy at sea. It is important to never leave any flame unattended. If you leave the room to go to the head, take the lantern with you to light your way and hang it on the wall in there. Don't set it down. The seas can get rough, very rough, and the lantern could roll and shatter."

Alice nodded in understanding.

There were two beds, one on each side of the room, and each with its own nightstand and wardrobe. A table and two chairs divided the sides of the room.

"Which bed would you like?" Casey asked.

"I guess that one," Alice indicated one of the beds. "Does it matter?"

"I guess not. I just thought that since you were here first, you might want to pick the bed you liked best," Casey replied, unslinging her satchel from his shoulder and placing it on the bed.

"Here first?"

"Oh," said a soft, feminine voice from the doorway.

Alice turned to see the Duchess standing at the door dressed in a fine light blue dress with a matching parasol. Her dark, doe-like eyes large with surprise at seeing Alice. Behind her Alice could see the black furred face of Mister Cooper and at least two other rabbits.

"Excuse me, Duchess," Cooper said as the Duchess stepped aside to allow him to enter the room. Behind him two rabbits, each holding one end of a large brown trunk and laboring under the weight, huffed and puffed as they struggled to carry it through the narrow doorway. Cooper noticed Alice's pack on the one bed and gestured toward the other, "Set it down over there boys."

The two rabbits grunted and strained as they carried the heavy trunk over and set it down beside the bed. When they stood upright, Alice thought they looked like a tremendous weight had been removed from their shoulders. They stretched their necks and rolled their shoulders before nodding to Mister Cooper as they made to quickly leave the room. However, both sailors stopped in the doorway, then slowly back peddled, their eyes riveted to the hallway beyond as a sleek, black form emerged from the darkness.

The jaguar's paws were nearly silent upon the wooden planks of the floor as it entered. Intense yellow eyes flicked toward the two sailors, "Don't worry boys. The only rabbits I eat walk on four legs."

The two sailors laughed at the gest, though the nervousness in the sound was unmistakable. Cooper remained impassive but Alice noticed his back and shoulders had visibly stiffened at the sudden appearance of the powerful predator. Even the normally unflappable Casey moved to place the table between himself and the jaguar.

"Lady Cheshire," Alice smiled and dipped her head respectfully. "Will you be joining us on the voyage?"

"The Red Queen directed me to accompany the Duchess on her diplomatic mission, much to the chagrin of Hatter when he saw me come aboard," Lady Cheshire flashed her teeth in what Alice took to be a wide smile, though the two sailors took another step back at the sight of the large teeth.

"Well, I am delighted to have you with us," Alice grinned, pleased at the thought of anything that caused Hatter distress.

"Thank you, Alice. Perhaps this journey will give us the opportunity to catch up."

"I would like that very much."

The jaguar's feral eyes softened and her voice lowered in the slightest, "And Alice, I would be grateful for any news of my daughters you could share with me. I was not permitted to visit them."

"Yes, of course, Lady Cheshire," Alice grimaced, her mind snapping to the image of the two jaguars pacing anxiously as Alice filled the dungeon with smoke. "I was only with them a short while, but they seemed to be well cared for."

"Well, that is good," Lady Cheshire responded, clearly disappointed at the paucity of information. However, a smile quickly returned to the jaguar's lips, the faux expression of pleasantness that comes with years of court politics and countless social functions with your rivals and detractors.

Lady Cheshire slowly swung her large feline head studying the room, observing one bed and then the other. The grin slipped from her face and her yellow eyes flashed with anger as she looked toward Cooper, "There are only two beds and three occupants to this room."

"The Eaglet does not have any female crew. This is normally the room I share with Mister Jakers as the two senior officers after Captain Suarez. He had us move to the crew quarters so that the ladies could have separate accommodations during the journey."

Alice was impressed that Cooper met Lady Cheshire's gaze unwaveringly.

"I understand that," Lady Cheshire nodded her feline head, "but there are only two beds, and I see Alice and the Duchess have already claimed those. So where am I to sleep?"

"We were only just informed of your presence on this voyage, Lady Cheshire," Cooper explained.

"Couldn't you just curl up on the floor like a . . ." one of the sailors began, then stopped mid-sentence when his companion elbowed him sharply in the ribs and gave him a stare that Alice easily interpreted as 'shut up.'

"Like a what?" Lady Cheshire took a menacing step toward the sailor, a low growl rumbling deep in her throat. "Curl up on the floor like a cat?"

The sailor looked nervously from Cooper to his companion, who had taken a noticeably step away from him. He opened his mouth to speak, then closed it and glanced desperately from face to face.

"Do you crawl into a rabbit hole to sleep at night?" Lady Cheshire stepped so close to the sailor that Alice could see the brown fur on his arms fluttering from her breath.

"What?" the sailor stammered.

"Do . . . you . . . sleep . . . in . . . a . . . hole?"

"No," the sailor shook his head, "I sleep in a hammock."

"Do you expect me to curl up and sleep on the foot of the Duchess' bed?"

"Oh, I don't think there would be enough room," the Duchess' distress was visible as she stared at the small bed. Alice shook her head. The Duchess was quite beautiful, in a vapid, Victorian sort of way; however, she was also exceedingly daft.

"Lady Cheshire, you can have the bed. I will gladly sleep in the crew quarters," Alice offered. "Mister Cooper, I presume there is enough room for one more?"

"There is room," Cooper nodded, "but I don't think it would be appropriate for you to reside with the crew."

"Relax, Mister Cooper, I'll not be walking around with my tits out," Alice nodded toward her pack. "Casey, please grab my gear and show me to the crew quarters."

"Yes, Alice," Casey responded, quickly moving to grab her things from the bed. He had a faint smile upon his face and there was something in the way that he avoided Alice's gaze that made her think he was picturing her walking around in just such a state of disrobement.

"Thank you, Alice," Lady Cheshire nodded appreciatively and the sailor exhaled a deep breath, relieved to have the jaguar's attention off of him.

Sounds of shouts on the main deck drew their attention. They sounded angry and Alice was certain she heard both Captain Suarez's and Hatter's upraised voice in the mix, though she could not make out the words.

"For Mother's sake, what is it now?" Cooper looked toward the ceiling, as if he could see the fray beyond the wooden planks above. He quickly turned to the Duchess who gasped and dramatically clasped her hands to her chest at his use of such foul language. Alice rolled her eyes at the woman's theatrics. "I'm sorry Duchess, I meant no offense."

"Let's see what trouble has come our way now," Alice headed for the door and all four rabbits followed quickly behind her, eager to be away from the intense yellow gaze of the jaguar.

As Alice ascended the stairs to the main deck of the Eaglet, she blinked to let her eyes adjust to the bright sunlight. She immediately noticed that all work on the deck had ceased and the Eaglet's crew were intently watching an argument between Hatter and one of the Queen's guards who was trying to come aboard.

"I don't care what you've been told," Hatter barred the man's way onto the ship and pointed down the gangplank, "take them back."

"Hatter, you never said anything about bringing giants aboard my ship!" Captain Suarez stood atop the rounded roof of the stern cabin, his brow furrowing as he glared at Hatter.

"They're not coming aboard the ship," Hatter shot back at the Captain then turned back to the guard. "Turn around and bring them back to the dungeon or dump them in the bay, I don't care."

"Queen's orders," the guard growled back at him. "Now move out of the way or I'll have my men put a musket ball through your gut. Makes no difference to me. I'm delivering them to the ship either way."

"The giants are with me," Alice spoke up above the fray and all eyes turned toward her.

"What?" Hatter looked incredulous, "When did this happen?"

Alice walked to the railing of the boat. The giants stood impassively on the gangplank, their hands and feet manacled and chained together in the same manner hers had been. Both men were clad in loincloths and leather vests that left little of their scarred, muscular bodies to the imagination. The long-haired giant glared angrily around at the sailors on deck and the people gawking at them from the pier. His muscles were tensed like iron cord beneath his dark skin and Alice had little doubt that he would wreak havoc among the onlookers if he broke free of his restraints. However, his companion stood as relaxed and at ease as if he was in a quiet meadow, his bald head upturned to let the warm sun shine down upon his face.

Alice's eye drifted to the half dozen of the Queen's guards standing behind the giants, their muskets lowered and ready to fire. Another dozen guards lined the pier with their rifles trained on the giants. They were not taking any precautions. She grew concerned that if the confrontation lasted any longer, a trigger happy guard might fire a musket ball into one of the giants.

"The giants are with me," Alice's voice rose above the fray as she turned to face Hatter and the guard. "Last night, the Red Queen assented to the giants coming with us."

"You didn't think to mention this to me?" Hatter hissed, his eyes narrowing in anger.

"No," Alice gave him a hard stare, "not even for a moment."

Hatter threw his hands up in exasperation and turned away from her.

"Bring them up," the guard yelled back to his men.

"I have no room for giants aboard the Eaglet," Suarez glared down at her. "We would have to leave much needed supplies to make room for them in the cargo hold and I will not do that."

"Captain," a deep voice, heavily accented but speaking the Queen's tongue called out.

Alice turned to see the bald giant had stopped atop the gangplank and stared at Suarez. The guards looked anxious and uncertain what to do about the delay.

"Yes?" Suarez answered, equally as surprised as Alice to hear the giant speak in their language.

"I am Rebeck, son of Cormoran; this is my brother, Bore, and we respectfully request permission to come aboard."

Rebeck stood proudly despite the manacles and chains, his shoulders squared and unbowed by captivity. Alice thought he looked very much the son of a king.

Suarez walked to the edge of the cabin's roof and stared down at the giant, "Rebeck, son of Cormoran, do I have your word that you and your brother will bring no harm to my ship and crew?"

A murmur of conversation passed among the ship's sailors. Alice could see Casey, his eyes wide with terror, and knew the towering visage of the giants must have brought back terrible memories from his childhood.

"You would take the word of a giant?" Rebeck asked, his face registering mild surprise.

"My thoughts exactly," added Hatter.

"I would take the word of Rebeck, son of Cormoran," replied Suarez.

Rebeck dipped his head, "Before the Mother of the Sea, I swear it. You have my word that we will bring no harm upon your ship or your crew."

Suarez stared at the two giants and then nodded, "Then permission granted."

The Captain turned to yell to his crew. "All of you get back to work. Guard, you can remove those chains. Mister Begley, perhaps our new guests can assist with getting some of these crates stowed."

"Remove the chains? Are you mad, Captain Suarez?" Hatter stepped in front of the guard to block him from unlocking Rebeck's manacles. "Chain them to the base of the mast and post a guard or you'll wake up with your throats cut!"

"There'll be no men in chains on my ship, Hatter," Suarez pointed a white-furred finger at the gunslinger. "Half the men in this crew spent time in chains, myself included, and I will not abide such things as long as I am the captain."

"They are giants," Hatter implored. "They killed two of the Queen's guards just yesterday."

"Then I like them already," murmured one of the sailors. Alice could not be sure but she thought it was Begley's voice.

"Captain Suarez, they killed those men while aiding me in the Queen's dungeon," Alice countered.

"They gave their word before the Mother of the Sea; there's not a man on this ship that takes such a thing lightly," Captain Suarez touched two fingers to his lips and several of the sailors aboard followed suit. Alice had seen the gesture before. It was common among sailors and represented the spray of the ocean upon their lips. It was a sign of reverence for the goddess that watched over them at sea.

"Wonderland is full of liars and dishonorable men. I suspect the giants' land is no different," Hatter stepped aside to let the guard unlock the manacles from Rebeck's wrists.

"My brother and I are neither liars nor dishonorable," Rebeck glared at Hatter as he rubbed the skin around his wrists, raw and chafed from the manacles.

"Thank you, Captain," Alice spoke softly and gave Suarez a small smile as Mister Begley directed the giants toward several large crates that needed to be taken below deck.

"If they are not true to their word, I will have them both thrown into the Great Wide Open and not lose a moment's sleep," Suarez cautioned in a hushed tone.

"If they are not true to their word, I will throw them in myself," Alice replied, watching the hulking form of the giants make their way down the deck.

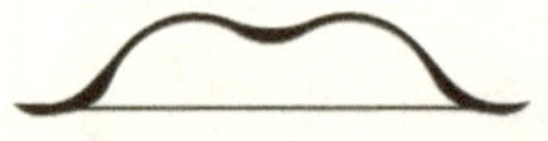

They had all assembled on the deck of the Eaglet as the sloop drifted away from the pier and into the open waters of Queens Bay. The salt air felt cold and fresh upon Alice's face. There was a cleansing feeling in the ocean air and she closed her eye and let the wind caress her face.

"They call that the Mother's Touch," a voice said quietly beside her.

Alice opened her eye to see Casey standing beside her, a gentle smile upon his face. He had largely avoided her after the incident with the giants and Alice suspected he resented her for their presence.

"The feeling of the wind from the Great Wide Open upon your face like that, sailors call it the Mother's Touch," Casey explained. "It is the fingers of the Mother of the Sea welcoming you on her ocean."

"It's incredible," Alice breathed in the briny air.

"When I am up there in the crow's nest," Casey gestured to the barrel strapped to the top of the mast that served as the ship's lookout position, "when we're at sea, all you can see for miles around is ocean. I can feel the wind all around me. It's like the Mother of the Sea has me in her embrace, keeping me safe. A lot of the others don't like it up there but I love it. That's why I am the ship's barrelman. Once we get out in open waters, I would like to take you up there if you're not afraid."

"I would love that, thank you," Alice smiled at him. "Casey, about the giants. I know . . ."

A range of emotions crossed Casey's face all at once, both so human and leporine at the same time, then he appeared to steel himself, "It is ok, Alice, I know what happened to my parents is what happens in war. They were just in the wrong place at the wrong time."

She nodded but could not hide the pained look on her face, "It does happen in war, but that does not make it acceptable. We need Rebeck and Bore's help, but that does not mean what happened to your parents is forgiven or forgotten."

"Rebeck and Bore are the sons of Cormoran, it was the giant Galligantus and his men who destroyed our village. I won't blame them for the actions of someone else, even if they were all giants. Captain Suarez taught me better than that; you judge everyone by their own weights and measures."

"Thank you, Casey," Alice smiled.

"But I won't be their friend," he added quickly.

"Of course, not."

Casey smiled back and shuffled his feet nervously, "I need to get up to the crow's nest."

Alice nodded to him and the young rabbit climbed up onto the rail of the ship and took hold of the ratlines, the horizontal ropes tied between the shrouds of the ship, forming a makeshift ladder to climb to the top of the mast. Casey scampered up the ratlines as easily as someone ascending a flight of stairs and swung himself up into the barrel. He looked down smiling, pleased that she had watched him ascend, and waved. Alice waved back, flattered by the young man's infatuation.

"It seems you have developed quite the admirer," Clodword commented looking up toward the crow's nest as he approached. There was no mockery in his words. Alice could tell he meant it purely as an observation.

"Well, he had slim pickings on this journey. I am the only woman on this trip who is not a big cat or imbued with a pole up my ass taller than the masts."

Clodword chuckled and looked over to where the Duchess stood, parasol clutched in her hand to shield her from the sun's rays. Beside her, the Lady Cheshire had leapt up so that her front paws sat upon the rail and her hind paws upon the deck, "The Duchess is just used to a sheltered life. Maybe this journey will . . . loosen that pole up a bit."

The off-color remark caught Alice by surprise and she caught Clodword's sly grin and laughed, "Clodword, I do believe that is the first improper thing I have heard you say."

"Who is that?" Alice pointed to a heavy-set bald man with a thick black mustache standing on the other side of the Duchess. The man's scowl etched deep lines on his face."

"Ah, that's the Duchess' cook. A rather tiresome and unpleasant fellow. He's sharing the room with Hatter and me."

"I trust he was displeased with the arrangement?"

"Oh, most certainly, and he will gladly tell you of it! I see your giant friends have settled in nicely," Clodword looked to where the two brothers sat talking on two barrels as they worked the knots out of some tangled ropes.

"Yeah, well, if The Pan is anything like I have heard, we'll need their muscle to get through this."

"I fear you're correct," Clodword took the bowler hat from his head and ran the brim through his fingers.

"Hatter is still sulking over the giants?" Alice nodded toward where Hatter stood alone on the bow of the ship looking out toward the open sea.

Clodword pursed his lips then sighed, "Hatter is sulking over a great many things."

Alice waited for him to say more but Clodword had fallen silent. The ship was approaching the mouth of the bay and the narrow channel that led out into the Great Wide Open. The towering walls of the castle loomed off the port side of the ship and Alice averted her gaze. The heads of the White Queen and her court adorned the top of the wall facing the sea.

So The Dark could see who truly ruled in Wonderland, the Red Queen had said.

Captain Suarez was in his usual place atop the curved roof of the cabin, Mister Cooper standing beside him. The Captain was peering through a telescope, studying the walls of the castle. Alice watched as he slowly withdrew the telescope and looked down as if composing himself, a bitter expression on his face.

Is he troubled by the sight of the White Queen's head?

He slowly walked to the edge of the cabin's roof and looked out at the passengers spread out on the deck.

Suarez cleared his throat and announced, "Passengers aboard the Eaglet, please grant me your attention."

The Duchess, the cook, Lady Cheshire, Hatter, and even the giants, turned their eyes to the Captain who stood stoically atop the cabin. He slowly looked from face to face, in a drawn out effort to make sure every newcomer to his vessel was paying close attention.

Hatter harrumphed loudly and folded his arms; Alice heard him mutter something about sea captains and theatrics. Alice was almost inclined to agree with Hatter, but her eye caught an irregularity in Captain Suarez's demeanor. The captain glanced toward the castle. It was the slightest of movements, a quick darting of his eyes without any inclination of his face in that direction. She had thought nothing of the first time Suarez had done it, but then he did it a second time as he looked toward where she and Clodword stood.

Alice had been in enough sword fights, won enough sword fights, to know the eyes were an opponent's tell. Captain Suarez was overly concerned about the castle.

No, that's not right. Suarez had been watching the castle through the telescope just moments before; if he was concerned about the castle, he'd be keeping a keen eye on it.

Then Alice felt a cold chill down her spine.

Suarez did not want them looking at the castle. He saw something he did not like and now he was trying to distract them. She glanced toward the castle but with Clodword standing beside her, Alice's right eye could not see it without craning her neck to look past him and that would alert Suarez.

"Let me familiarize you with the Eaglet. As you know, I am her Captain, and I have three other officers onboard. Beside me is Mister Cooper, my second-in-command. Mister Jakers, who you can see here at the helm, is our Chief Navigator." Suarez gestured toward Jakers, who stood with his hand on the large, spoked wooden wheel that controlled the ship's direction. Then he pointed toward the large grey rabbit examining the wooden supports of one of the cannons, "And that is Mister Begley, our Master of Guns. The bespectacled gentleman arriving late as usual is Mister Alistair, our ship's physician. If you find yourself taking ill on the journey, please feel free to seek him out."

Suarez's words caught the doctor in mid stride as he walked up the stairway from the lower decks. Nonplussed by the sudden attention, Alistair gave a slight bow and wave of his hand.

"I have all the finest spirits known to man. They'll cure all your ailments and bring you good health, long life, and make your ears stand tall!" Alistair announced with a wink and a smile, inducing a hearty ripple of laughter among the crew and a familiar scowl from Suarez.

Alice noticed the Duchess' immediate interest in the doctor, though she doubted the woman registered the doctor's bawdy remark. Even before Alice's unsavory business with Duke Enderton, the Duchess was widely known throughout the court for her frail constitution. Though, it was generally acknowledged by all but the Duchess that her near constant conditions were a manifestation of an over active imagination rather than any physical malady. Ava took a kinder view of the Duchess, as was in her nature, and once told Alice that she thought the Duchess' illnesses were the result of being ill-suited and ill-equipped to deal with the stress and responsibilities placed upon her by her station. Some people were made for the intrigues and machinations of court life, and others simply were not.

"Thank you, doctor," Suarez sighed with clear irritation and the laughter quickly quieted.

"Captain, you called the Eaglet her; how do you know the ship is a woman?" the Duchess asked.

A few of the sailors snickered at the question but Captain Suarez silenced them with a stern look.

"Duchess, excellent question. All ships are referred to in the feminine," Cooper answered her, his voice full of diplomatic politeness.

There it was again. Alice caught the Captain's eyes flick toward the castle and then back to the Duchess.

Alice wanted a look at the castle and took a step backward to see past Clodword but her back immediately met with resistance. She nearly cried out in surprise, there had been nothing behind her moments ago.

A deep voice spoke in the giants' language, followed by soft chuckling. Alice glanced back to see Rebeck and Bore standing less than a foot behind her and Clodword. The two brothers were easily able to see over their heads to watch Captain Suarez. She felt a mixture of annoyance and respect for the giants. It was not often someone snuck up on her and she did not like it. However, the brothers moved remarkably quietly for such large men and that impressed her. Bore was directly behind her and, from the smirk on Rebeck's face, had made a snide remark.

"What did he say?" Alice asked.

Rebeck leaned down toward her, "My brother said the yellow haired one has one eye in front and no eyes in back."

Alice gave Bore a withering look, "Tell him, I would have turned around if I thought there was anything better looking than a donkey's ass to look at."

Rebeck translated her words for his brother. Bore's eyebrows shot up in surprise and then his face broke into a broad grin as Alice winked at him. The giant ran a thick, gnarled hand through his long hair and made a hushed braying sound like a donkey.

"Does the big fellow have a question?" Captain Suarez's voice was sharp and angry.

"Just a translation issue, Captain," Alice replied back with a wave. Suarez glowered at them then continued with an explanation to the Duchess of the difference between the bow and the stern of the ship.

"Rebeck, can you see the castle?" Alice spoke quietly without turning.

"Yes."

"What do you see? Is anything unusual happening?"

The giant was quiet for a moment and then Alice felt his warm breath against her ear as he leaned down to whisper, "They are adding a new head to the wall."

Alice's stomach knotted with fear as she thought of Ava alone with the Red Queen.

"Can you see what the head looks like?"

"No, I cannot. The battlements are blocking any view of the heads."

Confirming her suspicions, with the Eaglet now past the castle and moving deeper into the channel, Suarez had wrapped up his impromptu lesson and was looking toward the bow of the ship to get a better view of the ocean before them. Bore gazed about the ship and shook his head as he said something in the giants' language.

Rebeck quickly translated when he saw Alice questioning look, "My brother says that this is how all adventures begin; heroes assembled and confident of victory. None think they will end smashed like waves upon the rocks."

"Well, that's a grim outlook," Clodword pursed his lips.

"Captain," Casey shouted from the crow's nest, "Dead Man's Shoal. Thirty degrees off the starboard side."

"Mister Jakers, Dead Man's Shoal. Thirty degrees off the starboard side," Cooper yelled back to the helmsman, withdrawing the brass telescope from his pocket. The largest section was covered in leather and the sea captain extending the length to the full five brass tubes before bringing it to his eye.

"Aye, Aye, Captain. Dead Man's Shoal. Thirty degrees off the starboard side," Mister Jakers repeated as he turned the helm to swing the ship closer to the port side away from the deadly shoals.

"What is this 'Dead Man's Shoal?'" Rebeck asked, his forehead furrowing in concern.

"It's a submerged ridgeline," Cooper answered, approaching the group. "Nasty, jagged rocks. Could tear the bottom right out from under a ship. Any vessels coming in have to sail within cannon range of the castle in order to avoid Dead Man's Shoal."

Rebeck translated for his brother and the two exchanged heated words with Bore clearly upset.

Hatter grinned, "It looks like Tweedle Dum and Tweedle Dee here cannot swim."

"Captain, black sails off the port bow, closing quickly," Casey yelled pointing to his left.

"It's the Lory," Captain Suarez yelled as he swung the spyglass toward the approaching ship. "Mister Jakers, we need to get clear of the shoals before the Lory enters the channel."

"It's going to be close, Captain. The wind's in her favor," Jakers shouted back.

"Casey, what's happening?" Alice called up to the crow's nest

"That ship's a bloody black sail," Casey leaned over the edge of the crow's nest barrel and pointed toward the ship, his long ears twitching nervously. "It's one of the Red Queen's longfish ships."

"I don't understand," Clodword's forehead wrinkled in confusion, "isn't the channel wide enough for both ships?"

Hatter eyed the tense posture of the crew, "Clockwork, something tells me the issue is not nautical."

Alice instantly recalled the confrontational nature of Grech and his fellow sailor and a bad feeling brewed in her gut. There was a tension in the air that reminded her of the moments before a battle, the sense that bloodshed was imminent as both sides moved into position.

"Clodword, please go escort the Duchess and Lady Cheshire below deck to their quarters," Alice gestured toward the Duchess with her brightly colored parasol, craning her neck to view the approaching ship.

"Yes, Alice," Clodword nodded as he headed toward where the Duchess and the jaguar stood.

"Do you expect trouble?" Hatter gave her a sidelong glance.

"You've been in enough battles. Don't you?"

Hatter nodded then called after Clodword, "Clockwork, maybe leave the cook up on deck."

"Damn, the Lory's forcing the channel." Suarez cursed under his breath then yelled to the helmsman, "Jakers, take us hard to starboard. We'll give her wide berth to pass."

"That'll take us dangerously close to the shoals, Captain," Jakers responded as he turned the wheel, adjusting course.

"Understood. Casey, keep a sharp eye out and give a yell if we get too close."

"Aye, Aye, Captain," Casey responded, his eyes fixed on the waters ahead.

Alice watched as Clodword ushered the Duchess, cook, and jaguar below deck. Leaning over the rail, she eyed the approaching ship. The Queen's red flag fluttered in the breeze from the tallest of the ship's three masts, the same flag that flew atop their mast. The ship was fully rigged, each mast stepped with three square black sails. She counted eleven shuttered ports along the ship's gun deck; there would be an equal number on the starboard side of the ship and two more aft, in the rear of the vessel.

Twenty-four guns.

The Lory entered the channel just ahead of them, sailing on a parallel course. The channel was wide enough for both ships to sail past each other easily, though Alice could see they would be close enough to make out the faces of each other's crew without needing a spyglass.

The two giants had walked to the starboard side of the ship and were noting with alarm the closeness of the shoals as a jagged edge of rock broke the water's surface scant yards away from the ship. Bore, in particular, was looking increasingly uneasy at the prospect of damage to the ship.

"Hold her steady, Mister Jakers," Suarez moved to the very tip of the bow, scanning the waters for any sign of rock outcroppings.

The two ships were directly across from each other when Alice heard the telltale pop of a musket and the whizzing of a lead ball through the air. She immediately dropped to the deck. Hatter did the same beside her as more pops rang out.

All along the deck the sailors crouched low or took shelter behind barrels or boxes. A musket ball pinged loudly off the barrel of the cannon where Mister Begley huddled and the Master of Guns swore profusely.

"We're flying the Queen's flag, why are they shooting at us?" Alice called to him.

"Because longfish ships do as they please and this amuses them," Begley spat with disgust. "May the Mother of the Sea take them all to the deep."

"Are you going to return fire?" She already knew the answer before the Master of Guns shook his head in disgust.

"The Queen's justice will fall on any who hinders or harms a black sail," Cooper answered.

Alice heard one of the giants grunt and she saw Bore grimace and clutch his right thigh as they crouched, red blood flowing slick over his dark fingers.

"Are you okay?"

"He'll be fine," Rebeck replied as he pulled his brother lower onto the deck.

Jakers swore loudly and Alice saw that he too had been struck by a musket ball, his left hand dangling as he struggled to keep the helm steady with one hand. The tan fur of his left arm darkened from rivulets of blood running down from the shoulder of his vest. Alice leaped to her feet, a musket ball whizzing so close by her head she felt the rush of air against the tip of her nose, and ran to aid the wounded helmsman.

"We need Alistair up here!" Alice yelled as Jakers tried to wave her away.

"Already on my way," she heard the doctor call from behind her.

"I'm fine, we'll see to it later," Jakers replied through gritted teeth.

There was another loud crack of a musket, followed by the telltale grunt and thud of a body hitting the deck as the projectile found its mark.

"The Docs been hit," one of the sailors yelled among the cacophony of musket shots.

Alice gasped as she turned to see Alistair sprawled on his back, his medicine bag still clutched in his hand as a dark stain spread rapidly across the front of his waistcoat. She felt a sinking feeling in her stomach as the doctor's free hand moved slowly to clutch at his wounded chest.

At least he's still alive, for now. Chest wounds from a musket ball could be a gruesome affair.

The doctor's hand emerged from his waistcoat holding a silver flask, a large round hole in the middle leaking the last remnants of an ochre liquid. He shook the flask and the musket ball within rattled around like a child's toys.

"Mother-cursed savages," the doctor swore as he tossed the flask away in disgust.

Alice did not know whether to laugh or roll her eyes at the sight. Alistair caught sight of her gaze and flashed her a knowing smile.

"I told you my tonics were a lifesaver!"

Another shot rang out, sending a musket ball so close to Alice's head that it nicked the top of her left ear. It felt as sharp as a bee sting but did little more that draw a small trickle of blood.

"Alice, get your ass down," Hatter screamed at her. "You'll get yourself shot."

"It won't matter if we wreck upon the shoals," Alice yelled in reply then grasped one of the wooden spokes of the helm. She looked to Jakers, his teeth gritted against the pain in his shoulder, "Tell me what to do."

"We just need to hold her steady and we'll clear the shoals."

"I'll be your left arm." She gripped the wheel, standing shoulder-to-shoulder with the helmsman as another musket ball struck the wall behind them with a loud *thwack*.

In her periphery, she could see the Lory was almost past them; the sounds of musket fire already beginning to die down. She could feel Mister Jakers' body trembling from the pain in his wounded shoulder and the effort it took to hold the helm.

"We've cleared the shoals," Suarez called from the bow and a low cheer emanated from the crew.

Beside Alice, Mister Jakers exhaled deeply as the wide blue expanse of the ocean lay before them. A few scattered muskets sounded from the rear of the Lory, but it appeared the danger had passed as crew members emerged from their hiding spots to check the riggings.

"Well, that was unpleasant," Hatter stood brushing dirt from his legs and arms.

"Thank you. We should be okay now," Jakers nodded to Alice as an auburn-furred sailor came to assist with the helm and an older gray-black furred rabbit with round spectacles and a leather bag of medical supplies came to examine his wound.

Another musket report sounded from the Lory, this one more distant than the last, as the ships sailed further apart. Alice heard a low cheer emit from the other ship.

The final taunt of a bully.

Then she heard the sickening sound of a body hitting the deck. The unmistakable sound of bone breaking and flesh striking unforgiving ground.

No. Her heart sank at the sound. A body makes a noise like that only when falling from a great distance and there was only one sailor that high up on the Eaglet.

Casey.

Alice turned to see the crumpled form of the boy lying motionless beside the mast. His fellow sailors turned to look in stunned disbelief as Alice rushed toward the fallen sailor. Several voices called out for Mister Alistair to come quickly.

"Alice, wait," Hatter tried to stop her but she batted away his hands and fell to her knees beside Casey's body.

Casey's eyes were open and bloodshot, staring unseeing at the clear blue sky. Pink blood coated the teeth of his open mouth and ran down the corners of his mouth, darkening his fur and feeding a growing crimson pool beneath his head. His legs lay at an impossible angle, unable to be contained by a shattered hip, and his arms lay wide as if he was about to give someone a great big hug.

Alice raised a trembling hand to touch his cheek. Casey's head lolled lifelessly at her touch, revealing a ragged hole behind his head where the musket ball had struck. The crew had begun to gather around her and the enormous shadows of the giants cast her and the fallen boy in a wave of sudden shade. She felt the blood pounding in her head and the sound of Suarez's voice was distant in her ears as he ordered the men to make preparations for the body.

"No, no, no, no," Alice had not even realized she had been saying the words repeatedly as she pressed her hand against the hole at the base of Casey's skull, a futile attempt to staunch the flow of blood.

She felt the jagged shards of shattered bone and the wet squelch of brain matter against her fingers. Every broken blood vessel in Casey's eyes looked like a crimson root spreading from pupils blown incredibly wide.

"No, no, no, no."

Strong, white, fur-covered hands closed about her shoulders and Alice realized that Captain Suarez was kneeling beside her.

"He's gone child," Suarez whispered softly. "He's at peace. They can hurt him no longer."

The Captain gestured a sailor to come with the blanket they had brought to cover Casey's body. The sailors stepped forward, solemn and grief stricken, but waited quietly for Alice to step aside. Alistair came running up with the medicine bag gripped tightly in one hand, but slowed at the sight of Casey's broken form. There was no tonic in his bag that would cure this. Alice met the doctor's gaze and saw the depth of sorrow in his eyes. They had lost a member of their ship's family.

Alice moved her hand from the wound to untie the neckerchief around Casey's thin neck, holding it close to her chest as she stood. Captain Suarez stood as well, gesturing for others to help the sailor with Casey's body.

Deep within the core of her being, Alice felt a raging fire burn the grief she felt upon her heart. The fury within her burned so fiercely Alice thought she could taste ash in her mouth. She moved toward the railing of the ship, the very spot where a short time ago she had watched Casey scurry up the ratlines, grinning and waving to her.

"Alice," Hatter's voice was soft and consoling as he approached but Alice waved him away, turning on him with such rage etched upon her face that Hatter took a shocked step back and raised his hands in a calming gesture.

"Oh no," Alice heard Clodword utter as he approached and spotted the sailors wrapping Casey's body in the blanket. "Miss Alice?"

Alice ignored him and jumped up on the railing, seizing hold of the rigging lines and swinging her body around to grasp the ratlines.

"Clockwork, grab her!" Hatter yelled, but Alice was already scampering up the ratlines heading toward the crow's nest with Casey's bloody neckerchief clutched in her hand.

She stopped briefly as her knee throbbed with the effort of climbing. On deck, Alice could see the upturned faces of Hatter, Clodword, and the crew staring at her. Rebeck walked over too, with Bore limping behind him, a questioning looking on his face. Alice wondered if they thought her actions were that of an impetus child running from the adults amidst a tantrum.

Alice doing Alice things.

Alice resumed her climb until she reached the crow's nest and swung her body into the barrel. She gasped as she looked around; behind the Eaglet the castle and the Wonderland coastline quickly receded and before her stretched an endless sea of blue. In that moment, Alice truly understood why they had named it the Great Wide Open. She closed her eye, letting the fresh ocean breeze caress her skin, and raised her face to feel the warmth of the sun. The light was bright against her eyelids, interrupted only by the shadow of the flag that fluttered from the mast.

She retrieved the knife from her boot and opened her eye to stare balefully at the red and black-trimmed flag of the Queen. Alice grabbed a handful of the fluttering flag, the fabric rough against her fingers, and sliced the rope halyard. The flag flew free in the wind for a moment, then fluttered down from the sky. The sailors watched it descend like a red bird falling from the sky to land in the ocean.

Alice watched it drift upon the tide and then sink beneath the waves. Then, with great reverence, she tied an end of Casey's neckerchief to each of the halyards and let it loose. The wind caught the neckerchief and it flapped proudly in the wind.

"This is the only flag we fly under now," Alice yelled down at the upturned faces.

She could see Captain Suarez nodding his head appreciatively. It was Rebeck who pumped his fist into the air and gave a feral shout. Bore immediately followed suit. Soon they were joined by the crew of the Eaglet and even Clodword raised his fist and shouted defiantly. Only Hatter and Cooper stood motionless, their faces impassive and unreadable, as they stared at her, though Alice could read Hatter's mind as clearly as if she had heard his thoughts.

Alice doing Alice things.

CHAPTER 9: REQUIEM FOR THE DEAD

"Have a seat," Suarez gestured toward the long table.

Alice recognized the room as the one she had eaten in with the crew. The long wooden table and chairs dominated the room except for the kitchen area that contained a fire hearth with a chimney to funnel smoke to the weather deck. The hearth sat on a layer of sand and bricks to keep the hearth's heat away from the wooden planks of the floor. Large round pots sat in round holes on the top hearth for boiling meats.

Suarez followed Alice's gaze and gave a wry smile, "We don't much use that anymore. We're more a vegetarian lot these days."

Alice slid out one of the seats and sat down at one end of the table, keeping her eye averted from the place where Casey had sat beside her. Hatter took a seat across from her as Suarez slipped through a door beside the hearth. The room was silent except for the gentle slapping of waves against the wooden hull outside. She could tell Hatter was trying to catch her eye but Alice was not in the mood for any conversation. Her hands were stained crimson with Casey's dried blood and she rubbed at it absentmindedly.

"You'll have to scrub that off with soap and a good rough rag," Hatter offered, his voice soft and consoling, absent of all of his usual flippancy.

"I've had blood on my hands before," Alice replied flatly, not bothering to look up from her hands.

Alice caught sight of rows of supplies in the room beyond as Captain Suarez reemerged, a bottle of dark liquid in one hand and three glasses in the other. The Captain walked to the table and placed a glass before each of them including one at the end of the table where he sat down hard. He pulled the cork from the bottle and filled each of their glasses with three fingers' worth of the dark liquid, then sat back in his chair.

"Whiskey," Hatter smiled as he lifted his glass to his nose and sniffed.

"The very best," Suarez said as he gently swished the whiskey around in the glass. "I used to save it for happy occasions, but we don't have many of those anymore, so now I use it to chase away the bad days."

Alice raised her glass, "To Casey."

"To Casey," the others repeated as they raised their glasses and took a sip. The whiskey was strong with subtle hints of vanilla and Alice loved the warm feeling it gave her as it went down. Almost immediately her cheeks felt warm and she was certain they were probably flush.

Suarez ran his tongue along the inside of his cheek. His eyes narrowed as he looked from Alice to Hatter, two dark coals amidst the white fur of his face.

"Do you know why the Red Queen made us all rabbits?" he asked.

Alice looked toward Hatter but the gunslinger slowly shook his head.

"The Red Queen made us rabbits because rabbits are prey," Suarez took another swig of the whiskey. "Her Highness wanted all of us to know that if we disobey, all the world will be our enemy and whenever they catch us, they will kill us. Your Lady Cheshire, she's a jaguar—a predator—but we're just prey."

Alice took another sip of the whiskey. Across from her, Hatter just set his down on the table, staring at the dark liquid, lost in thought.

"There are no laws in Wonderland against killing a rabbit, not those who walk on four legs and certainly not those who walk on two," Suarez continued. "What you saw today, what happened to Casey, that was sport. That boy's life meant nothing more than that of a duck in a field."

"Lady Cheshire's curse is no different than your own," Hatter stared down into the whiskey then tossed his head back and downed the remnants in one gulp.

Suarez looked ready to argue with Hatter but the door to the galley burst open and the Duchess' cook rushed in.

"We're having a conversation in here," Hatter glared at the man.

"The Duchess needs her food prepared," the cook replied with a dismissive wave.

"The Duchess can wait until we're done talking," Hatter's voice took on a tone that Alice recognized as his 'this is about to get bloody' voice.

"No, she cannot," the cook rounded on Hatter, his deep set eyes and bushy mustache gave him the appearance of an angry walrus to Alice. "The Duchess needs to eat her meals at appointed times during the day or she will feel unwell."

"Fuck the Duchess," Hatter snarled, ready for a fight.

"Fuck yourself," the cook responded as he turned and began noisily moving around the pots on the hearth. "This kitchen is ill-equipped!"

Hatter started to stand but Suarez put a restraining hand on his arm and shook his head. The Captain poured a splash more whiskey in Hatter's drink and gestured toward the glass. Behind him the cook grumbled a continuous stream of complaints and disparaging remarks about the inadequate cooking conditions.

"Inadequate! Inadequate!" the cook grunted.

"I have to share a room with that horse's ass," Hatter pointed angrily toward the cook.

Alice caught the sly smile Suarez gave her before sipping his whiskey and she almost laughed out loud. The whiskey felt hot in her belly and she thought she would like nothing more than to continue draining the Captain's stock when a sobering thought hit her.

"Captain Suarez," Alice put her glass down, "what was it about the castle that you did not want us to see?"

Suarez looked surprised and then very grim. He downed the last of the whiskey in his glass, then set it down on the table and sighed heavily. Hatter seemed surprised, though whether by the question or the Captain's reaction Alice could not tell.

Suarez made a sucking sound with his teeth and glanced sidelong at Alice, "You're a very observant, young lady."

He was about to say more but paused as the cook noisily banged around several pots.

"He's doing that on purpose," Hatter growled and shot the cook a hateful glance.

"You were saying Captain?" Alice was not going to let Suarez off the hook.

"I saw activity on the wall and when I looked with my spy-glass," Suarez paused, staring at his empty glance, "they were adding another head to the wall."

Alice felt her stomach knot with fear. *Ava was still in the castle.*

"Who was it?" Hatter asked, finally less interested in the cook.

"It was the White Knight."

Hatter sat back hard in his chair, a look of profound sadness on his face. Alice felt guilty that her initial feeling was one of relief for Ava's well-being, but it quickly gave way to grief at the loss of the White Knight. Tinker had been kind to her and Ava, from the moment of their arrival at the palace, and in time had become a fatherly figure to her.

"I know his son is traveling with you. I did not want him to chance a glance and see his father like that," Suarez added.

"Thank you, Captain, that was very kind of you," Alice offered and Suarez nodded his head slightly in acknowledgement.

Hatter rubbed his hand across his top lip, deep in thought, oblivious even to the ranting of the cook. When he looked up, Alice was surprised to see his eyes looking glassy and on the verge of tears. He nodded, more to himself than anyone else, "I'll tell Clockwork."

"Maybe he should hear it from someone more sympathetic," Alice suggested.

"I said, I'll tell him."

A knock at the door ended the discussion as Suarez gave permission to enter.

A crewmember with reddish-brown fur stood in the doorway, "Captain, the body is ready for burial."

Suarez pursed his lips and gave a slow nod, "Let us go lay young Casey to rest."

As Alice followed Captain Suarez onto the main deck, she could see the crew of the Eaglet assembled in a horseshoe shape, each holding a torch even though the midday sun burned high in the sky. Beside her, Hatter pointed toward where Clodword and the giants stood off to the side of the crew.

"Where are the Duchess and Lady Cheshire?" Hatter asked as they approached.

"Lady Cheshire is below deck with the Duchess," Clodword grimaced. "The events of today have the Duchess flummoxed."

"Flummoxed?"

"Flummoxed. The Duchess' word," Clodword smiled slightly as Hatter shook his head.

Alice glanced at Clodword but said nothing. She always had difficulty dealing with death. Doling it out she could do all day, however, handling the loss of someone close to her or consoling someone else in their moment of grief was a challenge. Alice never knew what to say or how to act. Family friends said she was just in shock when she stood stoically holding her father's hand at her mother's funeral, and when their father died, Alice told herself that she was being strong for Ava. *Be the rock.*

The thought of her father brought the Red Queen's words rushing back. *One of your parents was from our world and one was from Wonderland. Was my father's whole life a lie? Was he even really dead? No bodies returned to England. Did he truly lay beneath one of those cairns in Isandlwana?*

Alice quickly pushed down the feelings of shock and betrayal. *Now is not the time.*

"How is your leg, Bore?" Alice pointed toward the giant's bandage thigh. The man looked down at the leg and then met Alice's gaze and nodded.

"I have been watching the crew prepare the boy's body," Rebeck's dark face looked contemplative as he studied the group of sailors. "They wrapped his body within the hammock he slept on and sewed it closed with a cannonball at the feet. They said it is to weigh the body down when it is placed within the sea. This burial at sea is a very interesting custom."

"How do your people bury their dead?" Clodword asked. Ever the scholar, he appeared genuinely interested.

"We burn our dead so that their breath and shadow may return to the sky."

"There is something oddly comforting in the thought of ending in a ball of flame," Hatter added. "No worms to burrow into your skin; no fish to peck out your eyes."

"Fascinating!" Clodword continued, ignoring Hatter. "So you believe a soul is comprised of breath and shadow?"

"I do not know what a soul is. My people, the *Be'ena'a*, those you call giants, believe that when we are born the Great Goddess breathes life into our bodies and when we die we return that breath to her," Rebeck explained. "She gives us a shadow to watch all that we do and to speak of our deeds when we die. If our breath is worthy, she will breathe it into another *Be'ena'a* when it is born and our people will live on."

"And if she does not find it worthy?" asked Clodword.

A look of great sadness crossed Rebeck's dark face, "Then she leaves the breath on the wind and my people are diminished. It is important to my people to always act with honor, to guard against the day when there are no more worthy breaths to be returned and we cease to exist."

"So if it has a shadow and breath, your people consider it a creation of the Great Goddess?" Clodword asked and Rebeck nodded his head in affirmation.

"Ah, and what is more honorable then sliding down your kudzu stalks and killing every man, woman, and child you find?" Hatter pointed to the sewn canvas enshrouding Casey's body, "That boy was an orphan because your people honorably killed his parents."

"You speak to me of honor?" Rebeck's countenance grew stormy and Bore edged closer, alarmed at his brother's sudden change in demeanor. Bore did not speak the Queen's tongue, but he easily read Rebeck's body language. "We welcomed Jack Spriggins, the man who you call the Red King, into our halls as a guest and what did he do? He stole our most precious possession. We only went to war to get it back."

"What are you talking about?" Alice did not care much for souls, shadows, and final breaths, but war was another matter. "Your three kings invaded our lands."

Rebeck laughed a mirthless laugh, "You call the war the War of Three Kings, but to my people it was the Harp War."

"The Harp War?" Alice was confused but Hatter had grown suddenly quiet.

"The Harp of the *Be'ena'a* was a gift to our people from the Great Goddess. To pluck the strings of the harp was to make the Goddess' voice heard. It is what made our crops grow and raised kudzu to the clouds. Your Red King stole it like a thief in the night. All he saw was the harp's gold and he sought it as a prize for the Red Queen. But to us, the harp was life. Without it our crops did not grow and our people starved; I watched my own daughter waste away and die. We had no choice but to make war upon you to retrieve it."

"That is why the kudzu stalks do not grow back," Clodword rubbed his chin, deep in thought.

Bore spoke quickly in their native tongue. Alice could not understand him but she knew from his tone and expression that they were harsh, angry words. Rebeck raised a hand to silence him, his eyes glaring at Alice; two dark coals in a sea of white. "Yes, we raided your farms and plundered your countryside, because we needed food to send back to our people. Now the *Be'ena'a* are at the mercy of your Queen. I cannot fathom how many have perished since you defeated our armies and cut down the kudzu stalks. The crops will not grow in our land without the Harp of the Goddess and there are no kudzu stalks to climb to carry them food. My brother and I will help you retrieve the Red King and then we will ask your Queen to return the harp to save our people."

"Rebeck," Alice shook her head, "I have never heard of this harp."

"I have." Hatter stared down at the deck as if recalling the image in his mind and then met Rebeck's stare, "I have seen it in the Queen's chambers. That flying rat, Hooka, was plucking at its strings in jest until the Red Queen threatened to have him strangled with one of the cords."

"So it still exists," Rebeck's features softened in relief. "I feared it may have been melted down for its gold."

"Yes, it exists, but the Red Queen is not one for mercy," Hatter cautioned, "and giving the giants back the capability to regrow the kudzu stalks and invade Wonderland again is going to be a tall ask."

"She would have my solemn word that no *Be'ena'a* would ever return to Wonderland."

"Yeah, that's not going to work with her," Hatter gave the giant a smile that reminded Alice of a poker player bluffing a bad hand. "If she is to return your harp, you're going to need something in trade. Alice here already made a deal for bringing back the Red King and The Pan is little more than a nuisance, but if you were to rid the Red Queen of The Dark, well now maybe *that* would give you a chip to play in the game."

"If that will save my people, my brother and I will give our lives to kill this Dark." Rebeck spoke something to his brother in their language and Bore nodded and clutched his closed fist to his breast in a gesture Alice took to be an oath.

"I believe Captain Suarez is about to start," said Clodword, pointing to where the sea captain had come to stand beside the enshrouded body of the fallen sailor, his back to the placid blue waters of the Great Wide Open.

The crew of the Eaglet stood in a semi-circle around Suarez and the body, each silently and solemnly bearing a flickering torch. All were in attendance except for Mister Jakers who continued to man the helm of the ship. Suarez looked to each of the assembled sailors and then knelt beside the body and placed a white-furred hand on canvas. From the rounded shape beneath, Alice could see that Suarez was laying his hand on Casey's head. The captain closed his eyes and bowed his head, his leporine mouth quietly speaking words Alice could not hear.

The Captain had rescued Casey from the streets after the death of his family and given him a new life aboard the Eaglet, Alice thought the boy's death had to have wounded Suarez deeply though he kept any visible emotion deep beneath his rigid demeanor. Alice knew the heartbreak of being an orphan, and she found some solace that Casey had found a good home here among the crew during his short life. What was it Alistair had said to her? If the boy did not have bad luck he would have no luck at all.

Suarez rose and turned to face the sea, "Great Mother of the Sea, you who calm the oceans and raise the raging waves; we ask you to receive our shipmate, Casey, into your arms and grant his spirit fair winds and following seas to the hereafter."

The Captain paused for a moment and Alice wondered if the normally stoic sailor was getting choked with emotion. Then Suarez continued, his voice clear and strong, "He was born into a time of strife, but he stayed loyal to his Queen and he never turned his back on his ship or his crew. He stood his watches and was an able seaman."

Suarez turned and faced the crew, "You who sailed with him; do you have any complaints to state before the Mother?"

"No, Captain!" the crew shouted in unison.

"Very well," Suarez nodded to the men, "light his path to the Mother."

"Yes, Captain!" the men once again shouted in unison; then each end of the semi-circle filed slowly toward the railing of the ship and the sailors cast their torches into the sea. The procession continued until all the men had returned to their original positions in the semi-circle. Mister Begley, his dark gray ears fluttering lightly in the wind as he stepped forward and faced the Captain, raised his right hand to his head with the edge of hand slanted slightly downward, saluting Suarez.

"Sir, the way is lit."

Captain Suarez returned the salute and Begley stepped back into line with the other sailors.

"Boatswain, standby to pipe the side," Suarez addressed a young, light gray rabbit standing to his right and looked out at his crew, "As Captain of the Eaglet, I give the order; commend the body to the deep."

As two sailors stepped forward from each side of the assembled crew, the young rabbit raised a small metallic tube tipped with a round metal ball to his lips. Alice recognized it as a bosun's whistle. Her grandfather had a similar one as a keepsake from his time in the Royal Navy. With two sailors on either side of the body they gently raised Casey and carried him to the rail of the ship.

The boatswain blew a high note on the whistle followed by a low note as the sailors carefully slid the body overboard. Alice heard the body make contact with the water. It was not the noisy splash of an object tossed into the water, it was the perfect swooshing sound a diver makes when he plunges from the high board into a pool. She supposed the cannonball sewn into the hammock ensured Casey entered the water properly.

Suarez turned to address Alice and her companions, "Hatter, the boy died on your mission; would you like to say a few words?"

"No, I think your sendoff was fitting enough."

"I would like to say a few words," Alice stepped forward and immediately felt all the eyes of the crew turn toward her.

"Go on, speak your peace," Suarez nodded to her.

Alice looked at the crew—all rabbits. They were of different hues and combinations of brown, gray, white, black, and reddish fur. Many were older seasoned veterans of the sea while some were nearly as young as Casey, but all were rabbits. The price they paid for loyalty to the White Queen, a curse placed upon them by the Red Queen to cower and belittle them.

"When I was young, my sister and I grew up on a farm in Hampshire, England," Alice began. "We had a dog, an old a black Labrador retriever, who loved nothing more than to chase rabbits out of mother's garden."

Suarez's eyes narrowed as Alice spoke and several of the sailors shifted their feet uncomfortably. She could see the muzzle of Begley's gray muzzle rise in a subtle sneer.

"Maybe you should have picked a different story," Hatter whispered out of the corner of his mouth.

"I hate to agree with the little cowboy . . ." Rebeck whispered in a low rumble.

Alice ignored them and continued, "One day, he saw a group of rabbits eating clover atop a hill out in the fields and went charging off after them. He was growling and barking something fierce. The rabbits saw him running at them and they all turned and ran down the hill . . . all except one."

Alice raised her finger and paused. She could see that the crew was now watching her with rapt attention and Captain Suarez was studying her closely, seeing where this was all going.

"Now that one rabbit didn't run; he turned and faced the charging dog. It was as if he was saying 'dogs aren't dangerous, I'm dangerous.' That dog went running up that hill and that rabbit leapt at him; I could see the rabbit's teeth bared all the way from the porch. The two of them crashed into each other midair and tumbled down the other side of the hill and out of sight. I waited and waited, and when the dog finally came limping back over that hill. His paw was bleeding, one ear was torn, and he nearly had his eyes scratched out. It took the veterinarian three hours to stitch all of his wounds closed. When we got home, I walked up over that hill and looked for that rabbit. But I couldn't find him. There was plenty of blood, and at least a good amount of it was the dog's, but no rabbit. I don't know if he crawled back into his rabbit hole and died, but I like to think he lived. I do know this though, that dog never chased another rabbit again. He learned that rabbits are dangerous."

Alice finished and looked at the sea of leporine faces staring at her, their tall ears swaying slightly in the ocean breeze like a field of wheat. Dark eyes silently watched her from faces covered in fur of every hue from black, gray, and reddish-brown to pure white.

"Alright, everyone back to your posts," Captain Suarez broke the silence, his voice booming with command.

The assembled sailors quickly dispersed back to their duties. Mister Begley, his thick arms folded across his chest and his expression unreadable, was the last to leave. The giants returned to their ropes, speaking quietly in their native tongue, while Hatter had peeled Clodword away from the group and was walking with him toward the bow of the ship.

He's going to tell him about Tinker.

Alice did not like that it was Hatter relaying the news of the White Knight's death to Clodword. Hatter teased and mocked the man every chance he could, calling him Clockwork, yet she had to admit that there seemed to be a sincere friendship between the two men.

Clodword's not the booksmart, shrinking violet he appears to be. He killed those two guards without a moment's hesitation or remorse.

"Interesting story," Captain Suarez glanced sidelong at her as he walked past.

She watched the sea captain make his way back toward the helm, nodding encouragement to some of the sailors he passed, giving directions to others. The sailors responded well to Suarez and seemed to have genuine affection for him. These men had seen great hardship together and sacrificed greatly by staying true to the White Queen. Men like these did not give their loyalty easily and the high esteem they held their sea captain in was a testament to Suarez's character and leadership.

That was the kind of leader Danavi was. No, that is the kind of leader Danavi is.

This mission was as much about finding and freeing Danavi as it was about prying Ava from the clutches of the Red Queen.

My two loves, Danavi and my sister. I will not fail you.

Alice craned her neck to get a better look at Hatter and Clodword. The two men stood talking at the bow of the ship; she could not make out the words at this distance but Hatter looked grim as he spoke. Clodword held his bowler hat in his hands, his face downtrodden as he listened and nodded slightly. He appeared to thank Hatter, if Alice read his body language correctly, and turned to leave. She wanted to intercept him on his way back to his room to see if he was okay, but when Alice turned she found herself face to face with the Duchess. The woman's large, doe-like eyes appeared to grow even larger as they looked at Alice.

"Alice," the Duchess offered an awkward smile.

"Duchess," Alice nodded her head in greeting. Over the Duchess' shoulder she could see Clodword heading down the stairs to his quarters.

I'll have to catch him later.

"I know we have never been friends." The Duchess appeared so nervous Alice was certain if she yelled 'boo' the woman would leap overboard in fright. Then she gave a sad laugh, "In truth, I cannot say I have ever really had many friends. And I know there was that ugly business with my husband . . ."

Duke Enderton had plotted outright rebellion against the Queens while the bulk of their forces were fighting the giants. He had married the Duchess, the youngest daughter of one of Wonderland's wealthiest wine merchants, securing a hefty dowry, and planned to depose the Queens and start his own dynasty. Among his many flaws, and having met the man on several occasions, Alice thought they were indeed legion, the Duke bragged to his many mistresses of the gifts he would bestow upon them once he sat upon the throne. It was not long before word reached the Queens.

The Red Queen wanted to annihilate the Duke's entire household as a warning to any who would plot such crimes in the future. However, the White Queen's cooler head had prevailed and Alice was sent to surgically resolve the Duke's betrayal.

The Duchess had taken his death very poorly, though Alice doubted the old, fat, grey-haired Duke Enderton showed her any affection beyond his carnal desires. By all accounts, the Duke spoke very poorly of the Duchess, disparaging her as a dimwitted tart and vapid doll, sometimes even in her presence. Still, the Duchess placed significant stock in being the wife of one of the most powerful men in the kingdom and Alice killing the Duke directly threatened that status.

The White Queen had permitted the Duchess to remain in her position and likely had intended to find a suitable suitor for her once a worthy nobleman could be identified to assume the role of Duke. However, Alice admitted she was surprised to see the girl had survived the Red Queen's consolidation of power, especially without the added accoutrement of rabbit ears. Maybe there was more to the Duchess than she had given her credit for.

"We can be friends, if that is what you're asking, Duchess," Alice replied.

"Yes, that would be very nice. I would like that," the Duchess smiled, then looked slightly alarmed. "Though it is probably best that we keep the sleeping accommodations as they are."

"I am very comfortable in the crew quarters," Alice assured her.

"Good, that's very good," the Duchess smiled nervously, "It's just that I don't want to upset Lady Cheshire. You saw what a fuss she made."

"Of course, Duchess." Alice extended her hand, "Friends?"

The Duchess stared down at the offered hand, her doe eyes registering confusion, and then she reached out and squeezed the tips of Alice middle three fingers in her small, soft hands before quickly letting go.

"Friends," the Duchess smiled, the relief evident on her face. Then she quickly turned and headed back to her quarters.

Alice watched the Duchess walk down the deck and shook her head.

What a strange woman.

She looked up and saw Hatter standing alone at the bow of the ship, his back to her, facing out toward the sea. Alice was loathe to talk to Hatter but she was concerned for Clodword and wanted to know how he took the news. Intruding on Clodword's mourning down in his cabin seemed too invasive so that left her little option.

As Alice made her way from where she stood amidships to the bow of the Eaglet, she noticed several of the sailors glancing at her and silencing their conversations as she approached. The men would curtly nod their heads in greeting or appear too engaged with their work to notice her.

Perhaps that had not been the best time to tell my Bob story.

Hatter leaned heavily on the rail, his dark hair blowing lightly in the ocean breeze. In his hands he held the pocket watch that Tinker had repaired for him. The watch's golden chain was wrapped around his left hand to secure it from slipping into the ocean. The front case of the watch was open and Alice could see the white face and dark hands of the clock within. Curiously, she noticed the watch was stopped at four o'clock.

"Not like Tinker to not fix something correctly," Alice quipped as she approached.

He glanced back at her and slipped the pocket watch back within his vest as he stared back out over the Great Wide Open, "The watch works just fine."

"Oh, is it four o'clock somewhere in Wonderland?"

Alice thought he would snap back with a witty retort but Hatter just stared contemplatively out over the water.

"How did Clodword take the news?" Alice leaned her back against the rail and stretched her sore knee.

"Tinker was more than just a father to Clockwork. How do you think he took it?" Hatter did not attempt to mask the bitterness in his voice. Then his tone softened, "But Clockwork is as resilient as they come. He'll be back to asking the giants a million questions about their homeland in no time."

"Maybe I'll see if we can pry that bottle of whiskey away from Suarez; let Clodword send the White Knight off with a proper drink."

"Clockwork doesn't drink," Hatter did not even glance in her direction.

"Oh," Alice looked up at the Eaglet's sail, the heavy canvas catching what little breeze was in the air.

"The White Knight," Hatter said it almost to himself. "So much fucking death."

Alice glanced sharply at him then looked away, controlling the biting comment that strained to be unleashed. Hatter caught her sudden movement and turned to her, his face flushing red with anger.

"What? What was it you were going to say?" he demanded.

"Nothing, I'm going to my quarters."

Alice pushed off from the railing and started to walk away but Hatter grabbed her arm. She yanked it from his grip and turned on him, enraged at the affront of Hatter placing his hands upon her.

"What was it you were going to say? Spit it out Alice. I have never known you to be shy," Hatter gritted his teeth.

"I was going to ask, and who's to blame for all that death? But why ask when we all know the answer," Alice glared into his dark eyes. "You are."

"Ha!" Hatter's laugh was short and harsh. "You know a lot for someone who has been asleep for a year."

"That's rich, coming from the man who shot me off that bridge."

"I never intended to shoot you, Alice." Hatter's eyes narrowed and his voice got low, "That catapult shot was going to kill the whole lot of you bunched together there on the bridge. I had one chance to try and knock one of you off the bridge, to try and save one of you. You were my friend Alice, but the White King was my liege lord; I took my shot and tried to save the king, but Danavi hit my hand and the shot went wide and hit you instead."

"Why would Danavi do that?"

"I have no idea and the Red Knight offered me no explanation," Hatter shook his head, "But whether it's thanks for saving your life or blame for your injuries, both lay with Danavi. If I could have saved you both somehow I would have, however, if I had to do it over a thousand times, I would always choose my king."

Alice gave a derisive laugh and sneered at the gunslinger, "And where was that loyalty when you killed the White Queen?"

Hatter blanched and recoiled as if struck by a physical blow. To Alice's surprise, when he met her gaze his eyes brimmed with tears and his voice broke, "Killing Indira took every ounce of loyalty in my body."

"Loyalty to who? I noticed you were in the Red Queen's bed chambers when you saw Hooka playing the harp."

"I was in her bed chamber, not her bed, Alice. When it became clear the Dodo was not going to return, the Red Queen sequestered herself in her room for weeks. The White Queen sent me with messages when she could not go to her sister herself."

"Is that when the Red Queen turned you to her cause? Did you see a chance to become the next Red King?"

This time Hatter's face hardened with resolve and Alice could see anger brewing behind his eyes, "Think what you wish about me, Alice, but my loyalty to Indira never wavered."

"Right up until the moment your blade sliced through her neck?" Alice's eye grew cold. She wanted to provoke Hatter, turn this confrontation physical. All he had to do was go for his gun and Alice would slice his gut wide with her shortsword and tumble his body back into the sea before his pistol left its holster. Her fingers itched to close around the hilt of the sword, to draw the sharp steel, but she needed Hatter to make the first move.

"Your blade," Hatter's eyes glanced down at her sword and then back to her face.

"What?"

"I used your sword. The one on your hip there. Indira insisted," Hatter could read the shock on Alice's face and he gave her a smug smile. "I told you, Alice, you don't understand anything that happened while you were unconscious."

Alice felt a wave of revulsion course through her body. The instrument of the White Queen's destruction lay nestled against her hip. The blade might as well have been a writhing serpent. She felt disgust at its touch and needed it away from her. Reaching down she grabbed the hilt, the touch of the familiar sword in her palm now filled her with loathing and she desired nothing more than to cast it into the sea.

"Wait," Hatter's hand closed over hers, preventing her from drawing the sword. His voice was soft now, "that's not what Indira wanted."

Alice's mind reeled, however, when she looked into Hatter's face she saw an earnestness there she had not seen in a long time.

"The Red Queen's attack was a surprise to us all. The speed and ruthlessness of her forces overwhelmed us; many of the White Queen's people were slain in their beds. I was ready to make my stand beside Indira, give my final breath defending her if it came to that. I implored her to surrender, let the Red Queen take her prisoner and buy time for Lord Cheshire to rally her forces," Hatter shook his head, grief turning his face grim. "Indira was certain the Red Queen was intent upon her death. There was no convincing her otherwise. She did not want to die at the hands of those who meant her harm, men who would parade her through the palace like a prized pig before taking her life. The White Queen did not want to leave this world surrounded by those kind of men."

Alice's legs felt weak and she sank down to deck until she was sitting on the cold wooden planks. Her imagination filled her mind with images of Indira's final moments as Hatter spoke.

"The White Queen bade me to bring your blade," his voice was soft and choked with emotion. "When I returned with the sword, she took it in her hands, closed her eyes, and spoke in a language I had never heard her use before. It was the only time I had ever seen her use magic. Before Indira handed the sword back to me, she ran her palm along one edge and drew blood. She told me that the blade's magic was now hidden so that even her sister would not detect it."

"What magic? It's just a sword," Alice glanced down at the weapon sheathed at her side.

"It's not just a sword, it's a key," Hatter explained. "If you touch the blade to the shards of the Looking Glass it will reform. The White Queen's dying act was to provide you and Ava a way home, so don't go throwing it in the ocean just yet. You know the rest of what happened so I am not going to rehash that fucking nightmare. In the end, Indira said the Red Queen would have no need for any more carnage after she was dead and asked me to save who I could—and that is all I have ever done"

"Including betraying Lord Cheshire?" Alice glanced sidelong at Hatter and saw his spine stiffen at her retort. He rounded on her, his face reddening with a fresh surge of anger.

"Oh, come now Hatter," a voice purred, "we're in the middle of the Great Wide Open on a suicide mission to the Cursed Isles, just tell the girl the truth."

Alice turned to see Lady Cheshire approaching, her large black paws moving silently along the deck. Hatter's demeanor quickly transformed from angry to chagrined as if Lady Cheshire had scolded him.

"There is no need to discuss matters of the past in front of Alice," Hatter responded but his voice had lost its conviction.

Lady Cheshire's yellow eyes moved from looking at Hatter to rest upon Alice. The eyes looked deep and soulful to Alice, the glint of predatory danger for the moment subsiding.

"Lord Cheshire was already set upon by the Red Queen's forces by the time Hatter and the surviving guards were captured." The jaguar paused, moving its mouth in a way that reminded Alice of a person pursing their lips. "My husband was already dead and our castle surrounded by the Queen's fleet by the time Hatter bent the knee and swore his oath to the Red Queen."

"But it was Hatter who betrayed you to the Red Queen," Alice glanced from Lady Cheshire to Hatter, who had turned from them and stared out across the ocean.

"My dear girl, Hatter did not betray me; he saved me and my daughters. The Red Queen's fleet would have leveled our castle with their cannons until there was nothing left but a pile of stone and broken bodies. Hatter came to me and told me that he had made a bargain with the Red Queen for our lives. He asked only that I trust him."

"And you did?"

"I did and I do," Lady Cheshire sat down between them, glancing up at Hatter before turning back to Alice, her tail swooshing lightly across the wooden deck.

"But you and your daughters . . ." Alice's eye met the jaguar's gaze as she searched for the right words.

"We're a little catty these days?" Lady Cheshire's eyes sparkled mischievously at Alice's discomfort.

"Well, yes," Alice bit her lip and looked away from the jaguar.

"The Red Queen promised that if I swore allegiance to her and convinced the rest of the White Queen's forces to surrender, she would let Lady Cheshire and the girls live," Hatter gave a bitter laugh. "As the Red Queen pointed out later, the bargain was only for their lives; there were no terms placed upon the condition of their persons."

"If nothing else, the Red Queen does not lack self-awareness," Lady Cheshire added. "She knew that with her sister dead and the Red King and Danavi lost in the Cursed Isles, there were few left in Wonderland that could advise her and prevent her from making rash decisions. She knew that if she was to rule alone she needed to be more . . ."

"Magnanimous," Alice finished the sentence as her mind recalled the late night conversation with the Queen.

"Yes, magnanimous," the jaguar nodded. "The Red Queen transformed me because I had defied her in those dawning hours and that could not go unpunished. However, as you can see, she was kinder to me than to these sailors and the others who opposed her."

"She imprisoned your daughters. They were in the cell beside mine."

"She did," Alice could see the mention of her daughters caused the jaguar's eyes to tighten in the corners as if wincing at the thought. "They are being held to assure that I continue to serve the Queen faithfully."

"Hostages."

"Hostages," the jaguar nodded in agreement.

"But why did she not transform Hatter? Punish him too?" Alice glanced toward the gunslinger who was staring silently at the rolling waves.

"Alice, she may have punished him worst of all." Lady Cheshire glanced toward Hatter and Alice detected a tenderness in her gaze. "Anyone who supported the White Queen was turned into rabbits as punishment; well, except for Tinker, because she needed him to be able to utilize his hands—and Hatter. The only one to escape the Queen's wrath. The slayer of Queen Indira. They all came to the same conclusion that you did—he was a traitor."

"You don't believe that?"

"I don't, because it's not true."

"And you trust him?"

"With my life and that of my daughters."

"Then why are you here?" Hatter turned, his voiced laced with bitterness and resentment, "If you trust me, then why are you not back at the castle with the girls? They've already lost so much, do you think they could bear losing you too?"

"All that matters anymore is getting their freedom. You made your deal with the Red Queen and I made mine, my love."

My love.

The words left Alice thunderstruck. She looked at Hatter who stared at the jaguar with his mouth agape. His eyes drifted toward Alice and reflected the dread of seeing that she had heard it too. However, Lady Cheshire looked at them with an expression of casual amusement.

"Lady Cheshire," Hatter breathed the words, his shoulders sagging with resignation as he braced himself with a hand upon the rail.

"Hatter, all who would harm us already know our secret. There is no reason to hide anymore from those who would be our allies. We will need Alice's help if we are to free the girls," the jaguar spoke to the gunslinger in a soft soothing tone before turning earnest yellow feline eyes upon Alice. "Hatter is the father of my two girls; he has been my lover for many years. One of the reasons the Red Queen transformed me into this magnificent beast was to steal from us that level of intimacy. It was a cruel bargain."

"But Lord Cheshire," Alice's mind reeled with yet another revelation. Since awakening, everything she seemed to know of Wonderland, and even her father, had been turned on its head. She had been unconscious for a year, but to her the battle on Cormoran's bridge and the world as she knew it then was just a day ago.

It's no use going back to yesterday, I was a different person then.

"He knew and approved of the relationship," Lady Cheshire assured her with a slight smile, "I may have been a beautiful woman before this, but that was never going to matter to Lord Cheshire. Our love was more akin to that between a brother and sister. He was a good and kind man; and he truly loved the children as if they were his own. In public, we were the Lord and Lady Cheshire, however, in private we discreetly followed our hearts. It was an arrangement we made when we chose to join our two great houses for the good of the realm. I had

Hatter and Lord Cheshire had his knight. They died side by side, defending each other from the Red Queen's treachery."

"Do your daughters know the truth?"

"No," Lady Cheshire shook her head. "We all thought it best not to tell them until they were older. Hatter was their gallant and adventurous surrogate uncle and long-time friend of their mother."

"The Red Queen may be half mad these days, but she is as shrewd as they come," Hatter added. "She knew about us. The girls were a bargaining chip. As long as she held them, Lady Cheshire and I were hers until the day came when we would negotiate their release.

"Did Queen Indira know?" Alice asked and Hatter nodded. A dawning realization came over her. "When she told you to save who you could, she was referring to the Lady Cheshire and your daughters?"

"Yes," Hatter nodded again then looked over to Lady Cheshire and gave her a faint smile. "It is all that ever mattered to me."

"The Eaglet was already yours to command and Tinker was working on devices for this mission before I ever woke up. Had you already struck a new bargain with the Red Queen?"

"I am not so sure Suarez would agree with you about command of the Eaglet," Hatter laughed. "But, yes, I had already struck a bargain with the Red Queen. If I stopped the Dark, she would free the girls."

"Oh, Hatter," Lady Cheshire shook her head. "You should have told me."

"You wouldn't have let me do it."

"Can the curse the Red Queen placed upon them be reversed?" Alice asked, "Can they be returned to human form?"

"No," Hatter shook his head. "I do not understand how the Queen's magic works, but I have heard her say that what is done cannot be undone. I know there are some like Cooper that hold out hope that their newfound loyalty will be rewarded with a reprieve from the curse, but it is beyond even the Red Queen's magic."

"Did you also make a bargain with the Queen?" Alice looked to jaguar and was struck by how much emotion her feline eyes expressed.

"Last night the Red Queen agreed to free the girls if I helped return the Red King," Lady Cheshire replied.

Hatter's face screwed with frustration, "You did not need to do that. Alice had already agreed to bring the Red King home. You're needlessly jeopardizing your life."

"Hatter, all that matters is the girls. If any of us succeed, our daughters will be free of that horrible dungeon."

Alice stood and both pair of eyes, human and feline, turned toward her. "I swear to you. The three of us, we'll kill the Dark, whatever the fuck it is, retrieve the Red King, and free your daughters and my sister."

Alice doing Alice things.

CHAPTER 10: THE DARK

Alice let the cool morning breeze and bright sun chase away the last of her sleepiness as she breathed in a lungful of cool, salty air. The ship rocked gently on the morning tide, but appeared to be anchored in place. She looked out and was surprised to see a stretch of beach off the port side of the ship.

Where are we?

Captain Suarez was at his usual vantage point atop the cabin roof; he held a long telescope to his eye, surveying the beach intently. On the deck below the Captain, Mister Cooper also stared out toward the beach while Mister Jakers leaned upon the helm; with the ship anchored there was no steering to be done. He appeared to be conversing with Lady Cheshire who lay sprawled upon the deck sunning her dark fur in the morning light.

A rabbit and a jaguar chatting amicably. What a strange world we now live in.

Not far from where the jaguar lay, Hatter fiddled with the copper box that Tinker had given him while Clodword appeared thoroughly engrossed in conversation with Bore and Rebeck. Alice was pleased to see the giants assimilating well with the others. If what they suspected from the readings last night were true, the two hulking warriors would be valuable companions on the battlefield.

"It's true; rabbits are widely known as the best endowed of all mammals," a grizzled-looking, gray-haired rabbit said to his two companions, a pair of younger rabbits diligently cleaning one of the ship's cannons. Alice had no doubt that he had intentionally spoken loud enough for her to hear the crude remark.

"Last night when you got up to take a piss I saw the shadow of your formidable endowment," remarked Alice as she walked by the three sailors.

"Is that so?" The rabbit puffed up his chest and gave her a wink.

"It is," Alice returned the wink as she passed him, "of course, at the time I thought you had your thumb wedged between two small acorns."

The rabbit's shoulders dropped and his mouth gaped open as his two companions roared with laughter, drawing the ire of Mister Begley.

"The salt air's got you boys giddy," Begley scowled as he stomped over toward them. "Perhaps you'd find the air cleaning the bilge pumps more to your liking?"

"No, sir," the two younger rabbits shouted back in unison as they redoubled their cleaning efforts and the older rabbit joined them.

"Alice dear, so good of you to join us," Lady Cheshire's yellow eyes flicked to Alice as she approached. "Mister Jakers and I were just discussing how ridiculous it is for one to dress like a, now what was Hatter's word for it, ah yes, a "cowboy" on a seagoing vessel."

Mister Jakers snickered loudly and glanced toward Hatter, who had just pushed back the brim of his black cowboy hat in frustration as he adjusted the dials on the copper box in his hands.

"Alice dresses like a pirate and I don't see anybody giving her shit," Hatter grumbled and nodded toward Alice.

Alice looked down at her knee high boots, brown leather breeches, and white linen shirt.

I don't think I look like a pirate.

She scowled, "Here now Hatter, are you referring to my eye patch?"

"Don't worry Alice, wearing an eye patch does not make one a pirate," Lady Cheshire purred, "no more than a cowboy hat makes one a cowboy."

"Uggh, Clockwork," Hatter handed the box out to Clodword, "see if you can get this damn thing to work properly."

"Oh, of course, Hatter," replied Clodword stepping away from the two giants who exchanged nods of greeting with Alice and took hold of the copper box. "I was just having the most fascinating conversation with Rebeck and Bore. Apparently, when the kudzu vines reach the clouds they give off a pheromone that mixes with the water vapor to create a portal effect. We knew that they could pass between our world and theirs through some manner of portal associated with the vines, similar to the Looking Glass, but I had no idea it was such a naturally occurring process. The Looking Glass was created to be a portal, but the giants' portals are strictly botanical."

"So they don't live in a land in the clouds?" Hatter asked adjusting his brim back down.

"No. No, of course not," Clodword looked at Hatter perplexed, missing the sarcasm in the man's reply.

"Can you get that damn thing to work or not?" Hatter pointed at the box.

"Oh yes, you just need to flick this switch here," Clodword flipped a small black switch on the bottom of the box and then turn a small red dial seated among five silver dials and what appeared to Alice to be a compass, "and then turn this."

The box immediately made a whirring sound followed by three short clicks at even intervals. Hatter pursed his lips in annoyance as Clodword handed the box back to him.

"There you go."

"Captain Suarez, where are we?" Alice called up to the sea captain.

"We're in Chess Bay," Suarez responded without taking the telescope from his eye. His voice sounded more somber than usual, which Alice attributed to lingering sadness over Casey's death.

"Chess Bay? That's just over the rise from the Queens' castle." Alice was shocked that they had barely gone further than a morning canoe trip from Wonderland. "Why aren't we further out in the Great Wide Open?"

"All in due time, Alice," Suarez again responded without taking his attention from the beach.

"What is he staring at?" Alice asked the helmsman.

"See for yourself," Cooper averted his gaze from her as he slipped a cylinder from a pouch on his belt and, with a flick of his wrist, extended it into a three-sectioned telescope before handing it to Alice.

Alice held the telescope to her good eye; the magnification was momentarily disorienting until her vision adjusted. She scanned the beach; nothing but empty white sand and then she paused.

"Are those children?" Two sandy haired boys no older than ten played in the sand with a red-haired girl about the same age. The boys appeared to be carving a moat in the sand while the girl shaped a round mound into a crude castle.

"Human children," Cooper agreed. "You see, the Captain and your friend Hatter believe The Dark works on a cycle, coming every thirteen days."

"We think it takes The Dark thirteen days to recover from its forays here," Hatter explained. "It attacks and disappears, then thirteen days later it's back again."

"What do the children have to do with this?"

"They're the bait," Hatter said, looking back out toward the beach. "The Queen's agents left the children on the beach and placed a small button on the children's clothes. The contraption in Clockwork's stubby fingers can track them once The Dark takes them."

"What?" Alice stared from face to face, but only Mister Jakers would meet her gaze albeit with deep sadness in his eyes. "This is monstrous."

"If it makes it any better, they are orphans. They'll be no families to miss them if they are gone," Jakers added, the corners of his mouth dipping into a frown, as if even he did not find any solace in the thought.

"I'm a fucking orphan," Alice sneered back at him and the helmsman held up his hands in a gesture of apology.

"And you call my people monsters," Rebeck commented, a look of distaste on his dark features.

"You are all okay with this?!" Alice stared at them in disbelief.

"Alice, there is no other way," Hatter looked grim as he spoke. "Believe me, no one likes this."

"He's right Alice," Clodword briefly met her gaze then looked back down to the copper box as Alice gaped at him in disbelief.

Lady Cheshire was suddenly on her feet "Hatter, how could you do this?"

"I'm only doing what is necessary for this mission to succeed," Hatter hissed in response, his voice bearing an uncharacteristic edge to it."

"But at what price? Those are just children," pleaded Lady Chesire.

"There is no price too high, Lady Chesire," Hatter snapped back at her with such venom that she took step back. "You of all people should know that."

Lady Chesire gave a menacing growl, deep and guttural, as she turned away from him.

"How do you even know The Dark will come here?" Alice gestured toward the beach "There are children all over Wonderland."

"Because this is where The Dark took Captain Suarez's children," Cooper said in a harsh whisper, looking up to the Captain's silent vigil. "His little boy and girl."

"We have to stop this thing or it will keep taking children," Hatter said, his voice full of remorse. He pointed out toward the three children playing in the sand. "The sacrifice these children make will save hundreds from meeting a similar fate."

"Captain Suarez," Alice was prepared to cut the man to the bone. "Casey was an orphan just like those children. What would he think of this?" She pointed toward the beach. "What would he think of you?"

She saw the Captain's spine stiffen at her words and fully expected a hot retort, but his words sounded only sad and tired.

"I would hope that Casey would ask the Mother to have mercy upon my soul," He replied without turning from the beach.

A horn, long and mournful, sounded in the distance. Several of the sailors noticed and halted their activities, listening intently to see if their ears had betrayed them, hoping that it was just a trick of the wind. Alice noticed that even Suarez had finally lowered his telescope and had turned toward the sound, his eyes scanning the horizon.

"Wha—" Alice began to ask but Hatter held up a hand for silence.

The horn sounded again, unmistakable this time, and closer. Then another horn, even closer.

"Raise the anchor," Suarez bellowed. "Prepare the ship to sail."

Suddenly the deck all about her was a flurry of activity as the sailors of the Eaglet sprang into action. Alice could hear the clanging of the anchor chain as it was winched off the ocean floor.

"It's the warning towers, the Red Queen had them built all along the coast," Hatter explained "They've spotted The Dark."

"Hatter, is your damn fool device ready?" Suarez called down to them, his face the impassive mask of command of a hardened leader.

Hatter looked to Clodword, who nodded, "The tracking device is picking up the signal from the beach."

The beach. Call it what it is; the signal from the children.

The sanitization curdled Alice's stomach. They were damning innocent children to some hideous fate; the least they could do is acknowledge their action. She knew that dire times bore tough decisions, but sugar coating them was never her style.

A horn blared again, this much closer than the ones that had preceded it, and Alice could hear the distant rumble of cannon fire accompanying the horns.

“It’s the castle guns. They’re firing at The Dark,” Hatter yelled.

“Will they harm it?” Alice asked.

“They never have before,” Lady Cheshire replied. “I am going to head below deck and see to The Duchess.”

The jaguar gave a forlorn look toward the beach, then to Hatter before turning away. Alice watched the sure-footed jaguar easily walk along a deck that rocked at the mercy of the waves now that the Eaglet was freed of its mooring, and thought Lady Cheshire had a world-weariness to her stride. As a mother, with both her daughters imprisoned in the Red Queen’s dungeon, Alice knew Lady Cheshire felt outrage at placing the children in harms way more acutely than any of them.

“The land around the bay is too high for us to see toward the castle,” Cooper cursed as he scanned the surrounding hilltops.

“Off to port, thirty degrees,” the lookout called down from the crow’s nest.

Alice turned her head in the direction of the others and there in the distance she could see a black streak in the sky. Its blackness was so impenetrable it looked as if a crack had opened in the clear blue sky.

“Mother of the Sea, that thing must stretch all the way to the Cursed Isles,” Cooper observed through the telescope. “It’s like a giant arm reaching all the way back to the horizon,”

The steady sailor’s voice cracked, just for a moment and only slightly, but Alice heard it. She wondered if the emotion was for the children on the beach or for his own children taken by the monstrous force slithering across the sky—likely both she decided.

Multiple horns were sounding now and the rumble of the thundering cannons was nearly constant. A collective gasp arose from the crew as a ribbon of darkness rose from over the hilltop; even the stalwart Captain Suarez took an involuntary step backward.

Rebeck and Bore were suddenly beside her; their towering forms, muscles taunt and ready for battle, flanking her on either side. Alice squinted her eye to get a better look at The Dark. It appeared as ethereal as smoke but with a darkness that was impenetrable. The sun's light seemed to disappear within it rather than illuminate its shape.

It rose higher into the sky, clearing the hills in a wide arc, as would a diver preparing to plunge downward. The obsidian band of smoke blocked the sun, casting a shadow that stretched from the beach to the ocean, enshrouding the Eaglet in a dark eclipse of sunlight. Like Suarez, Alice raised her telescope to her eye and scanned the beach.

The three children cowered, their sandcastle thrown into ruin as they huddled close together. Alice wanted to scream out for them to run but there was nowhere for them to go. The inevitability of the jaws of the trap closing about the three youngsters clenched at her heart. She could not bear to watch and lowered the telescope.

Alice noticed that Suarez did not look away; he held the telescope close to his eyes with a shaky hand. Whether the sea captain felt a personal responsibility to not shirk from watching the doom he played a part in consigning these children to, or if it was out of a desire to witness the fate his children had experienced, she did not know. For a fleeting moment, Alice pictured Suarez, tormented in the dark of night with visions conjured in his imagination of his children's final moments.

Alice turned back to The Dark. It had begun a downward trajectory toward the children and, for the first time, she got a good look at the forefront of the entity. She was struck by the lack of noise the thing made. The Dark was an utter absence of light and sound.

A gasp escaped her lips. The forward tip of The Dark began to take shape as it moved inexorably toward the children. Dark whisps fluttered like tendrils of hair blown backward by a strong breeze, the front of the ribbon of darkness taking on the unmistakable shape of a woman's face.

Clodword shot her a fleeting glimpse, "Do you see that too?". Alice nodded, transfixed.

"By 'that' do you mean the face of that banshee in the cloud? I think we can all see that!" Hatter gawked at the cloud.

"What's a banshee?" asked Jakers.

"That," Hatter pointed toward the face.

"There have been reports of others seeing a face in The Dark, I . . . I just thought it was hysteria, but this . . ." Cooper's words trailed off as he shook his head in apparent disbelief.

As Alice stared at the face, dark pits sank inward to form hollow eye sockets, the clear lines of the jaw opening to reveal a gaping maw. The creature's mouth opened impossibly wide, too wide for the proportions of the head, and Alice was gripped by the mental image of a snake swallowing an immense prey.

Alice could not hear the children on the beach but she knew they were screaming in terror as that mouth closed down around them. There was no cataclysmic collision with the earth as The Dark's mouth closed about the children, but then, like a rubber band that had stretched to its full length, The Dark began to recede. For one fleeting moment Alice's eye locked with those of the Dark and then it was gone, retreating along the path it had come.

The beach where the children had been only moments before was unmarked by their passing, as if they had simply vanished. A loud whirring and clicking punctuated the air, snapping her out of her horror.

"I'm getting readings," Clodword shouted, looking down at the copper box. "North Northeast."

"Mister Jakers, set sail, North Northeast," Suarez yelled, hopping down from the cabin top and landing alongside the helmsman.

"Aye, Aye, Captain. North Northeast," Mister Jakers answered as the Captain moved briskly among the crew, giving orders to move the sails to fully catch the wind.

"Does that mean the children are alive?" Alice asked.

"It just means we are receiving a signal," Hatter replied, his usual roguish bravado dampened by the horror of what they had just witnessed.

Bore said something to Rebeck in their native language. Alice could not fathom the words but she understood the ominous tone. *We're all going to die.*

CHAPTER II: CURIOUSER AND CURIOUSER

The hammock rocked slightly from side to side with the motion of the Eaglet upon the ocean. Alice had to admit that it was not an altogether uncomfortable feeling. In fact, she found it rather soothing as she lay in the darkness of the crew quarters.

Each crew member had his own hammock and a place beneath to store a chest or footlocker with his personal belongings. Most of the sailors hung their clothes on a peg beside their hammock, slipped into their canvas bed in their skivvies, and then rolled out of bed and threw the clothes back on in the morning. Laundry was an infrequent occurrence and Alice supposed the room would smell quite ripe before the end of their journey, assuming rabbits sweated the same as people did. She was not quite sure.

One thing she was certain of was that rabbits snored. It was not the gentle snore of the large white rabbits her grandfather had raised in her youth that would drift off to sleep in her lap as she pet them. The rabbit sailors of the Eaglet snored as if they were bellowing challenges to the sea; loud, wood sawing sounds punctuated by occasional snorts and farts.

Still, she preferred these accommodations over sharing a room with the Duchess. The two women had reached an uneasy detent in their long standing discord and Alice was fairly certain the Duchess would be mortified at the notion of snoring or making any other bodily noise, however, Alice had always made a point of sharing as much of the hardships of campaigns as the soldiers, and now sailors, she went into battle with.

The only exception she had made was the night before and after each battle; those she spent in Danavi's tent. There was something about the desperate sense that it could be their last night together that just made the sex otherworldly; not to mention, it calmed Alice's nerves before a battle. The night after a battle, exhausted, they would expend the last of their energies in the throes of ecstasy and then collapse into each other's arms and examine their cuts and bruises.

Alice bit her lip to hold back the emotions conjured by memories of their last night together, the night before the battle on the bridge. They had never gotten to their after battle ritual; they may never again.

Alice exhaled deeply and pushed the thoughts from her mind; there would be time to deal with that later.

I'm coming, Danavi. You better not be dead. Not you too.

She could not get the horrific images of those children on the beach out of her mind. Every time she closed her eyes she saw that monstrous female face in the clouds, the expression on it a reflection of pure malice. Alice did not want to think about what the children experienced being swallowed by the heinous maw, or the countless children it had already taken. The few moments of restless sleep she did manage was marred by dreams of Ava being snatched up and swallowed by The Dark.

Maybe I need to see if Alistair has a tonic to help me sleep. No, she needed to stay sharp and ready for whatever horrors this nightmare had in store for her. Drowning your sorrows only dulled the senses and got you killed, and she needed to stay alive for Ava and Danavi.

There was a knocking at one end of the crew quarters and Alice heard the muffled thump of someone hopping out of their hammock and stumbling across the wooden floor planks. She heard the squeak of the door hinge and then muffled voices, too quiet to make out the words above the cacophony of snoring sailors. Alice closed her eye and concentrated, trying to drown out the noises and focus on the two voices.

She nearly jumped in surprise when a hand lightly shook her shoulder. Her eye sprang open as her hand reflexively slid beneath her pillow and grasped the knife she had secreted there. A young rabbit stared down at her, still blinking the sleep from his eyes and stifling a yawn with one furry hand. His fur was jet black except for one large white patch around his left eye and Alice immediately recognized him as one of Begley's gunner's mates. Her grip slackened on the knife hilt though she did not remove her hand.

"Alice, there is someone at the door for you," the rabbit spoke in a hushed tone. "It's that Clockwork fellow."

"Clodword," she corrected. "What does he want?"

"I don't know. Go see," he replied as he turned away and headed back into the darkness toward his hammock.

Alice pulled on her pants and slipped on her boots then quietly made her way to the door, careful not to jostle awake any of the sleeping sailors as she passed. She opened the door just far enough to slip her body through the opening, not wanting to let light stream in among the sleeping sailors. Clodword waited in the corridor, a hooded lantern in one hand and a book and some manner of belt in the other. She smiled when she spied the hooded lantern in his hand, cracked slightly to provide only enough illumination to see in the dark passageway.

Of course, Clodword had the forethought to not awaken everyone in the room with a blazing lantern. Hatter would have lit up the room like a sunny day to come find me.

A broad smile briefly crossed his cherub face then quickly retreated as a fretful look replaced it, "I'm sorry for disturbing you so late."

"It's okay, Clodword. Is there something wrong or do you make a habit of calling on young ladies in the middle of the night?" Alice gave him the slightest hint of a smile but that did nothing to allay his sudden look of alarm.

"Neither. I mean, nothing," Clodword stammered, searching for the right words.

Alice laughed. Clodword's awkwardness had a charm unto itself. "What have you got there?" she gestured to the book and belt.

"Oh this," Clodword's face lit up with clear relief at changing the subject. He handed the book to Alice, "This is from your sister. She requested I deliver it to you once we set sail."

Alice took the leather bound book from Clodword's outstretched hand. The cover had raised images of plants and trees intertwined along the cover and binding. She looked down at the gold lettering on the front of the cover and frowned.

Skaggit's Encyclopedia of Flora of the Royal Gardens.

"Ava wanted me to have this?" Alice could not hide her confusion as she looked from the ornate cover to Clodword's smiling face.

"Oh, yes. She was quite insistent I not forget and that I only give it to you once we departed" he nodded. "I thought after the events of today, maybe it would provide a welcome distraction for you."

She ignored his reference to the atrocity that occurred on the beach, Alice did not forgive his role, or at least foreknowledge, in what transpired.

"Is that for me too?" Alice glanced at the bizarre belt affixed with all manner of metal plates and straps.

"Yes. Yes, it is," Clodword looked momentarily perplexed, as if he forget he was holding the strange belt, then visibly brightened. "I made this for you."

"Oh," Alice tried to make her most grateful face though suspected she failed miserably. She was never good at faking emotions. "It's . . . wonderful?"

"It's for your leg; your injured knee," Clodword gestured toward her right leg with the belt. "May I?"

Alice nodded uncertainly and Clodword knelt down on one knee. He adeptly began to cinch the straps around her leg, constantly glancing up to make sure it was not too tight for comfort.

"There. How does that feel?" Clodword asked as he stood.

Alice looked down at her leg. A metal band ran down each side of her thigh and calf with a hinged joint at the knee. The device was affixed to her leg by four leather straps.

"How does it work?" Alice looked from her leg to Clodword.

"You just . . . walk."

Alice shrugged and took an uncertain step forward with her right leg. To her surprise, the hinge moved smoothly and impacted her normal stride minimally.

"It . . . it doesn't hurt at all," Alice could not hide her shock.

She took several steps around the corridor, moving quicker with each step. Remarkably, she felt none of the pain in her knee that she had begun to grow accustomed to. In fact, her leg felt strong. Clodword smiled as he watched her, evidently pleased with his craftsmanship.

"Clodword, this is amazing! How did you do this?"

"It's just some belts and metal straps from old barrels. When we get back to Wonderland I can make you a proper brace."

"Clodword, I don't know how to thank you."

"You don't have to thank me. We're friends. Friends help each other."

"Yes, we're friends, Clodword," Alice agreed and smiled when she saw how happy the response made him.

"Well, I will let you get back to sleep. This should provide just enough light to get you back to your bed without tumbling over half the crew." Clodword dipped his head in a slight bow and handed her the lantern, "The brace should be fairly easy to take on and off once you get used to it."

"Thank you again, Clodword. I hope you have a good night's sleep." Alice said as he headed down the hall.

"Oh, I doubt that will happen," he called over his shoulder. "Between the cook's snoring and Hatter's complaining, I think I will enjoy the night air on deck for a while."

Alice smiled and had to admit Clodword was growing on her. He was perhaps one of the few bright spots in this disorienting new Wonderland. She bent and unbent her right leg several times, marveling at the absence of pain.

He may not have Gryphon's fighting prowess, but he definitely inherited Tinker's genius.

The exhilaration of her newfound mobility chased away any thoughts of sleep. Alice lifted the lantern and looked down at the leatherbound volume in her hand.

Ava, I hope you picked one with lots of pictures.

She flipped the book cover open and frowned in confusion as she read the title on the inside page.

> *Addendum to The Complete Accounting of the Overthrow of the Yellow King, the Fall of Carcosa, and the Rise of the Queens of Wonderland by Myrddin Emrys, First Knight-Scholar of Wonderland.*

Alice flipped back to the cover of the book. The gold letters read *Skaggit's Encyclopedia of Flora of the Royal Gardens.*

"Clodword?" Alice called, hoping he had not already gone above deck.

"Yes, Alice?" Clodword replied. He sounded as if he was halfway up the stairs to the main deck.

"There's something wrong with this book."

She heard his footfalls coming down the stairs and toward her as she examined the cover. Alice turned the book over in her hands several times, examining the cover. As Clodword approached from the darkness, she handed him the lantern so she could examine the book with both hands. He held the lantern over the book and peaked curiously over her shoulder at the tome.

Alice read out loud for them both to hear.

> "After thorough study of the archival records in the Royal Library, as the ninth Knight-Scholar of Wonderland, I feel it is my duty to expound upon the histories detailed in The Complete Accounting of the Overthrow of the Yellow King, the Fall of Carcosa, and the Rise of the Queens of Wonderland written by Myrddin Emrys, First Knight-Scholar of

> Wonderland. This addendum should in no manner of interpretation be deemed as besmirching the completeness of my predecessor's work. Rather, in the centuries since the penning of his seminal tome, additional information has come to light that, hitherto, did not seem noteworthy in Myrddin Emrys' day but now appear critical to the understanding of the past history of Wonderland. This addendum is my humble attempt to add to the completeness of my colleague's work."

Clodword's brow furrowed in confusion as he looked from the book to Alice, "I thought this was a book on gardening?"

"That's what the cover says," Alice flipped the book closed to show him the title, then opened to the first page and pointed to the writing, "but see here, it says this is some kind of historical record."

"Can I see that for a moment?" He asked, handing her the lantern.

Clodword flipped through the pages, his eyes poring over the print. He examined the cover again, sliding his thumbnail between the paper affixed to the inside cover.

"Someone has replaced the cover with the binding to the gardening manuscript," Clodword declared handing the book back to her in exchange for the lantern. "This appears to be some manner of later companion volume to a history of Wonderland."

"Ava did not mention anything about this?"

"No," Clodword shook his head, "she was just very insistent that I give it to you . . ."

He paused mid-sentence as a piece of paper slipped from the book and fluttered to the floor like an oak leaf in autumn. They both watched it make its quiet journey until it came to rest on the wooden floorboards and then looked at each other.

"You've got to be kidding me?! What next, I rub the cover and a djinn appears?" Alice watched as Clodword knelt and retrieved the note, handing it to her as he stood.

Alice unfolded the paper as Clodword dipped the lantern close, "It's definitely Ava's handwriting but it makes no sense. It's just numbers and random words. It's gibberish. What good is this?"

"The book is an annotated compendium to a larger volume. Perhaps the numbers correspond to notations in the book?" Clodword offered.

"Clodword, don't let Hatter tell you otherwise, you are undoubtedly the brains of this operation," Alice smiled as she looked at the paper.

"We'll just keep it our secret," Clodword grinned.

With the hood of the lantern fully opened, the galley was brightly illuminated. They had decided the dining area would be the best place for them to delve deeper into the mystery of Ava's gift. Alice slouched back in her chair with the open book in her lap; Clodword sat across from her and carefully laid the note on the table.

"What's the first number on the note?" Alice asked.

Clodword peered over the paper, "Twelve and the words 'three queens.'"

Alice opened the book, flipping through the annotations until she came to note number twelve.

> "Note 12: An untitled document maintained by Carcosa's Master of Words, in the year 1345 of the Carcosian calendar, recorded a listing of entities who fled the persecutions and hunts of the servants of the Nailed God in the Otherworld. Among those granted permission by the Yellow King to pass through the portals and receive sanctuary in Carcosa is a notation identifying three sisters possessed with the ability of witchcraft, each with a different mastery over earth, sea, or air. This notation is believed to identify the entry into this realm of the women whom the Yellow King would elevate to the Three Queens of Carcosa."

"The Nailed God likely refers to the Christian religion of your world," Clodword offered.

"I believe you're right," Alice agreed. "I know Indira and Lairen came from my world, that is why they don't age here, but I have never heard anything about a third sister. And have you ever heard of this Yellow King or Carcosa?

"No, this is all new to me, and I have read extensively in the Royal Library," Clodword shook his head. "The portals must be similar to the Looking Glass you passed through. Could Carcosa be a more ancient name for Wonderland? It was my understanding that the Queens were the first rulers of Wonderland, but perhaps Carcosa was here first and ruled by the Yellow King?"

"Uggh, what good is this without the original text. This is just a fragment related to histories written by this First Knight-Scholar of Wonderland. I have never even heard that title used before."

"Let's try this next line," Clodword looked down at the note, "Fifteen, Peter the Pan."

Alice begrudging flipped the page and ran her finger down to note fifteen.

> "Note 15: Three lines after the Master of Words' notation of the three sisters receiving sanctuary in Carcosa, is an entry identifying the admission of three centaurs and a pan. As this is the only discovered record of a pan passing from the Otherworld to Carcosa, it can be concluded that this was likely Peter the Pan. The three centaurs are most certainly identifiable with the surviving sons of Eurytion, slain by the Yellow King and served to his guests at the wedding feast on the shore of the Lake of Hali after his betrothal to the Three Queens."

She looked up, "That seems fairly self-explanatory. The Pan came from my world as well, which explains why the Red Queen would still believe him alive after all these years."

"Now that's interesting," Clodword sat up straight as he pointed at the book. "That's a name I have seen before."

"Peter the Pan?" Alice frowned. "We have all heard of him, Clodword."

"No, not Peter. Well, yes, I have heard of Peter of course, but the Lake of Hali." Clodword's eyes took on a familiar excited glimmer, "I like to consider myself an expert with maps; I never forget a place. I remember seeing a map once that had a large lake far east of Wonderland and I am certain it was labeled Lake Hali."

"So Wonderland and Carcosa are separate places," Alice nodded. "One ruled by the Queens, the other by the Yellow King."

"But I don't think they existed concurrently. I think Carcosa came first. What was the name of the work by the First Knight-Scholar again?"

Alice flipped the book back to the first page.

> "Addendum to The Complete Accounting of the Overthrow of the Yellow King, the Fall of Carcosa, and the Rise of the Queens of Wonderland."

Clodword rose to his feet and started to pace, "This is beginning to make sense. The Queens overthrew the Yellow King and came west to establish their own land."

"Wonderland."

"Wonderland," Clodword nodded, then walked back to the table to look down at Ava's note. "Her next line is note thirty-three, Kraken a jailer not a guardian."

Alice quickly turned the pages until she found note thirty-three.

> "Note 33: It is important to note that Emrys' account of the Yellow King's granting of sanctuary for the Lord of the Forest and the Mother of the Sea to return from the Otherworld is factually sound. The sanctuary was granted upon condition that the Lord of the Forest accept exile to the Drowned Isles, later called the Cursed Isles, to which he assented. Documentation compiled by Silas, Third Knight-Scholar of Wonderland, significantly expounds upon the events of this time and the Pan's role in the imprisonment of the Lord of the Forest on the Cursed Isles. Silas recorded the story of a bard who Peter approached with a request to compose a song regaling his trickery of the Lord of the Forest and the Mother of the Sea. According to the tale Peter relayed to the bard, Peter returned to the Otherworld and convinced the forest god and the sea goddess to come to Carcosa where they would receive sanctuary until the purges of the Nailed God's servants subsided and it was safe to return. Peter confided that he not only

> had foreknowledge that the Yellow King intended to imprison the Lord of the Forest on the Cursed Isles by sending the Kraken to prevent his departure, but it was actually The Pan's idea. The bard described to Silas that Peter's motivations appeared to stem from a deep-seated hatred of the Lord of the Forest, however, whatever the origin of this hatred, Silas does not provide any additional details."

Alice looked up, "Is this the same Mother of the Sea that Suarez and his men worship?"

"I think it's very likely," Clodword agreed. "So the Kraken is there to keep those on the Cursed Isles imprisoned, not to keep others out."

"But it has been known to attack ships approaching the isles."

"Very true. There are multiple accounts in the histories of such attacks. I would assume it's just an unfriendly creature to all who encounter it."

"Great, a fucking angry octopus," Alice swore then looked down at the page. "Clodword, listen to this next entry.

> "Note 33A: To clarify my statement on immortality in the Otherworld in Note 33, beings who pass from Wonderland to the Otherworld do not become immortal as they can still be killed. However, they do remain ageless until returning to Wonderland. Conversely, beings who come to Wonderland from

> the Otherworld will not age in Wonderland. This has been documented in each of the thirty-two Otherworlders who survived the fall of Carcosa. The only notable exception is the Yellow King, who inexplicably did not appear to age in either world. Silas in his *Study of the Yellow King* theorized that since the Yellow King was already of advanced age he may have come from a place other than either Wonderland or the Otherworld and thus aged in neither world. Bran, Fourth Knight-Scholar of Wonderland, refuted Silas' theory in his *Treatise on the Yellow King* and believed the Yellow King had mastered a magic that prevented him from aging. A third theory was developed by Andrus, Sixth Knight-Scholar of Wonderland, in his *Reign of the Yellow King* claiming the Yellow King was neither living nor dead, but permanently existed in a state somewhere in between. Although there is no clear evidence to support any of the theories regarding the Yellow King's longevity, Andrus' theory is generally considered to be the least plausible, though not impossible."

"So that seems to confirm that Carcosa was destroyed." Clodword rubbed his chin. "The next line says forty-two, Pan crazy."

"Wonderful," said Alice as she flipped through the pages. "Here it is."

> Note 42: An entry in Emrys' personal journal indicates he provided the White Queen details of a thorough study he conducted of the medical journals in the Royal Library and provided a conclusive statement that the madness inflicting the Pan has no known cure or treatment. Emrys expresses frustration that his recommendation to the White Queen to reverse her judgement of banishment of The Pan and decide in favor of the Red Queen's request for execution was dismissed. The Complete Accounting of the Overthrow of the Yellow King, the Fall of Carcosa, and the Rise of the Queens of Wonderland does not include any information regarding the mental affliction ailing The Pan, the reason for the Red Queen's request that he be executed, or the White Queen's clemency. Emrys' record states only that in the fifty-fourth year of the reign of the Queens the Pan was exiled to the Cursed Islands."

"So an angry octopus and a mad pan," Clodword smiled as he sat back down into his seat.

"I'm so glad this amuses you." Alice threw him a mock ferocious stare. "I don't understand why Ava could not have just written this all out for us."

"Perhaps she didn't have time."

"Perhaps she didn't have time," Alice did her best imitation of his voice. "My sister basically shattered a glass vase into a million piece and told us to piece it back together so that we don't get killed by an angry octopus or a crazed Pan and get served to someone for dinner like the sons of Eurytion, whoever the hell they were."

"I believe they were centaurs, half-man half-horse," Clodword explained in a helpful tone that irritated Alice.

Alice glared at Clodword, "What's the next line in her note?"

"Forty-five, Pan Imprisoned."

> "Note 45," Alice read, "In his personal journal Emrys memorializes the date of the Pan's exile from Wonderland with an entry that simply states 'The Captain of the Gator confirmed that the Pan, with his company of trolls, was lowered into a longboat and rowed for the Cursed Isle. The boat cleared the boundary maintained by the Kraken without incident. The following morning the Gator's lookouts spotted the boat with several arrows protruding from the hull and mast. The ship's company appeared to have been significantly reduced by the unknown attackers, however, the Pan and at least seven trolls remained. No further sighting was made of The Pan or his vessels. Good riddance.'"

"So there are other hostile inhabitants on the Cursed Isles? We'll have to make sure Captain Suarez is aware of this," Clodword added.

"Hostile to the Pan at least. Peter had this Lord of the Forest imprisoned there. If he still lived, I don't imagine he would be all too happy to see Peter."

"The Lord of the Forest returned here from the Otherworld, or more precisely your world, but he is a creature of this world." began Clodsword.

"So he would not be ageless here like the Pan and the Queens."

"Correct. If he still lives he may prove an ally to us," Clodword contemplated the point for a moment, "though he may be no friend of the Queens either. It appears from these notes that, at least at some point, the Queens may have been aligned with the Yellow King."

"Great. We'll add vengeful forest god to the list with crazed Pan and angry octopus. Hopefully the next entry has some good news."

Clodsword moved his finger down the page to the next line, "I don't think so. It says sixty-nine, Queens' power."

> "Note 69: This paragraph significantly deviates from Emrys' meticulous citation of written or verbal accounts in describing events during the reign of the Yellow King. His statement that the Yellow King enhanced the powers possessed by the Three Queens to more effectively rule and maintain order

> in Carcosa is generally agreed upon by most scholars. However, Emrys' assertion that the Yellow King altered their powers so that it was in some manner shared between the Three Queens is unsupported by any surviving account. Further, his assertion that the power was imbued within the Queens in a manner that if any of the Queens were to die her power would be redistributed to the surviving Queens equally is wholly uncorroborated by any surviving sources of documentation."

Alice looked up from her reading, "Clodword, does that mean that the Red Queen is twice as powerful because she killed Indira? That could explain the new powers she has evidenced. It could also be why she killed her sister."

"Possibly," Clodword leaned back in his chair, a contemplative look on his face. "The Red Queen was certainly concerned about the threat posed by Peter and The Dark. Assuming the original entry from Emrys is correct, and that is by no means a certainty based upon note sixty-nine, then it is conceivable that the Red Queen killed Indira to consolidate the power within herself."

"If Emrys is correct, then why would the Red Queen wait centuries to act?"

Clodword shrugged, "It is hard to be certain of any of this. Our information is fragmentary. I suspect all of the authoritative works were removed and likely destroyed or secreted away at the order of one or both Queens. This book was disguised as a garden encyclopedia; I assume Ava found it by sheer happenstance. Perhaps there are others hidden in the Royal Library."

"Uggh," Alice tossed the book on the table with disgust. It thudded heavily on the hard wood. "We're grasping at straws. Without the original histories it's just a trail of breadcrumbs to nowhere."

She leaned her head back and rubbed at her eyes. A vicious headache was beginning to form in the back of her head.

"Hmm," Clodword looked down at the note.

"Something interesting?" Alice squinted at him. The light from the lantern felt like needles prodding her burgeoning headache.

"The next entry, seventy-two, Azure Queen," Clodword read over and slid the book toward him. He opened it and thumbed through the pages until he found the entry he sought.

> "Note 72: This is Emrys' first reference to the Queens by color—Red, White, and Azure."

"Azure Queen?"

"Alice, this seems to confirm that this Azure Queen is the third queen and a sister to Indira and Lairen," Clodword poked one thick thumb down at the page.

Alice leaned forward, placing her elbows on the table, as Clodword picked up the note and flipped to the next entry on Ava's list. His eyes scanned the page then he looked up excitedly.

"Listen to this." Clodword seemed almost giddy with excitement.

> "Note 132: This entry marks Emrys' first mention of the Queen in Yellow in the histories of Carcosa. It is also noteworthy that from here forth there is no mention of the Azure Queen or her fate. Andrus' *Reign of the Yellow King,* a work of highly speculative scholarship, draws a conclusion from this that the Queen in Yellow and the Azure Queen are one in the same. While Andrus is correct in stating there is no further reference to the Azure Queen in the histories hereafter, it is critical to denote that Emrys never makes this assertion, either explicitly or implicitly. Before his passing, Talos, the Eighth Knight-Scholar, stated to me personally that Andrus' claim remained unlikely. He cited that while the Queens led the rebellion against the Yellow King, the histories clearly show the Queen in Yellow stood in opposition and ruled as the de facto sovereign of Carcosa when the Yellow King crossed into the Otherworld. The drugging of the Queen in Yellow's wine by the Red Queen is considered to be the first act in the rebellion against Carcosa."

Clodword did not even look up at her before he was moving to the next note on Ava's list.

He's actually enjoying this.

Watching Clodword so engrossed in the mysteries of the book reminded Alice of Tinker, so consumed by working on his creations that he would not eat or drink, sometimes for days. Thinking of the White Knight brought up emotions she could not deal with at the moment and she pushed them back down, down into that chest of things she would have to unpack and deal with one day, but not today.

"Note 159," Clodword read, the excitement clear in his voice.

> "Emrys' addressing of the fate of the Queen in Yellow with a single sentence appears deliberately incomplete, though as to why has never been successfully discerned. However, following the death of Emrys, Clovis, his contemporary and chief scholarly rival, wrote *The Fall of Carcosa* which expounds upon the final days of Carcosa before the destroyed city was abandoned. Both works are largely similar in their description of the sequence of events that occurred with two notable exceptions. Unlike Emrys, Clovis details that after the Green Knight was dispatched to the Otherworld to hunt for the Yellow King, the two Queens destroyed all of the known portals between the worlds except for one which they transported with them from Carcosa. Although Clovis provides no physical description of the portal, historians are of a consensus that this was most certainly the Looking Glass. The second point of departure between the two works is Clovis'

description of fate of the Queen in Yellow. After the Queens, through some manner of witchcraft, place the Queen in Yellow in a state of interminable sleep, they have her body placed within the hold of a crewless schooner and set her adrift. According to Clovis, this is the Queens' final act before leaving Carcosa. The bardic tale *Curse of the Red Queen*, author unknown, tells of a ship cursed by the Red Queen to forever sail upon the tide, never reaching land. As the tale is roughly dated to the time period of the destruction of Carcosa, it has been surmised by some that the cursed ship of the song refers to the one carrying the unwaking body of the Queen in Yellow. While Emrys only states that the life of the Queen in Yellow was spared, there is no accounting of the reason for this decision by the Queens or the disposition of the Queen in Yellow after this judgement. As Clovis' work is generally considered to be authoritative, and no substantive errors have been disclosed in his text, it is therefore reasonable to discern that his description of the Queen in Yellow's fate is factual. Andrus takes great liberty in his *Reign of the Yellow King* to theorize that the reason the Queens spared the life of the Queen in Yellow was because she was in fact the Azure Queen, though he postulates that their mercy was not born of sisterly love, but as a bulwark against treachery on the part of either sister. Building upon

> Emrys' unsubstantiated claim that the Yellow King altered the Queens powers so that it was shared between them, Andrus asserts that if the White or Red Queen were to betray and kill the other, the slain Queen's power would go to the surviving sisters. Andrus believed this redistribution of power would be sufficient to awaken the Queen in Yellow/Azure Queen, creating a vengeful rival with equal power to the surviving Queen. Thus, he claimed the Queens' motivation in allowing the Queen in Yellow/Azure Queen to survive in stasis was a check against either Queen committing sororicide."

Clodword sat back in his chair and exhaled deeply; he did not meet Alice's gaze.

"Well, this Andrus person was clearly wrong." The pain was moving from the back of Alice's head to the front; she would need to get to bed soon and hope the pain subsided by morning.

"Alice, don't you see, Andrus was correct," Clodword looked at her with haunted eyes.

"That makes no sense. Why would the Red Queen risk awaking the Azure Queen and confronting her like an equal?"

"What if the Azure Queen was already awake and seeking revenge?"

"Already awake?" Then Alice felt her blood run cold with the sudden realization, "The Dark."

Clodword worked the dynamics out in his head, "Three sisters, each with dominion over earth, land or sea. Indira had power to affect the land and Lairen the seas."

"The Dark comes by air."

Clodword nodded slowly. "Peter must have found a way to awaken the Azure Queen. It is why the Red Queen felt so threatened by The Dark; she recognized it for what it was."

"Ava must have figured this out. What is her next entry?"

Clodword leaned forward and looked down at the paper, "There is only one more notation."

"What does it say?"

Clodword's brows furrowed, "It says last page, tea cup." He flipped the book to the last page, stared at it with visible confusion, and then examined several of the other final pages before returning to the last page again.

"Well?"

"I don't understand her meaning," Clodword frowned and spun the book around so that Alice could see.

Alice leaned forward and read the final page:

> *As Knight Scholar, it is my solemn duty to record the events of our histories for posterity without bias or undue influence. I have endeavored to make this addendum as comprehensive as the surviving records have allowed. The one significant foible to this work is that it is wholly reliant upon the previous writings and scholarships of other men. I cannot attest that there has been no effort to obscure, misinform, or*

misrepresent details by the architects of these histories. Those who put pen to paper were mortals, subject to the same flaws of ego, avarice, and ambition of any who wishes to leave their mark upon this world.

Thus, I join the expedition to locate the Green Knight. If he still lives, it is my deepest desire to learn from one who observed these events firsthand the veracity of details only speculated at by my peers. Some will say it is my own vanity that drives me to achieve the most comprehensive accounting of our past, but to those naysayers I protest that it is my duty to the realm as Knight Scholar to leave no stone unturned in the fulfillment of the duties bestowed upon me by my Queens.

Very Respectfully,
Udel
Ninth Knight Scholar of Wonderland

The world seemed to spin as she finished and Alice braced herself against the table with both hands. A wave of nausea rose up in her gut and the nascent headache in her brain flared brightly.

"Does it make any sense to you?" Clodword asked, looking at Alice as he rose to his feet in alarm. "Alice, are you okay?"

It did make sense to her and she was far from okay.

He had called it his 'tea cup', the way he placed a small c-shape on the side of the 'U' like the handle of a cup when he wrote his name. It was what made his signature *his* signature, he would always say.

Damn you, Ava. This why you wanted Clodword to wait until we were at sea to give me the book.

Ava would have recognized it the moment she saw it, the same way Alice did. It had been the U in Upton the last time they had seen it, but it was unmistakable. It was the way their father signed his name.

CHAPTER 12: THE TEA PARTY

Alice watched as the cabin steward, a young rabbit with black and tan brindled fur, set a teacup before each of the attendees in the Eaglet's galley. Captain Suarez sat at his usual place at the end of the table with Cooper on his right seated across from Jakers and Begley. Alice and Clodword took the seats next to Begley while Rebeck and Bore chose to lean up against the wall rather than bother with chairs clearly not designed with their hulking frames in mind

Hatter chose a seat at the far end of the table and he shrugged nonchalantly when Alice threw him an inquiring look. The reason behind his decision became all too apparent when there was a light thudding at the door. The steward quickly moved to the open door and jumped back in surprise as Lady Cheshire walked into the room and leapt onto the seat of the chair at the end of the table opposite Suarez.

The captain raised an inquisitive eyebrow in her direction and the jaguar flashed him a grin full of razor sharp teeth. By then the steward had returned to the table and had leaned over to fill Suarez's cup with hands that shook and splashed tea on the wooden table.

"I believe young Harry is quite unnerved by Lady Cheshire's grin," Jakers offered, winking over at the jaguar.

"Will the Duchess be joining us as well this evening?" Cooper asked as the steward moved to fill Jakers' and then Begley's cups. "I have not seen her above decks in the three days since we left Chess Bay."

"She is resting in her cabin; apparently she feels a little unwell after the . . . incident . . . with her dinner," Lady Cheshire replied.

Hatter snorted a laugh. "She's lucky that damnable cook did not go overboard with her meal."

"I'll make no apologies for my actions," Begley thumped the table with a fist. "What was that damn fool thinking cooking a rabbit stew on this ship?"

"No one thinks you were in the wrong, Mister Begley," Alice tried to calm him.

"And then to wave his ladle at me and call me uncouth. Uncouth!" Begley continued unabated.

"Well, you are an ill-tempered shit," Jakers stoked the fire further, poorly concealing his smile.

"I should have beat him senseless with that ladle," Begley railed.

"He is an unpleasant sort of fellow," Clodword nodded in agreement

"Ahh, the pleasant night of sleep I would have if you did," Hatter stared off dreamily, as if he could imagine the pleasant slumber.

"That's enough," Suarez rapped his knuckles against the table. "We have business to conduct."

Jakers and Begley fell silent. Alice and Clodword waved off the steward's offer of tea and Alice was shocked to see Hatter request a half cup. She had not thought him a tea drinker at all. The gunslinger then reached into his vest and withdrew a flask, filling the remaining half cup with rum despite Lady Cheshire's disapproving stare.

"Trust me, if you knew what Clockwork was about to tell everyone, you would drink too," Hatter winked at her as he took a sip. "Oh, that's good."

Clodword reached into a bag at his feet and placed the leatherbound volume on the table. He tapped it contemplatively for a moment and then placed his hand back on the table. The steward took a seat beside him, a log book in his hands.

"I seem to have come unprepared. Were we all supposed to bring a book to this meeting?" Hatter glanced from the steward to Clodword.

"Hush, Hatter," Lady Cheshire scolded, bringing out the gunslinger's roguish grin.

"It's a log book, sir," the steward explained. "I record the events of the captain's meetings."

"Mister Jakers, please begin," Suarez interjected, visibly annoyed at the chatter around the table.

Jakers stood, "Sir, the signal from the tracking device seems to have stabilized due east. We have set course in that direction and will continue until we reach the Cursed Isles or the signal changes."

"Clodword, how do you explain the signal's behavior? Has The Dark dropped the children into the ocean?" Suarez asked, his tea untouched.

"That's possible, but unlikely," Clodword nodded. "We believe that The Dark returned to its point of origin by the afternoon of the first day. In the two days since we have not detected any changes in direction or distance. Based upon calculations, if the wind continues to blow in our favor, we could reach the islands within a fortnight."

Suarez gave a harsh laugh, "Are you a sailor now, Clodword?"

"Uh, no," stammered Clodword.

"Well, let me tell you something every sailor knows: the wind never continues to blow in the direction you need it."

"Unless the Mother of the Sea wills it so," Alice interjected much to Clodword's relief.

Suarez's face visibly softened and the captain nodded, "Yes, unless the Mother of the Sea wills it so."

Begley looked at Alice and gave her a little wink that she took as "well played."

"Sir, we cannot rule out that The Pan has detected the beacon and is leading us into a trap," Cooper offered as Jakers took his seat.

"Mister Begley, what is our condition if we need to fight a ship?" Suarez turned to the Master of Guns.

Alice glanced over at the steward who continued to dip his quill pen into a little inkwell and take copious notes before looking over to Hatter. The gunslinger stared almost disinterestedly into his cup of tea and rum as the sailors spoke, glancing up only to give Lady Cheshire a half smile. The jaguar returned the smile, but Lady Cheshire's eyes watched the meeting with keen interest.

"Well, sir," Begley stood to make his report, "we have one hundred and fifty cannonballs for the three-pound guns, twenty-five balls per cannon. However, we detected a crack in the number two cannon on the starboard side."

"Can it still be fired?"

"No, sir. The crack is too deep. I have reallocated the guns cannonballs to the remaining guns; each cannon now has thirty balls. All six of the swivel guns are in working order, each with ten rounds of grape shot."

"Mister Begley," all eyes turned toward Lady Cheshire. She spoke in a calm measured tone, her yellow eyes radiating intelligence, "my great uncle was the First Mate aboard the Charybdis when she and the Stallion encountered the Kraken. Those were fourteen gun brigs with six-pound guns if memory serves me correctly, and he relayed that they did no damage to the beast. Of course, the Stallion was in a better position to see if the Kraken received any wounds from the six-pounders, but as you know, the Kraken destroyed the Stallion with all hands on board."

"Aye, you are correct Lady Cheshire," Begley nodded, glaring at Hatter. "We have sixty nine-pound balls as well, but we never received the cannons to fire them."

Hatter rolled his eyes in exasperation. "The crew has affixed the White Knight's siren to the bow. If we encounter the Kraken, he felt certain the siren would deter the creature from approaching the ship."

"How could he be certain?" Cooper asked as the Master of Guns sat back down. "Had he ever encountered the Kraken before?"

"The Kraken is believed to be a giant Cephalopoda," Clodword began. Then he saw the confused looks on the faces of those around the table and chose a less scientific explanation, "A giant octopus. My father tested the siren on several species of octopus and squid that inhabit the local waters with excellent results. In every case the creatures were repelled by the sound. He believed this effect would be replicated on the Kraken . . . theoretically."

"Theoretically?" Begley asked.

"Well, yes," Clodword conceded. Suarez pinched his eyes closed and rubbed his forehead as if a headache was coming on.

"No, not theoretically," Hatter interjected, leaning forward so abruptly he nearly upended his teacup. "The Dodo was equipped with a similar siren."

"For fucks sake, here we go with the pigeon again," groaned Jakers.

"Yes, here we go with the pigeon again," Hatter sneered back.

"Our guns won't hurt this thing. So we're going to bet our lives on something tested upon a bunch of little fishies? No offense to your father, Clodword," Begley began.

"None taken," Clodword gave the Master of Guns a grim smile and nod.

". . . and a pigeon that flew home?" Begley looked around the room.

Hatter looked ready to retort when Lady Cheshire spoke up, "Clodword, I believe you have uncovered information you feel pertinent to the success of this journey?"

"Yes. Yes, I have," replied Clodword awkwardly, rising to his feet and tapping the leatherbound book.

Her father's book.

The thought lanced through her heart; the family she had loved and mourned was a lie. Alice had lay awake for hours, her mind descending into dark places.

Did my mother know the truth? Of course she must have. My father would not have aged a day in all their time together.

Ava maintained a romantic notion of her father as a gallant hero, something that had grown legendary since his death. Alice had to admit that perhaps he even was a hero, despite his deception; he certainly died a hero's death that January afternoon.

Is he truly dead or was this another deception?

Did his body really lay beneath a cairn on the battlefield of Isandhlwana with the rest of the men of F Company, 1st Battalion,

24th Regiment of Foot? Or is he out there, even now, hunting for evidence the King in Yellow still stalked the Otherworld, plotting a return to Carcosa?

She knew Ava would say their father concealed the information to protect them and died before he could reveal the truth. Even if he still lived, Ava would hold the unshakable belief that he faked his death to hide their existence from the King in Yellow, who would undoubtedly seek to discover the Looking Glass.

Girls and their fathers.

"This book is an annotated companion to the histories of Wonderland. More specifically, it deals with the overthrow of the Yellow King, the fall of Carcosa, and the rise of the Queens of Wonderland, as its title states," Clodword explained.

Alice saw Bore turn to his brother and speak in a hushed tone. The tone of his voice sounded alarmed, and though she did not speak the giants' tongue, she clearly heard Bore say "Carcosa." Rebeck nodded gravely but gestured for his brother to stay quiet so he could listen to Clodword. His eyes briefly met Alice's gaze and an unspoken acknowledgement passed between them that the exchange had not gone without her notice. They would talk about this at another time.

Clodword reviewed his findings for the assembled group. Ava's breadcrumbs had proved very thorough and he had not gleaned significantly more information than where she had led them. Captain Suarez leaned forward and placed his elbows on the table, his nose resting against his folded hands as he listened intently to Clodword. Beside him, Begley and Jakers grimaced and groaned at each new detail. When he finished, Clodword nodded to the captain and took his seat while the steward feverishly continued scribing the details into the log book.

"So you think Peter and the Azure Queen are somehow in league and The Dark is a manifestation of her powers?" Cooper asked, leaning back in his chair and folding his arms across his chest.

"I do, sir," nodded Clodword.

"What do you men think?" Suarez's gaze moved from Begley to Jakers.

"I don't know, Sir. If these waters are truly the home of the Mother of the Sea, maybe she will intervene on our behalf. I'm just a simple sailor. These matters are all too great for me. They hurt my head to even contemplate," Jakers shook his head.

"If the Kraken is some kind of prison warden, it may not harry us on the way in, but it may give us a hell of a fight on the way out," Begley blew out a deep breath.

For the first time since Alice had known him, Captain Suarez stumbled upon his words, no doubt fighting back some emotion, "Clodword, did you discover anything concerning why the Azure Queen would be taking the children? What she is doing with them?"

"No, sir. I'm sorry, I did not," Clodword quickly averted his eyes from the captain's gaze.

"Well, if you ask me, there is some good news in what Clockwork found," Hatter slapped the table, almost merrily. "If The Dark is truly the Azure Queen . . ."

"I believe the Azure Queen was the woman's face we saw in The Dark during the attack on the beach," Alice interjected and Clodword nodded in agreement.

Hatter looked at them both and sighed , "If The Dark is the Azure Queen that is good news for us. She may be ageless like her sisters, but then she is mortal too; she can be killed."

"The Dark's incursions into Wonderland became more brazen after the death of the White Queen," added Lady Cheshire, "so we can assume that her powers and reach increased incrementally with the death of her sister, just like the Red Queen experienced."

"And the Red Queen still fears for her life. So, they can still be killed," Hatter tapped on the table to accentuate his point.

"Hatter, my dear, you're missing my point." Lady Cheshire's yellow eyes slid toward the gunslinger, "When we kill the Azure Queen, all three Queens' power will become consolidated within Lairen. We will kill a queen and create a goddess."

CHAPTER 13: MOONLIT NIGHT

The sea was calm, the waves barely a ripple on the glass-like surface of the Great Wide Open. Alice had never been out to sea and she was struck by how small it made her feel in the world. The night sky was dark, except for the crescent moon, the solitary light in the blackness of the ocean. She could not tell where the horizon met the ocean and, when combined with the gentle rocking of the Eaglet, it gave Alice a disorienting sensation as if tumbling through a blackened void. The crescent moon was her anchor and Alice kept glancing up at it to keep her bearings.

The meeting had broken up shortly after Lady Cheshire's revelation. Captain Suarez gave instructions that the ship was to proceed on a war footing. Begley was to increase training drills with his gunners from one to three times a day; the crew would arm themselves with pistols, shortswords, and axes. The ship's four sharpshooters would operate in two shifts with two riflemen on deck at any given time. Suarez wanted the men in a combat mindset so they would be prepared for any nasty surprises that may lay ahead.

The giants had slipped out of the meeting once it had broken up and Alice scanned the deck until she saw the two hulking forms standing by the mast in the middle of the ship. They were facing away from her but as she approached she could see they were watching Hatter strolling alongside Lady Cheshire. They made an odd pair, the gunslinger and the jaguar, walking side by side in the moonlight. Alice thought it was a bitter irony that after so many years of keeping their relationship a secret, even from their own children, that they should now have the freedom to step from the shadows together. It was an unnecessarily cruel turn that the Red Queen had transformed Lady Cheshire and her daughters, perhaps borne out of jealously with her own Red King lost.

Danavi always warned her that the Red Queen had a hard heart and even seemed to gain some measure of pleasure from the unhappiness of others. How unlike the White Queen she truly was. It was one of the reasons Danavi was so intent on their relationship remaining clandestine, the Red Queen would find pleasure in inflicting heartache on the two lovers. Queen Indira could provide some modicum of protection to Alice, but as Red Knight, Danavi was beholden to Queen Lairen.

Alice heard the brothers talking as they watched the couple walking. Bore was saying something that caused Rebeck to chuckle. She had spent enough time around men to know that whatever was passing between the brothers was likely crude.

"Care to let a girl in on the joke?" She said as she walked up to them. The brothers started slightly, surprised to have been approached at unawares.

Alice doing Alice things.

Bore did not meet her gaze, embarrassed at whatever had passed between the two brothers, which confirmed her suspicions. However, Rebeck greeted her with a wide smile.

"My brother was just asking if I thought Hatter and Lady Cheshire maintained carnal relations."

Bore's eyebrows furrowed and he playfully struck his brother on the shoulder, followed with an angry retort in their language.

"They had two daughters together before the Red Queen turned her into a jaguar, so I am certain they had carnal relations a plenty." Alice glanced over at Bore, "Does your brother understand any of the Queens' tongue?"

"Oh, no," Rebeck chuckled, "but we are brothers and it does not take language skills for Bore to know I told you what he had said. Back in our father's court we were always trying to embarrass each other in front of female suitors."

"Female suitors?"

"Yes, the Queen Mother was to decide who would marry her sons, so female suitors would come to convince her that they would be a good match."

"And you had no say in this?"

"No, of course not," Rebeck shook his head. "The mother always decides who their son will marry, if the woman will agree. Much to our mother's consternation, my brother and I went to great lengths to make the other look a fool in front of the suitors. She would get very angry that we chased off all the best suitors with our foolishness."

"So neither of you have wives?"

"My brother, no. But I have a wife and son at home, if they still live." Rebeck's face briefly clouded with concern, "They likely think me dead. She will be ruling as the dowager queen until my son comes of age to be king."

"You will return home, Rebeck; I promise you," Alice laid a hand on his arm. It looked small and childlike against his branch-thick limb.

Rebeck smiled, a sad sort of smile, "I do believe you mean that in your heart, but you cannot promise such things little lady. I was in that meeting. I know what we face before us."

"That is what I wanted to speak to you about. You both seemed to recognize the mention of Carcosa," Alice began.

"Carcosa?" Bore interjected, looking from Alice to Rebeck.

Rebeck said something to his brother in their language and it seemed to calm Bore, but his face was grave when he looked back to Alice, "Yes, we know of this place."

"From the histories that we have seen, Carcosa was the bastion of the King in Yellow but was destroyed by the Queens millennia ago." Alice explained.

"This may be true. I remember it as little more than a story to scare misbehaving children when I was young. However, our histories describe Carcosa as once a place of great evil. I have not heard its ruler referred to as the King in Yellow before, but when they speak of Carcosa they say it is a fearful thing to fall into the hands of the Living God. I believe that is who they speak of."

Bore looked at Alice and spoke emphatically in his language.

"My brother says it is considered ill-advised to speak of this place. We need to heed the old saying amongst my people that when you look for Carcosa, Carcosa looks for you," Rebeck translated.

"Okay, well that brings me to my second request. I would like you to teach me your language." Alice could see the surprise register on his dark face.

"Learn the giants' tongue?" Hatter interjected as he and Lady Cheshire approached, returning from their walk on the deck. "Why in the world would you want to do that? There are only two giants left in all of Wonderland."

"As a matter of fact, I think we should all learn it." Alice explained, "The Pan and the Azure Queen speak the Queens' tongue. I believe it unlikely they would be familiar with the giants' language."

"This is true. My people have had no dealings with The Pan," Rebeck agreed.

"If ever the need arises to speak discretely, it would behoove us to have a method to do so."

"Alice makes an excellent point." Lady Cheshire appraised Alice with her feline gaze. "This could give us a tactical advantage if the need arises."

Hatter rolled his eyes in overstated exasperation and shook his head.

"I do not know if I am much of a teacher, but I will do my best," Rebeck bowed his head toward Alice.

"Thank you, Rebeck."

"Rebeck, I have been meaning to ask you something," Lady Cheshire asked with uncharacteristic hesitancy.

"Lady Cheshire, it is late we should all be retiring for the evening," Hatter interjected but bit his lip and fell silent as the jaguar cast him a withering gaze.

"Yes, Lady Cheshire, how may I be of service," Rebeck dipped his head respectfully, which Alice thought was quite a magnanimous gesture for as a prince, even one from a hostile nation, Rebeck held a higher station in society than Lady Cheshire.

"When you were held in the Red Queen's dungeon, did you by chance have any contact with my daughters?" Her yellow eyes looked wide and pleading.

Rebeck smiled wistfully and Alice thought he was choosing his words very carefully. "My Lady, our confinement was not in close enough proximity to communicate. However, I was able to observe them regularly. They always seemed to me to be healthy and to draw strength from each other. At all times they conducted themselves with honor, dignity, and fortitude. In happier times, I look forward to making their acquaintance and telling them myself, how I was able to persevere in my captivity through their ever present example of courage in the face of adversity."

A wide smile broke across the jaguar's face, and even Hatter's tension seemed to ease.

"Prince Rebeck, I, too, very much look forward to that day. Thank you for your kind words, they do a mother's heart good."

Rebeck once again dipped his head in respect.

They parted ways for the evening, the brothers choosing to sleep outdoors below the night sky. Alice accompanied Hatter and Lady Cheshire back toward the stairway to the lower deck. She could see Captain Suarez standing toward the bow of the ship, his face turned up toward the night sky with his hands clasped behind his back. The white of his fur seemed to glow in the moonlight.

"I think I'll stay up here a little longer," Alice excused herself from her two companions.

"Going to get a head start on your giant lessons?" Hatter flashed her that roguish grin.

"Hatter, I liked it better when I was planning to kill you."

"You're not anymore?"

"Not tonight at least," Alice looked from the gunslinger to the solitary form of the captain.

Lady Cheshire followed Alice's gaze, her own expression growing wistful, "That's a man with a lot on his mind."

"Have a good night Lady Cheshire," Alice dipped her head respectfully toward the jaguar. "Hatter, I hope the Duchess' chef snores like a banshee tonight."

Hatter frowned deeply at the remark and appeared ready to respond when Lady Cheshire nudged him to get moving down the stairs.

The captain stood at the farthest point forward on the Eaglet, where the ship's hull came to a point. Beside him, the crew had mounted the copper 'Kraken siren' to the railing. The device consisted of a metallic box with a rotating crank bar emerging from the rear. A tubular horn to amplify the sound pointed outward from the front of the device.

"Enjoying the night air, Captain Suarez?" Alice announced herself as she approached the sea captain.

"Just looking up at the moon, Alice," Suarez replied without turning to face her.

"A waning crescent, that's good. We should be close to a new moon when we reach the Cursed Isles. The dark night sky will mask our approach to the island," Alice observed.

"When we're young we look up at the moon with eyes wide open and full of wonder," Suarez replied. The ever present scowl on his face softened as he gazed at the night sky.

"Sir?" Alice glanced sidelong at him. The captain sounded unusually introspective.

"My children used to look at the moon like that; they used to look at a great many things like that." Suarez turned to face her, "You think me a monster for what I did to those children on the beach."

"I don't."

"You should. I do."

"Maybe we're all monsters, Captain, but it will take monsters to fight monsters."

"Perhaps," Suarez nodded and looked back out over the water. "The day my children were taken, I let my son take one of the rowboats and row his sister to the beach all by himself. He was so proud. I was too, truth be told."

Suarez sighed heavily, "That day broke me, Alice. What I allowed to happen to those children in Chess Bay, I did so that no other parent will have to live with this dark hole inside them like I do."

"Captain, you don't have to justify . . ." Alice began when Suarez turned to her, the softness in his expression was gone now.

"No, Alice, I don't," he gave her a mirthless smile, "but it is good to know who you are going into battle with."

"That it is, Captain." Alice agreed.

"Do you think this contraption will work?" Suarez inclined his head toward the siren.

"I trust Tinker knew what he was doing. If Hatter sleeps in again tomorrow, I say we fire it up and give it a try," Alice flashed him a genuine grin of pleasure at the thought of the blaring siren jarring the gunslinger from his slumber.

"I like your style, Alice," the Captain gave her a wink and turned away. "Have yourself a good evening."

"Absolutely out of the question!" Mister Cooper's shrill tone pierced the quiet night and Alice saw the Captain's shoulders sag slightly.

"Mister Cooper is an excellent seamen and officer, one of the best I have ever seen, but the man gets along as well with others as a bee in a balloon shop," Suarez squinted, trying to discern the commotion in the dim light.

"Was he always this way?"

"Do you mean was he this way before he was a rabbit?" Suarez glanced sidelong at her then shook his head. "No, before the Red Queen's handiwork, he was quite well-liked, especially for an officer. But ever since the change, there's him and then there's the ship. That's not the sailors' way. For a sailor, you and the ship are one. One for all, all for one."

They glanced down the deck to where the first mate was embroiled in a heated conversation with Rebeck and Bore as a miserable looking young sable-furred sailor stood amidst them. The sailor's eyes dotted nervously from Cooper to the giants. Rebeck placed a restraining hand against his brother's chest as Bore repeatedly pointed to his head and tugged at his hair. The giant's voice sounded angry.

"Excuse me, Captain, I'm going to make sure the giants don't toss Mister Cooper overboard," Alice stepped past Suarez and walked purposely toward the arguing men.

"No weapons for the giants. Do you understand me?" Cooper pointed his finger directly at the face of the young sailor who looked down at the deck and nodded.

"Mister Cooper, what is the trouble?" Alice asked as she approached.

The first mate turned to her, his expression a mixture of anger and exasperation, "One of the giants asked Ansel for a weapon."

Bore looked ready to continue his angry protests but Rebeck spoke up first, "Alice, that is not an accurate accounting."

"Are you calling me a liar?" Cooper rounded on Rebeck then took a step back as Bore looked ready to pounce.

"I am not calling anyone a liar," Rebeck shook his head, his tone calm and even. "My brother simply asked the sailor for a knife to trim his hair. We were not able to groom ourselves during our long months of captivity."

Bore glanced toward Alice, his face taking on a plaintive look as he reached up and jostled his long hair.

"Tie it in a ponytail." Cooper scowled. "He's not getting a weapon."

"This is not a problem I share with my brother," Rebeck gestured to his bald scalp, "but my brother is quite superstitious and likes to wear his hair a certain way when he is on campaign. He believes it brings him luck and good fortune."

Bore again jostled his hair.

"It sounds like a reasonable request," Alice replied, bending over to draw the knife from her boot. She handed it to Bore, who nodded gratefully. Alice pointed at the blade, "I want that back once he's done."

Rebeck translated for his brother, who nodded and asked a question in return.

"My brother would like to know if it's sharp enough to shave hair," Rebeck asked.

"Tell him to be careful. It's sharp enough to shave a man's finger from his hand—even a giant one."

Bore looked down at the knife and guffawed as Rebeck translated Alice's words.

"This is unacceptable," Cooper protested then looked over Alice's shoulder. "Captain Suarez, I must insist the giant return the blade immediately!"

"Let it go, Mister Cooper," Suarez replied. "The giants are members of the crew on this voyage."

Cooper threw Alice a baleful glare, "You'll get us all killed."

The first mate turned and stalked away as Ansel visibly relaxed and gave Alice a weak smile. Rebeck gestured with his head for Ansel to follow as the giants walked over to the edge of the deck and the sailor happily followed.

"I'm good, I'll stay right here," Alice said when Rebeck looked toward her.

Alice watched as several of the younger sailors gathered around the giants as Bore gripped a handful of his hair and sliced off a chunk of the long locks. He tossed it over the side of the ship. The clump of long, black hair fluttered in the breeze like an escaping crow and the assembled sailors gave a small cheer. Soon they were whooping and cheering wildly with every handful of hair Bore cut from his head. He handed the knife to his brother, who stepped in front of him obscuring Alice's view as he worked. Loud scraping sounds, like sandpaper slowly drawn across wood could be heard as Rebeck groomed his brother. Alice looked back toward Suarez who gave her a quick wink as he too watched the spectacle.

He's enjoying seeing his crew have a moment of levity.

A loud cheer rose from the sailors as Rebeck stepped back and Alice could see the sides of Bore's head, the skin dark and smooth in the moonlight. A short, thick patch of black hair ran down the middle of the giant's head in a mohawk style. The giant grinned wildly as several of the sailors slapped him on the back good naturedly and he dipped his head so a few of the taller rabbits could rub the bristling mohawk. Rebeck separated from the crowd and walked over to Alice.

"Your knife," Rebeck smiled and extended the blade back to her, hilt first.

"I wouldn't be surprised if half the crew sported mohawks by morning," Alice bent and slipped the knife back into her boot.

"Wouldn't that be a sight?" the giant gave a warm chuckle. "You know, a few days ago I would have said the prospects of ever leaving the Queen's dungeon alive were impossible. We have you to thank for that, Alice.

Alice smiled and stretched her arms to loosen up a knot in her back, "My friend, at this point, I see six impossible things before breakfast. Get some sleep, Rebeck. Who knows what impossibilities await us tomorrow."

"Man overboard! Man overboard! Starboard side!" the lookout shouted from the crow's nest.

One of the sailors began to ring the ships bell, three long rings followed by three short rings, in a continuous sequence. Alice could hear the sound of feet thudding upon wooden planks as the sailors streamed up from below deck at the sound of the alarm.

"Watch leaders account for your people, I want to know who is missing," Cooper barked at the arriving sailors.

"Mister Chambers, bring us fifteen degrees to the starboard side," Suarez yelled to the junior navigator who manned the helm while Jakers slept. "Mother, help him if that damn fool doctor has fallen overboard!"

"I'm right here, Captain," mumbled a groggy Alistair as he plodded up the last few steps to the main deck.

Alice and Rebeck joined the other sailors along the starboard railing of the ship as they scanned the water.

"Watchman fire the rocket," Cooper commanded as he up alongside her, a mix of worry and determination etched on his face.

He's clearly worried about his missing sailor.

There was a loud hiss as a large firework-like rocket was ignited and streaked into the sky. It exploded with a loud crack that Alice knew would light up the night sky like a sunburst. She had seen such flares used often enough on the battlefield that she closed her eyes until the rocket detonated in the sky to preserve her night vision.

A cry went up among several of the sailors as they spotted something in the water.

"There he is!" shouted one of the sailors.

"Helm, hard starboard!" Suarez ordered as several sailors readied ropes to throw down to the distressed soul.

Alice spotted the form in the water, dimly lit in the dying light of the flare. She could make out a torso and two short, stubby arms bobbing up in the water. Suarez's adjustments to the ship's course was going to bring the starboard side of the ship within a few feet of the distressed sailor.

A sailor came running up to Cooper and spoke to him in hushed tones. When the First Mate turned back to the bobbing form his brow was furrowed in concern.

"Something wrong?" Alice asked.

"All our crew is accounted for," Cooper replied.

"Then who is that?" she asked turning back to look out into the water.

"I don't know," she heard him reply in a low voice.

Alice could see Hatter, rope in hand, alongside Clodword and the giants at the bow of the ship ready to cast the lifeline down into the water and pull the poor soul up to safety. A hush fell over those on bow as the Eaglet approached the bobbing form and she saw Hatter and the others exchange confused looks.

She craned her neck to see the bobbing form bounce lifelessly against the hull of the ship. As it passed beneath her in the water she could see that the form was the upper half of an alligator, its snout pointed skyward, mouth slightly open as if in surprise to reveal a maw filled with viciously sharp teeth. Its front two legs outstretched, froze in the rigor of death. The creatures eyes were clouded and sightless as it bobbed in the water, and she could see that the rear of its body had been shorn off mid-section.

The sailors began to disperse, and Alice heard more than one murmur about bad omens as they headed back below deck.

"I'm sorry, Captain, it looked like a person in the water," the lookout yelled down from the mast.

"You did good, better safe than sorry," Suarez replied as he approached to confer with Cooper, glancing over the side to see the remains of the creature before it trailed off behind the ship and into the night.

"Captain, what would an alligator be doing this far out in the Great Wide Open?" Alice asked.

"Not an alligator, Alice, a crocodile," corrected Cooper, his countenance grim as he exchanged a look with Suarez.

"And that is some kind of bad sign or ill omen?"

"You could certainly call it that," Suarez knotted his brows, deep in thought.

Alice looked at the two officers in confusion, she felt growing annoyance they were not being more forthcoming.

"Did you see that thing floating by?" Hatter nodded toward the ocean as he approached with Clodword and the giants, then shook his head in disbelief. "That's got to be one of the craziest things I have ever seen!"

Rebeck looked disquieted by the occurrence and Bore, already noticeably wary of the ocean, looked positively horrified. Whether it was the thought of crocodiles in the water or that there was something large enough to bite one in half, Alice could not tell.

Clodword, of course, looked absolutely fascinated by the sight, "Captain Suarez, what could have done that to the crocodile? A shark?"

"That's part of the problem, these waters are too warm for any shark big enough to take on a crocodile that size. Whatever did that is something I never encountered before," replied Cooper.

"What's the other part of the problem?" Alice asked glancing at Suarez.

"Crocodiles are never naturally this far from shore. The only time they are is when they are used on longfish hunts to drive them up toward the surface so they can be speared," Suarez looked out over the ocean. "If there is a crocodile this far out, it means we have one of the Queen's black ships out here somewhere with us."

"Do you think they would attempt to waylay us?" Clodword asked as Hatter hissed a curse under his breath

"You saw what they did to us in the harbor. Out in the open ocean, a black sail might not show as much restraint," Cooper replied

The image of Casey, his body broken upon the deck, flashed in Alice's mind. She felt as if a cold, clawed hand suddenly gripped her heart, not in sadness but in simmering rage.

Neither may we.

CHAPTER 14: ROUGH SEAS

True to Suarez's prediction, the weather did not stay in their favor. By morning, the Eaglet was in the midst of a roiling storm that tossed and swayed the ship. The Duchess was the first to feel the effect of the sea's turbulence and stayed in her cabin throughout the four day storm, unable to keep down food or liquids. Hatter too, much to the consternation of the Duchess' cook, was largely confined to his bed with a terrible bout of seasickness. The cook complained incessantly about the malodorous stench in the room and frequently spritzed the air about the debilitated gunslinger with rosewater, demanding Hatter remove himself to the bathroom for the remainder of the storm. Clodword, unaffected by the violent movements of the ship, had to disarm Hatter to keep him from shooting their unsympathetic roommate.

The heavy winds and torrential rains proved too much for even Rebeck and Bore to withstand and the two giants moved into one of the storerooms on the third deck of the ship. There, surrounded by boxes of provisions and barrels of fresh water, they began their language lessons, teaching Alice, Clodword, and Lady Cheshire the rudiments of their native tongue.

By the morning of the fifth day, the storm had broken and the waters of the Great Wide Open had calmed considerably. The crew and passengers of the Eaglet emerged from below decks like bears awakening from winter hibernation, shielding their eyes from the shining sun.

Alice breathed in deep lungfuls of fresh sea air as she stepped onto the deck. The stale air below deck had felt stifling after so many days. She closed her eye and tilted her head up to let the warm rays of the sun shine upon her face. The back of her head brushed against the longbow she had slung across her back. Adhering to Suarez's guidance to the crew, she was dressed for battle with a full quiver of arrows and her shortsword in its scabbard on her belt. The sword invoked a wave of mixed emotions; Alice knew that Indira had imbued it with magic as a final gift to her, but it was also the instrument of the Queen's destruction.

She was surprised to find Hatter and Clodword awake and already on deck. The gunslinger was wearing holstered pistols on each hip and his lever action rifle across his back. Alice did not see any weapons visible on Clodword. Then she remembered the small pistol he kept secreted inside his vest. Hatter looked pale and drawn from his sickness, but he appeared to have regained some of his swagger in the fresh morning air.

Two sailors walked by the men and greeted Clodword cordially as they passed; he wished them good day in return.

Hatter glanced at the sailors then looked askew at Clodword for a moment, "Making friends?"

Clodword shrugged, "I can't really say I know those two fellows at all."

"Good morning," Alice said as she casually approached and then leaned over the side of the railing to peer searchingly into the water.

"Good morning, Alice," Clodword replied as Hatter nodded in greeting then furrowed his brow looking quizzically at her as she searched the water.

"Lose something?" Hatter peered over the side.

"No," Alice continued searching the water, "I was just checking to see if you threw the cook overboard."

Hatter groaned and shook his head but Clodword laughed. Alice noticed Hatter immediately straightened up and squared his shoulders as Lady Cheshire emerged from below with the Duchess. The Duchess looked positively awful from her episode. Always a frail young woman, the Duchess now looked positively wraithlike and so ephemeral that Alice wondered if a light wind might simply blow her away. She walked on shaky legs and braced herself with one hand against the Lady Cheshire's strong shoulders, giving her a slightly hunched appearance.

"Duchess, so good to see you well," Alice smiled.

"Thank you, Alice," the Duchess managed a weak smile in return and then her eyes trailed slightly upward. "Such a beautiful day."

"Hatter, I trust you're feeling better as well?" Lady Cheshire asked, the hint of a smile on her feline lips.

"Never better, Lady Cheshire."

"It seems Rebeck and Bore are getting along well with the crew." The jaguar glanced over to where the giants were assisting Begley and his gunners reset the cannons in their mounts after the ferocious storm. They watched as Bore lifted one of the heavy cannons, his thick arms straining as the sailors guided it onto the mount. "I guess being inhumanly strong makes you a very useful commodity."

"Yes, well, that's not too difficult on a ship full of rabbits," Hatter said with a noticeable bit of acidity.

Alice glanced at Lady Cheshire and the two shared a brief, knowing smile. Lady Cheshire had confided that despite his adamant objections to the contrary, Hatter was jealous of the time she spent with the giants learning their language. The jaguar let no opportunity pass to further needle him on the subject, a fact which greatly endeared the woman to Alice.

"I don't know, they seem rather brutish," the Duchess commented, her voice weaker and breathier than usual.

"I could not agree more, Duchess," Hatter agreed. Then turning to Lady Cheshire, "Brutish."

"Clodword," a sailor nodded his head in greeting as he passed and Clodword smiled and nodded back.

Hatter watched the sailor pass by barely acknowledging the others present then turned back to Clodword and narrowed his eyes, "What's going on here? Why is everyone being so nice to you Clockwork?"

"Captain, sail on the horizon, starboard side" the lookout called from the crow's nest, pointing toward the ship.

Alice could see Captain Suarez further down the deck moving to the rail of the ship and placing the extended telescope to his eye. She peered toward the horizon and thought she saw a faint speck, though she could not tell if it was her eye playing tricks on her at this distance.

"Are there other ships this far out in the Great Wide Open?" the Duchess asked.

"From the reaction of our captain, I don't believe we were expecting any," Hatter quipped.

"I'm going to go talk to Suarez," Alice said as she turned to Hatter. "You coming or are you going to stay and watch Bore carry cannons around the deck all day?"

"When you put it that way, how can a man refuse?" Hatter replied with a wry half-smile.

"Can I join you?" asked Clodword.

Hatter's reply oozed with sarcasm, "I wouldn't think to not bring the most popular man on the Eaglet. Come. Let's make it a party,"

"I think Lady Cheshire and I will stay here." The Duchess gripped the rail with white knuckles, "I'm still feeling a little unsteady on my feet."

"Mister Begley, I want all the cannons mounted by midday. Have powder and shot ready to be loaded and fired. Swivels guns too," Suarez called out as he lowered the telescope.

"Aye, Captain," Begley called from the other side of the deck then turned to his gun crew. "You heard the captain, get your asses in gear. Big fella, if you and your brother can keep helping out it would be a great help."

"We will assist with whatever you need," Rebeck nodded.

"Captain, is there a problem?" Alice asked approaching Suarez.

"There's a ship out there. She's still a ways off, but this is far out even for a fully rigged ship," Suarez looked grim and concerned.

"Fully rigged?" asked Alice, still getting up to speed on all the nautical terminology.

"She's got three masts, all of them square-rigged, all of them black; that means she's one of the Queen's frigates. I think it likely that was her crocodile we spotted the other night."

"Why in the name of the Mother is one of the Queen's longfish ships all the way out here?" asked Hatter.

"Aye, this is far out even for them. My guess is they got blown off course in the storm."

"How many cannons on a ship like that?" Alice looked to where Begley was directing his cannon crew.

"Twenty-four, all 9-pounder guns."

"Can you fight a ship like that?" Alice asked.

"I can outrun a ship like that."

"Captain, has she spotted us as well?" asked Clodword, looking toward the ship and squinting.

"We're quite a bit smaller and she's likely not expecting to encounter another ship this far out, so she may not be looking. But if her lookout is worth their salt, then he's spotted us, or soon will. But they'll be more concerned with finding longfish than bothering with us. Right now she's running parallel to us.

Let's hope she stays off in the distance, fills her hold, and turns home."

"Thank you, Captain. We'll leave you to your preparations," Alice thanked him and noticed Hatter seemed eager to get back to Lady Cheshire. They turned to leave but Clodword lingered behind.

"Captain, can I inquire as to how Mister Jakers is faring?" Clodword asked with genuine sincerity.

"He's resting but should recover quickly." Suarez's features softened into a rare congenial smile and he extended his white-furred hand toward Clodword, "I owe you a debt of gratitude, Clodword. We all do."

"Hey now, what's this all about?" Hatter rounded and turned back. "What with all this 'Good morning, Clodword, we owe you a debt of gratitude, Clodword,' nonsense?"

Suarez's features hardened into their usual scowl as he faced Hatter, "Mister Jakers nearly worked himself to death trying to keep the Eaglet from floundering in the storm. Have you ever manned the helm in a fierce gale, Hatter? Of course not, you prissy shit. That wheel could snap a helmsman's arms like twigs in a storm like that. In the pitch dark of night, the wind gusts and the rain is so hard it feels like shards of glass striking your face. You pray to the Mother of the Sea to hold on for just a minute longer and when that minute passes you pray with all your heart for another. The storm had already pushed Chambers, our other helmsman, to the point of collapse, so Jakers stood his post, fighting that wheel all day and into the night. He cried out to the Mother of the Sea to make it stop until he was hoarse, until there was nothing left of him but an empty shell. The way I hear it, that is when Mister Clodword here stepped out of the dark, fighting the wind and rain to get to Jakers' side. Clodword took hold of the helm and with his strength and Jakers' knowledge, they fought that bitch of a storm all night until the skies broke and the ship was safe. All while you were snug in your warm bed. So yes, we all owe him a fucking debt of gratitude."

Alice and Hatter stared at Clodword, mouths agape and speechless as Suarez shook Clodword's hand and patted him on the shoulder with a nod of his head, acknowledging a job well done. Then the sea captain turned away without giving Hatter a second look and shouted orders to his crew. Clodword turned to face them, a look of humble embarrassment on his face at receiving such high praise from the captain.

"You were sleeping and the cook was snoring something awful," Clodword shrugged as if that explained everything.

"I'm proud of you, Clodword," Alice smiled at him which seemed to grow his embarrassment incrementally.

Hatter remained dumbstruck; his mouth opened and closed several times but no words emanated forth. Clodword kept a straight face while looking at the gunslinger but Alice could no longer repress her laugh.

A sailor walked by, a black furred rabbit with flecks of gray about his face and ears. He squeezed his way through the little group, begging their pardon for his intrusion as he passed through. Then, spying Clodword, his face broke into a broad grin and he dipped his head in greeting, "Fine day to you, Mister Clodword."

"Oh . . . yes," Clodword fumbled awkwardly and dipped his head in return. "And a fine day to you too!"

"Oh for fuck's sake," Hatter threw up his hands and stormed off.

Alice could not suppress her laughter and Clodword quickly joined her; she laughed harder than she had laughed in quite a while. It felt good to laugh; like a pent up release expelling all of the horrors she had experienced since awakening in that cell. She'd seen enough battles to know to cherish these rare moments of joy before the killing started in earnest but that did little to fend off the dark thoughts that lurked in the deep recesses of her mind. The sound of the laughter could not drown out the voice in her head telling her this could be the last time any of them had anything to laugh about for a very long time.

CHAPTER 15: LONGFISH

For two days the mystery ship remained on the horizon, sometimes dipping out of sight for hours at a time, but never really seeming to get significantly closer or further from them. The tension began to ease and life on the Eaglet quickly returned to normal. They remained on a battle-ready footing and Suarez and the lookouts kept an ever watchful eye on the black sails on the horizon. The vigilant sea captain ordered cannonballs and kegs of powder to remain ready at each firing station with two sharpshooters on deck with rifles at all times.

Alice, Clodword, and Lady Cheshire returned to their lessons with Rebeck and Bore. Hatter begrudgingly joined them, though he put very little effort into learning the tongue and Alice suspected he was largely there to keep an eye on the brothers' interactions with the Lady Cheshire. Although the vocabulary of the language was completely alien to Alice, she found the language relatively easy to learn. Since giants were anatomically basically large humans, or she supposed humans were small giants, their brains were formed similarly for language, which meant that both languages had the same basic structure albeit differing words and grammar. Ava would have thrived in these lessons, while Alice had no doubt that when she spoke in the giants' language it was with the complexity of an elementary school child.

Rebeck proved a very patient teacher and constantly strove to encourage them, "I believe you're on the right track. What did you try to say?"

"I was saying 'take the knife and cut my rope,'" replied Alice. She caught Bore attempting to hold back a smirk, "Why? What did I say?"

"You said, 'take the cabbage and cut my nose,'" he explained, somehow maintaining his stoic demeanor.

The language lessons broke up the monotony of life aboard the ship. Alice quickly discovered that like military campaigns on land, a mission at sea consisted of days of endless boredom punctuated by what she expected would be moments of sheer terror. The panoramic beauty of the Great Wide Open had given way to feelings of isolation. They were a very small ship in a very large ocean; danger waited for them back in Wonderland, before them in the Cursed Isles, and lurking beneath those black sails just over the horizon.

The crew fell into a regular routine of working, eating, and sleeping which gave them little time to dwell on the less pleasant aspects of life at sea. Clodword seemed nonplussed by the journey and spent a great deal of his time learning. Whether it was about the giants' homeland, reading and re-reading her father's book, or observing the working of the ship's crew, the man had a ceaseless thirst for knowledge. Alice did not know when the man slept. Though he was not the only one keeping busy during the nocturnal hours. Alice briefly glimpsed a hint of scratches poking out the top of Hatter's shirt before he noticed her gaze and buttoned the top button. The cook was consumed with preparation of meals for the Duchess, who seemed to grow more withdrawn and rarely left her cabin, even to walk along the deck on sunny days.

For Alice, who thrived on the chaos of life, the boredom of shipboard life threatened to overwhelm her. Thoughts of her father and his secret life, worry for Ava back in Wonderland, and most of all, thoughts of Danavi, consumed her. In her mind she revisited every stolen kiss, every carnal interlude, and every wild night they had shared until their hunger for each other was satiated in sheer exhaustion. Against her better instincts, Alice held out hope in her heart that Danavi still lived, though her mind told her that Danavi was gone forever. There would be no Red Knight waiting for her at the journey's end, only the undeniable crushing reality that Danavi was truly dead.

With Danavi, Alice had laid bare every secret, intimate part of her mind and soul. There was no hope or fear they did not share with each other in the dark of night, safe in each other's embrace. They knew each other in a way that Alice would never know anyone again. They were airtight, nothing and no one could ever get between them.

In some ways, the incontrovertible closeness and clandestine nature of her relationship with Danavi eased the feelings of betrayal Alice felt toward her father. Had he felt the same way about her mother? They always seemed genuinely very happy and in love. Was his past life in Wonderland an airtight secret her parents shared? She supposed it was possible, even probable. The secret was just too big to hide from someone for so long.

Whoopf.

The muffled sound of an explosion roused Alice from her thoughts. She sat up in the hammock and looked around the room; in the dim light of the sleeping quarters she could see others sitting up and listening.

Whoopf.

A second explosion. There was no mistaking the sound.

The room about her burst into a flurry of motion as sailors leapt from their hammocks and quickly dressed and armed themselves. Bright light flooded the room as the door flew open, sailors quickly rushing out to get up to the main deck.

Whoopf.

The explosion sounded all wrong to Alice. It sounded too muffled to be cannon fire. Slipping on her boots, Alice belted on the shortsword and grabbed her bow and a quiver of arrows. She followed the sailors out the door and up the stairs onto the main deck, Hatter and Clodword joining her from their cabin.

"Any idea what's going on?" Alice asked.

"That's what we want to know too," Hatter shook his head. "Lady Cheshire is staying below deck with the Duchess."

They came up onto the main deck. The morning sun was shining upon an otherwise calm sea. Alice could see Mister Begley's gun crews, three men to a cannon, already at their stations with Rebeck and Bore standing by to assist in any way they could.

"There's the captain," Clodword pointed out where Suarez stood beside Mister Cooper at the railing, each with a telescope pressed to their eye.

"Oh, shit," cursed Hatter, following their gaze.

Alice did as well and felt her stomach drop at the sight. The black-sailed ship lay about a thousand yards off the Eaglet's port side, less than half a mile and easily within the cannon range of the vessel's nine pound guns. Two small whaling boats dotted the waters between the two ships. Each bore nine men in the black and red attire of the Queen's sailors: six rowing, two standing, and a man guiding the rudder in the rear. She watched as the man standing furthest forward on the boat closest to the Eaglet used the cigar in his mouth to light what appeared to be a stick of dynamite and toss it in the water. Behind him, the second man stood, armed with a three-foot metal harpoon with a length of rope affixed at the end. The man held the harpoon up around his shoulder, ready to throw.

Whoopf.

The dynamite exploded below the surface sending a geyser of water skyward.

"Captain, what's going on?" Hatter asked as they approached the two grim looking sailors.

"The black sail closed on us in the night," Suarez replied without removing the telescope from his eye.

"It doesn't seem like they are attacking. What are they doing?" asked Alice

"You've never seen a ship hunt longfish?" asked Cooper, handing her his telescope when she shook her head.

"It's barbaric and an offense to the Mother of the Sea," Suarez added with clear disgust.

Alice raised the telescope to her eye as Cooper explained, "When they spot longfish, the ship releases a pair of crocodiles into the water. The crocs swim down low, forcing the longfish closer to the surface. The men in the small boats stun them with the dynamite and then harpoon them when they float to the surface."

"Why don't the crocodiles just swim off?" asked Clodword.

"They are raised on the boat and the crew feeds them well; they swim back like chickens to a coop," answered Cooper.

Alice scanned the black-sailed ship, relieved to see the ship's eleven starboard-side cannon stations did not seem to be readying to fire. Toward the rear of the ship there were several men armed with wicked looking skinning knives the length of a machete and wearing long leather aprons that covered their torsos and legs. Attached to the mast above them were two large pulleys that Alice surmised they used to hoist up the longfish. She caught glimpses of a long thick fishtail as the men appeared to be preparing to lift and filet one of the fish.

Whoopf.

Alice lowered the telescope. The boat nearest the Eaglet had set off another stick of dynamite and a second geyser of water appeared by the further boat. She watched the ships maneuver, the rowers frantically pulling at their oars as the boats gave chase.

Harpoons, dynamite, and crocodiles, all to put a slab of meat on the Red Queen's plate.

She looked back to the black-sailed ship and felt her blood run cold. The men had hoisted the fish up into the air, a thick metal hook through its tail. From tail to the midpoint of the fish was approximately three feet, the body thick and covered in a smooth grayish skin that more closely resembled a dolphin than a fish. However, beyond that was the torso of a woman with white flesh, long red hair, and thin spindly arms that dangled downward. The head of a thick harpoon stuck through her shoulder just above her exposed breast causing rivulets of red blood to run down the pale flesh and drip from the shoulder. One of the men placed a thick copper pot below the drippings.

"What the fuck is this?" Alice felt her chest tighten and she could barely breathe for the horror. "They have some kind of woman . . ." Alice could not even finish her sentence. She had no words.

"She's one of the Daughters of the Tide," explained Cooper. "They are the servants of the Mother of the Sea and held as sacred creatures by all true sailors. Centuries ago poachers would hunt them as a secret delicacy for the nobles, but any ship sailing under the protection of the Mother would not abide such a thing. I've heard stories of vessels ramming poaching ships and even full on sea battles until the Queens intervened and prohibited Longfish hunts under penalty of death."

"That is until the Red Queen revoked that protection," Suarez added with disgust. "Now they are hunted like does in the wood by those cursed black ships."

Alice was stunned,. "Longfish?" was all she could manage as she turned to stare at Hatter and Clodword. "You knew?"

"Longfish are mermaids," Hatter looked genuinely saddened. "I'm sorry, Alice, I thought you knew that."

"But I thought that mermaids were like people except for their lower extremities?" Alice could not hide her disgust.

"They are," Suarez finally lowered his telescope. "They call them longfish to dehumanize them. They throw the human half to the crocodiles, but the blood and fish portions are considered a delicacy. Some believe they even possess rejuvenating properties."

"Barbaric," Clodword breathed.

Whoopf.

The geyser of water was so close that droplets of water sprayed them. Alice raised the telescope back to her eye, forcing herself to look back at the ship. It took her a moment to find the mermaid hanging suspended by her tail. The woman's eyes were closed and she dangled unmoving despite the pain the harpoon through her shoulder and the hook in the tail must have caused.

Maybe she's dead.

Alice did not know anything about mermaid biology but if they were as similar on the inside as they were on the outside that harpoon strike was close enough to the heart to be fatal. She groaned as one of the men walked behind the mermaid and jerked the harpoon backwards. The mermaid's eyes suddenly flew open and Alice could see they were an emerald green as the woman screamed and jerked on the hook. Alice was thankful they were too far to hear the mermaid's anguished cries, but the look of agony on her face was unmistakable. A second man stepped forward and sliced his long knife across her throat so deep that her head flopped backward. The man adjusted the copper pot with his foot to catch the crimson waterfall that gushed from her open neck as the man behind her gave a second hard pull that freed the harpoon from her spasming body. The men stood back laughing and joking as careless as if they were watching a barrel of wine emptying.

As the crimson blood flowed into the copper pot Alice remembered Ava's comment about the Red Queen's meals of longfish and sanguis. The thought disgusted her and she felt the bile rise in her throat.

"The lower decks of the ship are designed to keep the blood and flesh cold," Cooper pointed toward the black-sailed ship. "That's why all of the ship's cannons are located on the main deck."

Whoopf. Whoopf.

Each of the small boats set off a stick of dynamite in their pursuit of more mermaids. Alice glanced sidelong at the boats, a roiling anger building in her gut as she pictured the mermaids trapped between the snapping jaws of the circling crocodiles and the pursuing hunters.

She did not want to look back through the telescope at the savage practice being conducted on the ship, but something deep within Alice felt she owed it to the mermaid. The poor creature died alone on that ship, injured and surrounded by brutish men that mocked her pain. Alice would be the silent witness to the carnage inflicted upon the hapless mermaid, a vigil for a creature more human than those who butchered her.

Steeling herself, Alice looked back through the telescope toward the black-sailed ship and recoiled in horror as the air fled from her lungs. The men had sawed through the mermaid's torso. Only the dolphin-like extremity remained on the hook where one of the men was slicing back the gray skin to filet the meat.

One of the men, large and red-bearded, his apron slick with gore, held the upper torso of the mermaid like a dancing partner as he twirled around the deck to the merriment of the others. The mermaid's entrails dangled down like the tentacles of a sleeping octopus, swaying as the man danced her about. He turned her around and waved her lifeless arm toward one of the sailors and then grabbed her breast. The other sailor ran up and took the torso from him, grabbing her by the hair and lowering the torso so that he could simulate having sex with her mouth as all of the sailors laughed uproariously.

Alice could not bear to watch any longer. Equal parts sickened and infuriated, she moved the telescope away from the grisly scene. She was just about to hand it back to Cooper when something caught her eye. The brass plate with the ship's name emblazoned in black letters.

The Lory.

"That's the fucking ship that killed Casey," Alice seethed. The crew's murder of Casey and savagery toward the mermaid filled her with a rage so intense her eyeball felt hot.

"Aye, it is," replied Suarez, his voice grim and tinged with anger as he continued watching the ship's guns for any sign of preparation to attack.

A cheer went up from the closest rowboat and Alice saw that they had speared another mermaid with their harpoon. The long shaft had lodged itself halfway through the dark-haired mermaid's left bicep. The water around the mermaid turned crimson with blood as she frantically tried to dislodge the harpoon. She could not escape the small boat and flee to the depth of the ocean as the rope affixed to the ring at the tail end of the harpoon gave her no slack with which to maneuver. The mermaid screamed in pain and thrashed violently in the water as the men began to pull the rope back toward the small boat.

Alice had seen enough. She handed the telescope back to Cooper and stalked along the rail of the ship, unslinging the bow from her back.

"Hey, now," Cooper watched her with evident concern. "What are you doing?"

"Alice," Hatter called after her. "Alice, what are you doing?"

She could hear Hatter's feet moving hurriedly toward her as she drew an arrow from the quiver and moved closer toward the front of the Eaglet where she would have the best shot.

"Alice," Hatter yelled, "don't do this. You'll get us all kil—"

Hatter's words were suddenly cut off by a strangled cry and the sound of a body striking the deck with a loud grunt. She glanced back and saw Hatter sprawled on the deck, his eyes wide with the fear that he would never reach her in time to prevent disaster. Beside him, a sable-haired sailor, one of Begley's gunners, winked at her as he slid the long wooden pole used to drive home the powder and ball into the breach of the cannon from between Hatter's tangled legs. Cooper rooted in place, his face a mask of shock and disbelief, looked on in horror.

Her eye met Hatter's for the briefest moment and he knew.

Alice doing Alice things.

Alice drew back the bow, fixed on her target as she gentle released the breath in her chest, and let the arrow fly. The arrow flew true, slicing through the rope affixed to the harpoon. The mermaid felt the rope slacken and dove deep below the surface of the water as several of the men on the ship tumbled backward with the tension on the rope sudden gone. Angry shouts went up from the small boat and Alice could see one of the men pointing at her.

"Alice stop that immediately!" Cooper ordered.

She had already sighted her next target and nocked another arrow on her bow. The second ship was further away and winds over the ocean were notoriously unpredictable so she knew the shot would be more difficult. Alice drew the bowstring back and waited for her moment. The timing had to be perfect.

Alice watched the man in the second boat light the stick of dynamite, her eyes fixed on the movement of his shoulder. In her periphery she saw one of the men in the nearer boat draw a pistol and struggle to aim it at her as the small vessel rocked amidst the sudden chaos. The smart thing would be to eliminate the threat and kill the man with the pistol. He was closer and posed a greater danger. The men on the second boat had not realized their comrades had come under attack yet. She would have time to deal with them later. The man with the pistol used both hands to steady his shot.

Fuck it.

The arrow flew off the bow, sailing toward the man in the second boat as he reeled his arm back to throw the burning stick of dynamite. Alice did not watch to see if it struck home before she was nocking another arrow and pivoting to face the man with the pistol. The barrel of the man's flintlock pistol was like an unblinking eye focused directly upon her and Alice saw the slight upturn of the man's lips in a smile as his finger eased onto the trigger.

A roaring blast momentarily deafened Alice and she nearly let loose an errant shot as she involuntarily flinched. The man with the pistol fired harmlessly into the air as his body tumbled backward into a pink mist of his own blood, his chest torn open by three gaping wounds. The men about him screamed in pain and surprise while others tumbled over dead as shards of blood, bone, and splintered wood shot up around them.

Alice glanced back. Begley stood beside one of the swivel guns, a thin wisp of smoke rising from the barrel as the gunners quickly loaded another packet of grape shot and powder into the small cannon. The canvas packet consisted of nearly a dozen musket balls and Alice knew that at this distance the projectiles could penetrate multiple bodies before coming to rest.

"Cease fire! Cease fire!" Cooper screamed the order.

Begley gave her a quick nod and shouted over the blast of a second swivel gun, "Dogs aren't dangerous, I'm dangerous."

Alice flashed him a smile in return and watched as the grapeshot from the second swivel gun tore into the groaning and terrified men on the small boat. She glanced at the second boat and saw that her arrow had hit its mark. The man lay unmoving across one of the rowing benches, the long shaft protruding from the right side of his chest. The other men in the boat appeared to be frantically trying to climb over each other to grab the lit stick of dynamite and at least two of the men had jumped overboard into the water and were frantically swimming for the Lory.

The second boat disappeared in a spectacular blast that sent water, pieces of wood, and broken bodies sailing into the air, as the exploding dynamite ignited the remaining explosives onboard. Alice aimed her bow back at the closer boat but the second volley of grapeshot had turned it into a charnel house of broken bodies and dying men. She saw a bearded man treading water beside the boat, having jumped clear before the second round of grapeshot that claimed his mates. With mild surprise Alice recognized the man; Grech, the sailor from the market.

Well, it seems I get to kill you anyway.

Alice aimed; she would put the arrow right through the man's loud mouth. Then she stayed her hand. Behind Grech a long dark shaped moved slowly toward him. Drawn by the blood and flesh in the water, the crocodile quickly spotted the large man treading water. She saw it dip below the surface just behind him. Grech had only a moment to scream as the ferocious reptile sank its teeth into his lower extremities and pulled him beneath the waves.

"Captain Suarez, you cannot allow this! It is treason!" Cooper pleaded with him.

"Mister Cooper, either fight your ship or get below deck. Sharpshooters focus on the cannons. Aim for the gunners. Dead men can't shoot," Suarez shouted as the musket men fired a volley toward the Lory. The first pair of sharpshooters fired and then reloaded as the other pair fired at their targets.

Cooper stared in disbelief at Suarez, then crestfallen, walked toward the stairs to the lower deck. Several of the sailors shook their heads and murmured angrily as the First Mate slowly descended the stairs.

"Mister Jakers take her directly abeam. We've got the wind over the bow quarter. The Lory will only be able to get to a beam reach in these conditions. We can try and outrun her."

"Aye, Captain," Mister Jakers shouted in reply as sailors scrambled to rig the sails to maximum efficiency.

Alice saw that Hatter had drawn his lever action rifle and taken up a position kneeling along the railing. He was able to fire and load in much quicker succession than the muskets and the bullets Tinker designed proved to have significantly better accuracy.

I hope you're smiling down right now Tinker.

"We'll never pierce their hull with these three-pounders. Aim for the main deck," Begley ordered the three gun crews manning the cannons. The men quickly made the adjustments.

The Eaglet rocked as the cannons fired. Alice saw a splash of water as one of the cannonballs fell short and a second thudded harmlessly against the hull of the Lory. The third shot sailed across the main deck of the ship and Alice hoped it wrought carnage in its path.

Begley yelled adjustments to his gun crews. They had caught the Lory by surprise and drawn first blood, but the Queen's sailors were responding now and musket balls were starting to whiz across the deck and thud into the wooden structure of the ship from the Lory's sharpshooters.

Her bow was useless at this distance, so Alice laid low on the deck and surveyed the scene. The giants were crouched low among Begley's gun crews passing along cannonballs for the men to reload. Clodword was over by Jakers holding up a barrel to shield the helmsman from the Lory's sharpshooters. Alice could not decide whether she thought he was being incredibly brave or foolish, though she had to admit Clodword lacked none of the bravery of his brother.

The air thundered as the Lory's cannons entered the fray. Alice counted eight loud booming reports from the ship.

Eight of eleven guns.

The Eaglet's efforts seemed to be having some effect, but they were still badly out gunned and those nine-pound cannonballs could easily wreak havoc upon the smaller ship. Geysers of water flew up all around the ship as the Lory's fusillade fell all about the ship but failed to land a direct hit.

Alice heard a grunt and one of the sharpshooters slumped over, a ragged hole in his gray-furred chest. She crawled over to where he lay and searched for a pulse in his neck. *Dead.*

Begley's three cannons fired back in response, rocking the ship. Alice watched as the cannonballs sailed across the space between the ships and crashed through the Lory's railing. She knew they would shatter the bones of any legs unfortunate enough to be caught in their path.

The swifter Eaglet was slowly outdistancing the Lory, which made it more difficult for the larger ship to bring its guns to bear against them. Suarez shouted adjustments to Mister Jakers and the crew to counter the Lory's maneuvering to position the ship to deliver a full broadside volley from its cannons.

Alice picked up the sharpshooter's musket. It was longer and clumsier than her bow, but had the necessary range to reach the enemy vessel. She could not see the targets clearly at this range, but she could discern moving shapes well enough. Bracing the musket against the railing, Alice took aim at a moving shape she spotted close to where the lower torso of the mermaid swung on its hook. Narrowing her eye and controlling her breath, Alice squeezed the trigger. The heavy musket bucked and slammed painfully against her shoulder, but she noted with immense satisfaction that the shape on the ship jolted violently and dropped.

She ducked down behind the heavy wooden side of the railing as musket balls from the Lory's sharpshooters flew past her or buried themselves in the wooden planks. Her hands searched along the dead sailor's belt, grabbing his bag of shot and powder horn to reload the musket. As she reloaded, Alice scanned the deck to see how the other's faired.

Hatter was also crouched down behind the railing about amidships reloading his lever action rifle. Their eyes met for a moment. The gunslinger's eyes blazed with the feral intensity of a seasoned soldier in battle; they narrowed slightly when they met hers and Alice knew there was a hint of anger there towards her. This was a fight of her doing.

Alice doing Alice things.

He finished reloading and lifted his rifle above the railing, aiming and firing off three shots in quick succession as his hand rapidly worked the lever to feed a new round into the rifle's chamber. Alice glanced at the Lory and saw three black and red clad shapes fall beside the cannon they were feverishly working to load.

Fucking impressive Hatter, I'll give you that.

The gunslinger ducked back down as musket balls from the Lory's sharpshooters sent shards of wood flying through the air all about him. Hatter rose and fired a single shot before ducking back down and moving further down along the railing. On the Lory, one of the sharpshooters tumbled from his perch atop the middle mast; a rope tied around his waist kept his body from plummeting to the deck. The man's body jerked violently to a halt halfway down the mast and pendulumed back and forth leaving a glistening crimson arc on the black sail.

Clodword was still at his post by Mister Jakers, barrel held in place to shield the helmsman. The barrel would occasionally rock backward as a musket ball slammed against the wood.

Rebeck swung down into the hold through a wide square hatch on the deck, presumably to get additional barrels of gun powder for the cannon crews. Alice saw Bore grab Begley by the shoulder and emphatically point toward the larger nine-pound cannonballs piled uselessly in a pyramid on the deck.

Begley shouted to the giant over the din of the battle, using his hands to explain what words could not, "They're too big for the cannons."

Bore's face frowned heavily as he stared down at the cannonballs. Then bending down, he lifted one of the balls. It looked like a child's ball in his large hands. He took one lunging step forward and with a primal grunt hurled it skyward toward the ship. Begley watched agape as the nine pound ball sailed through the air arcing down toward the Lory until it crashed into the deck amidship.

Begley whooped with joy, a wide grin spreading across his face, "Can you do that again, big fella?"

Bore grinned back, the first smile Alice had ever seen on his face and nodded.

The cannons of the Lory roared, spewing a cloud of smoke that momentary obscured the deck of the black sailed ship. The cannons fired in near unison and Alice counted only six this time.

Two more down.

Alice's eye opened wide with horror as a half dozen spinning objects spun out of the cloud of smoke. Chain shot. She had seen it used against the giants with devastating effect. Two halved cannonballs connected by a length of chain. The spinning motion made it less accurate than normal cannonballs but far more deadly as they were capable of cutting a wide swath of destruction in massed units of combatants. She knew that in naval warfare chain shot could be employed to shred the rigging and sails of an enemy vessel, but the Lory's gun crews had fired directly at the main deck of the Eaglet.

"Get down!" Alice managed to scream moments before the spinning projectiles struck the deck. Whether they heard her warning through the cacophony of battle or saw the incoming wave of death, Bore tackled Begley to the ground and Hatter, Suarez, and several other sailors sprawled flat against the deck seconds before impact.

One of the spinning balls and chain spun a few feet over Alice's head, missing the ship entirely and landing harmlessly in the ocean. Four others struck the middle of the main deck, slicing a swath of death and destruction among the gun crews. The chain shot tore through wood, bone, and flesh. One struck the number four cannon, knocking it from its mount to crush the leg of a black furred sailor, while a second round of chain shot decapitated the other two members of the crew before crushing a running sailor against the main mast. The remaining two whirling chain shots completely eviscerated the six members of the number five and six gun crews, tearing limbs and heads from bodies and severing whole bodies in half.

As they crashed into the decking, they propelled splintered timber into deadly projectiles that struck down several other sailors with knife-like lengths of wood protruding from soft skin.

The deck of the Eaglet was slick with blood from the wounded, dead, and dying. Sailors rushed to help their fallen mates while surviving gunners frantically tried to get the Eaglet's two remaining guns back into the fight. Bore rushed over and lifted the number four cannon from the wounded gunner's mangled leg. The sailor gave a strangled scream of pain and lost consciousness as the giant lifted the cannon free.

Begley hobbled over to Bore, a hand pressed around the large sliver of wood protruding from the Master of Guns right hip that was coating his trousers and the gray fur of his hand in a slick crimson sheen of blood.

"Get him down to Mister Alistair," he yelled, gesturing toward the procession of wounded sailors staggering toward the stairway. The giant nodded in understanding and rushed away with the unconscious sailor cradled in his arms.

Alice's heart sank as she saw the Lory maneuver to deliver another broadside shot that she knew would render the Eaglet relatively helpless to combat the onslaught.

This is the end. I'm sorry, Ava.

She heard the loud report of a musket firing and one of the gunner's mates on the Lory jerked backward a spray of blood blossoming out the back of his head as he toppled away from the cannon. Alice turned to see Cooper standing atop the stairs, a smoking musket in his hand. Rhys was beside Cooper handing him a freshly loaded musket and taking the expended one. The musket had barely touched the young rabbits hands before he was quickly reloading the weapon.

In one swift motion, Cooper raised the musket, sighted his target, and fired. The weapon jerked in his hand as a plume of white smoke mushroomed from the barrel. Across on the Lory, Alice saw another gunner's mate spin from the impact of the shot and pirouette over the side of the ship. She was damn impressed, the man may have been as good a shot as Hatter.

A ragged cheer went up from the crew at the sight of their First Mate fighting alongside them. Cooper looked toward Suarez for the briefest of moments as Rhys exchanged his musket for the reloaded one, giving the man a subtle nod of the head. Alice saw Suarez return the nod, the corners of his mouth upturned in just hint of a smile.

"Welcome to the fight, Mister Cooper."

"Just had to get my guns, sir," Cooper replied as he fired off a musket ball that sparked as it struck the top of one of the Lory's cannon and ricocheted into one of the throat of one of the gunners, The man clasped his neck with both hands as he dropped from sight.

The arrival of Cooper had momentarily buoyed the spirits of the embattled crew, but she knew it was too late for the Eaglet and its crew.

Alice had little doubt that the Lory would continue to fire upon the Eaglet until it was just shattered timbers and broken bodies upon the tide. There would be no quarter given. The hard, cold iron of a cannonball would shatter her bones and pulp her body or she would sink beneath the waters with the crew of the doomed vessel. There was no escape this time.

She heard the rumble of the Lory's cannons fire, eleven guns this time, each in quick succession, and a smoky cloud of expended gunpowder engulfed the enemy ship. Alice crouched low to the deck, heart sinking as she waited for the deadly impact. But it never came.

Instead, Alice heard what sounded like the screech of a barn owl yet so deafeningly loud that Alice felt it in her bones. The surviving members of the Eaglet's crew looked around in horror and confusion for the source of the noise and she saw true terror on their faces.

"Captain," the lookout, miraculously still alive in the crow's nest, cried out and pointed toward the Lory.

Alice chanced a look over the protection of the sideboards toward the Lory and was amazed to see the Lory fire off a second volley of cannon fire from their port cannons facing away from the Eaglet. The ship was engaging another foe.

Has a second ship come to our rescue?

The smoke from the cannon fire obscured visibility and Suarez quickly climbed atop the cabin roof and withdrew his telescope.

"Who is it?" Alice called up to the lookout but the young rabbit just shook his head.

"Sweet Mother of the Sea," Suarez gasped as he peered through the telescope.

Alice turned toward the Lory and was stunned to see the vaguely anthropoid outline of a creature rise in the hazy smoke about the vessel's sails; it appeared so massive that it dwarfed the black-sailed ship. She could make out what looked like an octopus-like head with a mass of tentacles surrounding a short, sharp owl's beak that gaped open to reveal a maw of massive teeth. Long, narrow wings, withered and boney, protruded from its back but looked incapable of providing flight to a creature of its immense size. It raised a massive arm into the air above the Lory and Alice could see its skin was the smooth dolphin gray of the mermaid's lower extremities and ended in a single thick talon.

"It's the Kraken," Hatter, his face streaked with blood from a half-dozen small splinter wounds, stared in awe. "The sounds of battle must have drawn it here."

The Kraken raised its head to the sky and screeched another of its deafening calls, then looking back to the Lory, brought the talon crashing down on the ship. The rear two masts shattered like twigs, crashing down among the terrified crew as the talon tore into the deck. A blow from its other taloned arm splintered the bow of the ship. Alice could see black and red clad sailors leaping into the ocean as the Kraken battered at the ship like an angry child with a toy until the spine of the ship snapped, severing the Lory in two.

The ocean rushed into the exposed innards of the ship, quickly pulling it into the depth of the Great Wide Open. The stern of the Lory angled high out of the water as the forward compartments flooded with the onrush of seawater as the bow, ripped loose from the stern by the Kraken's violent blows, quickly sank. The stunned sailors aboard the Eaglet watched as the stern of the Lory rose to an almost vertical position and then sank into the water. Sailors jumped from the remnants of the doomed ship as the last remnant sank below the surface.

The small shapes of bobbing sailors dotted the water as they desperately tread water or clung to debris. The Kraken eyed them. The tentacles about its beaked-mouth writhed like a dozen snakes as it bent low to bellow another screeching scream at the sailors. The force of its expended breath caused violent ripples and waves in the water that tossed the sailors about amid the flotsam and jetsam of their ruined vessel.

Alice held her breath, terrified at the sight of the unfathomable beast, and expected the creature to begin snatching up the sailors with its hideous tentacles and swallowing them down. Instead, the creature's yellow-green eyes turned to look at the Eaglet.

"Hatter," Suarez growled, "I think it's time to use your siren."

"Yes, right," stammered Hatter as he ran for the bow of the ship, jumping over debris and the bodies of slain and wounded sailors.

Alice watched as the Kraken turned toward the Eaglet and lurched through the water in their direction. The creature slunk steadily between the waves until only its octopus-like head remained above the surface of the water, its yellow eyes glaring malevolently at the ship as it rushed onward.

"You better make it quick, Hatter," Alice called, not taking her eyes from the onrushing behemoth.

A loud grating noise filled the air as Hatter cranked the handle of the siren.

"You've got to be fucking kidding me, Hatter," Suarez barked, a ferocious scowl on his face.

Hatter desperately cranked the handle again but only achieved more of the horrible grating noise. All eyes turned toward the Kraken, noting the creature continued to charge unabated by the siren.

"Is that what it's supposed to do?" asked Alice running over to join the gunslinger.

"I don't know," replied Hatter, his expression a mix of fear and confusion. "I don't think so."

"Here, let me try."

Hatter moved aside and Alice cranked the handle with all her might. The handle grinded in a stiff, clunky movement, emitting only more of the grating sound.

"Is it stuck?" Alice asked as she continued cranking the handle.

Hatter examined the siren, then his countenance fell and his shoulders sagged as a resigned look of defeat crossed his face, "Alice, stop."

"Why? What is it?"

"Look," Hatter pointed to the side of the brass housing unit. "It was hit by one of the Lory's sharpshooters."

"What? How could they know?" Alice leaned over and examined the ragged hole a musket ball had punched through the side of the housing.

"They didn't. It must have been an errant shot." Hatter peered down into the hole, "It looks all broken up inside."

Alice felt her stomach knot with despair as she looked up and met Suarez's gaze. She slowly shook her head and the sea captain lowered his white-furred face.

When he looked up, there was grim determination on his face. "Mister Cooper, get the men to the lifeboats."

"Sir, there is no time," the First Mate replied, looking from the oncoming Kraken to his captain.

"What's happening up h—", Lady Cheshire had ascended the stairs to the main deck, the sight of the Kraken stopping her in her tracks, mouth agape. She looked up at Hatter and the gunslinger flashed her one of his roguish smiles, but Alice could see there was little conviction behind it.

Alice walked over and retrieved her bow from the deck and slid an arrow out from her quiver.

"You really think that will do anything?" Hatter asked. "The Lory couldn't stop it with nine pound cannons.

"Maybe I can get an arrow past those tentacles and put out its eye, give it something to remember us by," Alice replied with grim determination.

Hatter reached into his vest pocket and withdrew the gold pocket watch. He popped open the casing and stared down at the watch face. Alice could see the watch hands still remained stopped at four o'clock.

"Checking to see the time of our death?" Alice quipped. Hatter gave a short snort of laughter as his finger ran almost lovingly over the watch's winding crown as if he contemplated winding the mainspring to get it running again.

The Kraken was now little more than a few hundred feet away and suddenly stopped its advance. The creature's tentacles flailed about its face as it glared malevolently at the ship, gusts of water splashing as it exhaled deep breaths. At this distance Alice could see its gray skin looked mottled and pockmarked. It looked ancient and Alice imagined it could be as old as the world itself.

"Why did it stop?" asked Lady Cheshire, mesmerized by the sight of the Kraken.

"I . . . don't . . . know," Hatter breathed quietly and looked to Alice who shrugged but lowered her bow.

"Do you hear that?" The jaguar cocked her head to one side.

"Hear what?" Hatter asked as he snapped closed the pocket watch and slipped it back into his vest pocket.

"Wait, I hear it too," Alice strained to listen, forcing her mind to dim the sound of the crashing waves and the creature's geyser-like breaths. It sounded like voices; very faint, but distinctly voices.

Captain Suarez must have heard it too and Alice watched as the sea captain slowly walked to the edge of the deck and peered out over the ocean. Cooper and a few of the ambulatory sailors followed their captain to the end of the deck.

"What the hell is going on?" Hatter gave Alice a questioning look.

Equally confounded, Alice walked to the edge of the deck and looked out onto the water. Her mouth opened into a surprised 'oh' as she saw a line of bobbing shapes in the water between the Kraken and the Eaglet. Nearly a dozen female shapes, mermaids, their dark hair wet and plastered down about their naked torsos, faced the Kraken. Alice could see the red, raw gaping wound on the shoulder of one of the mermaids and she knew that had been where the harpoon had pierced the woman.

"What are they doing?" Hatter asked as he and Lady Cheshire joined her.

"They're singing," Lady Cheshire replied. "I don't understand the words, but they are singing."

Lady Cheshire was right. Alice could hear it too. The mermaids' voices were raised in song. It was a more melodic sound than Alice had ever heard a bird or human throat make. She looked at the Kraken and could see the rage slip from the creature's yellow eyes, its monstrous countenance growing softer as the flailing of its tentacles grew less manic.

Then, without warning, the Kraken turned away from the ship and slowly slipped under the water and out of sight. As the creature disappeared beneath the waves, the mermaids too dipped beneath the ocean's surface without as much as a glance back toward the ship; only the one with the wounded shoulder looked back, locking eyes with Alice for the moment. Alice's mouth curled up in a slight smile of thanks and she thought the mermaid had done the same before joining the others under the sea.

Several of the sailors fell to their knees and cried out thanks to the Mother of the Sea. Even Suarez, the stalwart sea captain of a hundred voyages, looked visibly shocked and relieved.

"I can't believe that just happened," Hatter shook his head.

"Which part?" Alice asked. She felt so drained by the battle and the near certainty of death at the hands of first the Lory and then the Kraken that she felt like she could collapse to the deck and sleep.

"Any of it; all of it."

"I need to go check on the Duchess," Lady Cheshire excused herself.

"How is she?" asked Alice.

"She took one of Mister Alistair's tinctures." Lady Cheshire's feline face formed a slight grin, "She slept through all of it."

"Of course she did," Hatter shook his head.

There was angry and alarmed shouting coming from a small gathering of crew around the helmsman's wheel. Cooper seemed to be arguing with Mister Jakers as Suarez stalked over toward the group. Rebeck was standing beside his brother watching the display, then turned toward Alice and mouthed the word "Clodword" to her.

"Something's happened to Clodword," Alice said with no small modicum of alarm and started running toward the group before she heard their reply.

She sidestepped sailors helping the wounded and bounded over the overturned number four cannon. As she approached, she could hear Jakers arguing with Cooper and telling him to back away.

"Why are you men jaw jacking when we have wounded men that need tending to and repairs to be made?" Suarez's voice quieted the crowd as he pushed his way through the small knot of sailors.

Alice could see Jakers glaring angrily at Cooper but the helmsman blocked her view of Clodword. She only caught glimpses of him standing sheepishly behind the helm wheel.

At least he seems to be okay.

But Clodword was not okay. Rebeck and Bore fell in beside Alice as she approached the fray and the sailors quickly parted to let them through. Alice caught a look of suspicion from a grim faced Captain Suarez before she set eyes on Clodword. As she got a better look at her friend, Alice stopped and stared in confusion, unsure what she was seeing.

Clodword stood behind the helm wheel, his face looking miserable as he glanced at her. He had been wounded by a musket ball that struck his hand as he held the barrel up protectively to shield the helmsman. The wounded appendage was cradled in his arm. The skin had been badly torn back from where the musket ball had ripped through his flesh. The glint of metal shone off the myriad of metal rods and gears exposed by the damage done by the musket ball.

"Clodword?" Alice looked from the hand to her friend in confusion.

"Everyone calm down. I can explain everything," Hatter said as he walked through the growing crowd of sailors.

CHAPTER 16: LIKE CLOCKWORK

Captain Suarez's face bore its familiar scowl, though his white fur was speckled with droplets of dried blood as he sat with his arms folded in the galley. To his right, Cooper brooded in silence, not making eye contact with any of the others. Lady Cheshire took her usual spot at the opposite end of the table as Alice collapsed heavily into her chair, drained from the morning's events. Clodword, his hand held behind his back and head bowed, stood next to Hatter who scowled back at Suarez. Beside the gunslinger, Begley swayed on uncertain feet; his injured hip was bandaged but the dressing bore a red stain in the middle that seemed to be steadily growing in size. Rebeck, who had been knocked unconscious in the hold by a tumbling barrel of gunpowder during the fight with the Lory, had recovered enough to assist his brother with clearing the deck of debris.

"For the Mother's sake, Begley, take a seat before you fall on your face," Suarez gestured toward one of the vacant chairs.

"Begging your pardon, sir, but I would like to make my report than rejoin my men on deck," Begley replied through teeth gritted in pain.

Suarez exhaled deeply, "Very well, make your report."

The Master of Guns news was grim. Nine sailors were dead and six more badly wounded and likely to die without more extensive medical attention than Mister Alistair could provide. One of the ship's storage holds was being converted into a makeshift hospital for their care. Two of the cannons were now damaged beyond repair and the crew was working to get the remaining four guns ready for action.

Alice tried to catch Clodword's eyes as she listened to the report, but the man kept his head down. She was more perplexed that Clodword had hidden such a secret from her than by the revelation that his hand was other than flesh and blood.

Suarez thanked Begley for his report and the Master of Guns hobbled toward the door, almost colliding with Mister Jakers as the helmsman quickly strode into the room. The two men mumbled quick apologies to each other and Jakers clapped a reassuring hand on Begley's shoulder as the wounded sailor passed.

"I hope that Mister Begley will not be treated harshly for firing on the longboat," Alice watched the Master of Guns leave and then turned toward Suarez.

"I gave Begley permission to fire on the longboat," Suarez barked, his eyes narrowing in anger, "which is more than I can for your display of archery."

"Captain Suarez, I'm sor—" Alice began.

"Sorry, does not bring my sailors back to life, Alice, or fix the damage to my ship," Suarez's rebuke was scathing and

Alice wanted to break his gaze, but she would not show the sea captain that disrespect.

She caught sight of Hatter's smirk. He enjoyed someone finally taking her to task for her actions.

Alice doing Alice things.

"I understand your actions. Those bastards killed Casey and what they do to the mermaids is an affront to the Mother," Suarez's voice softened but his eyes remained hard, "but this is my ship and I choose if and when we go into battle. Is that clear?"

"Yes, Captain," Alice nodded.

"Good. If you subvert my authority again I will put you in one of our longboats and put you to sea. It's important that you understand, Alice, this is not a threat, this is a promise. I am the Captain of the Eaglet and my dominion aboard this vessel is absolute."

"I understand, Captain. It will not happen again."

Suarez glared at her a moment longer and then looked askew at his helmsman, "I was not expecting your report yet, Mister Jakers. Has the assessment of the ship's damage been completed already?"

"No, sir, Chambers is continuing to assess the damage to the sail," Jakers replied as he crossed the room to stand beside Clodword and placed a hand on the man's shoulder. Clodword looked up at the helmsman in surprise and Jakers gave him a reassuring nod. "I'm here to support Clodword."

"Yes, well, let us discuss that now then," Suarez looked at Clodword. "Clodword, please place your hand on the table."

"Yes, sir. Of course," replied Clodword in a low voice.

He placed his hand palm down on the table, one of the metal rods making a slight tapping sound as it made contact with the table. Alice noticed he appeared only able to move his thumb and forefinger; the mechanism controlling his other fingers seemed to be damaged by the musket ball that tore back the flesh on the hand.

Suarez's eyes narrowed as he looked at the hand and Alice was amazed at the intricate workings of gears, wires, and rods she could make out through the torn skin, though she noticed there was no blood. Everyone seemed mesmerized by the sight except for Hatter who watched with a look of mild indifference.

"Is it just the hand that's like this or is it the whole arm?" asked Suarez pointing at the hand.

Clodword stood straight and slipped the damaged hand into the pocket of his trouser, "It's . . . everything."

"Excuse me?" Suarez's eyebrows shot up in surprise, opening his eyes wide.

"It's everything. All of me," Clodword shrugged and looked down at the table.

"Clodword, are you saying your whole body is made of metal pieces?" Lady Cheshire could not hide her shock.

"Well, yes," Clodword nodded. "Metals, gears, springs, wires, rods, and something called hydraulics." Clodword momentarily appeared almost cheerful, as if he was about to engage in one of his intricate scientific conversations, but the smile quickly faded again.

"But that's not possible, Clodword. Are you saying you are some kind of giant clock?" Alice thought this had to be some kind of misunderstanding.

Clockwork.

Alice's eye shot to Hatter, barely able to suppress her anger as she pointed an accusatory finger at the gunslinger, "You knew about this."

"Of course I knew. And I don't see what all the fuss is about." Hatter waved his hand dismissively, "Clockwork is the same Clockwork he was this morning. What is the problem?"

"Sailors are a superstitious lot, having some kind of 'Gear Man' onboard could be viewed as a bad omen and that's bad for morale. But more importantly, you kept this from ship, it's a violation of trust." Cooper shot back.

Suarez glared back at Hatter, "Cooper is correct on at least one point, this creates a trust issue between us, Hatter, what little there was to begin with."

"Let's stop this witch hunt right now. This has nothing to do with Clockwork," Hatter seethed.

"How does it not?" Cooper's dark eyes narrowed.

"You can't bear the thought that we destroyed one of the Queen's black ships and you are taking out your anger on Clockwork."

"I have no love for the black ships, especially the one that killed Casey. I fought the Lory with the rest of the crew," there was more bitterness than pride in Cooper's voice.

You fought because you had to, not because you wanted to," Hatter sneered.

"No, I fought because you and Alice left me no choice. The Queen's justice will fall on any who hinders or harms a black sail," Cooper slammed his fist down on the table. "It is the Queen's law. You have sentenced us all to death."

"Cooper," Hatter shook his head and gave the first mate a pitying look, "you can follow all the Queen's laws for the rest of your life and she will never change you back. All we have are those of us on this ship, including Clockwork. The rest of the world is against us—especially the Red Queen. We may all fight and die together before this is done, but for the Mother's sake, don't die for the Queen. I have been on this ship for a few weeks and even I can see your own crew didn't believe that you were here for them and willing to die for them until you stood on that deck and brought thunder down from the mountain on the Lory. You were magnificent. You stayed loyal to the White Queen and the consequences were awful, I will not deny you that. But this crew needs you to be that man that refused to bend the knee to a tyrant."

Cooper opened his mouth to respond and then closed it. He averted his gaze from the gunslinger and stared down at the table top as the room fell into awkward silence.

"Captain," Lady Cheshire's voice was as smooth as velvet, "you are taking a jaguar, a cowboy, and two giants to kill an immortal queen that can steal children with a smoke monster on a ship crewed by human-sized rabbits; let's give your crew a little credit. Clodword's . . . internal workings . . . may have been a surprise, but I think it's hardly going to phase them."

"Captain, may I say something?" Jakers asked.

"Why not, Mister Jakers? It seems everyone has an opinion today," Suarez shook his head in exasperation.

"Whatever Clodword is, and I cannot truly say I understand what that is, he stood the helm in that storm and saved this ship," Jakers inclined his head toward Clodword. "He withstood conditions maybe no other human could. If what he is enabled him to do that, than I would sail with someone like him any day. I trust Clodword with my life. We all did during that storm and he did not fail us."

Jakers gave Clodword a curt nod of support and Clodword gave a hesitant, embarrassed smile as he returned the nod.

"I see," Suarez's voice was gruff as he leaned forward and interlaced his finger as he stared contemplatively at the wooden table top.

"Clodword, you are my friend, nothing changes that and I trust you too." Alice looked at him in earnest as she struggled to find the words, "I just don't understand. You just seem so real and . . . alive."

"Clockwork is as alive as you or me." Hatter exhaled deeply and looked at Suarez, "If you will indulge me, I think I can explain to everyone's satisfaction."

Suarez studied Hatter for a moment, then nodded for him to continue.

"Captain, I've said my peace. With your permission I will go help Chambers with the damage assessment," Jakers looked to Suarez who nodded.

"Permission granted." Suarez watched the helmsman walk to the door. "Mister Jakers, one more thing."

"Sir?"

"Thank you for your counsel; you are a fine officer,"

"Thank you, sir," Jakers failed to hide his smile as he left the room.

Hatter took his seat next to Lady Cheshire and Clodword sat across from Alice. She noticed that he conspicuously kept his damaged hand beneath the table. He gave her a nervous smile and she winked back at him. The gesture seemed to put Clodword at ease and Alice could see the tension ease in his face.

If he is a machine, how can he display so much emotion?

"As most of you know, Tinker, the White Knight, had a fascination with building and creating things to make Wonderland a better place to live. When he was a young man, one of the last royal librarians brought him back from the Otherworld copies of three manuscripts called the *Codices Forster* which contained detailed notes on engineering. He showed them to me once, but it was all math and gibberish to me. The damned things were even written in reverse and from right to left, so that you could only read them in a mirror," Hatter shook his head at the memory.

A royal librarian? Father?

"Well, with these books, Tinker got the notion that he could build a mechanical human being. It was just an idea he had; a flight of fancy really. Then his wife died and Tinker became obsessed with the notion of making someone who would never die and leave him. He worked on it tirelessly for months; the *Codices Forster* gave him the knowledge he needed to construct arms, legs, and the rest that could move like a person, but he could not figure out how to animate it and make it think."

"In time, his grief subsided and he set the project aside, though the thought was never far from his mind. One day, Tinker never told me how, he came into possession of artifacts from before the time of Wonderland. Two books, *Morryster's Marvels of Science* and the *Liber-Dalmation.*"

"*Liber-Damnatus,*" Clodword corrected.

"Right, *Liber-Damnatus,*" Hatter agreed. "Tinker said the books provided him a way to make his creation a real and living thing, but he thought whatever was in the books called upon terrible powers he did not fully understand so he again set aside the project."

Artifacts from before the time of Wonderland? Were these tomes from Carcosa? From the library of the King in Yellow?

"Everything changed when the Dodo failed to return from the Cursed Isles. The likelihood of Gryphon's death pushed Tinker's mind to the brink of insanity. Whatever was contained in those books, Tinker used it to bring Clockwork to life. He swore me to secrecy and I have kept that secret up until this day. As far as I know, I am the only person Tinker told his secret to, aside from Clockwork that is."

Alice caught Hatter's use of the word 'person' when referring to Clodword. Hatter was many things, most of them infuriating to Alice lately, but he was no fool. The gunslinger had chosen his words with careful intent and their meaning was not lost on any in the room.

"How Tinker was able to keep my presence hidden from the Red Queen for so long I cannot even begin to guess. Perhaps she was too preoccupied with bending Wonderland to her will that I was too trivial a detail to catch her attention. But I believe my father knew the Red Queen was growing impatient with him and sent me away with you to protect me," Clodword gave a wistful smile.

"It was more than that, Clodword. If Gryphon is dead, then you are his last living family member," Lady Cheshire added.

A knock at the door drew their attention, though Alice's mind was spinning with the possibility of yet another potential intersection of her father in Wonderland.

"Come in," Suarez barked. Alice noticed the sea captain looked mildly surprised to see the helmsman walk through the door before his expression grew dark, "Is there a problem, Mister Jakers?"

"No, sir," the helmsman's face was a mix of excitement and disbelief. "It's the lookout, Captain; he's spotted land. We've reached the outer banks of the Cursed Isles."

The wind was favorable to them and blew the ship steadily toward the outer chain of islands. They all stood on deck their eyes fixed on the thin slivers of land sitting on the horizon like a fleet of unmoving ships; even the Duchess and her cook had emerged from their cabins to see. Alistair was there, his eyes red-rimmed and haunted. Alice had seen that look before, on the faces of other battlefield physicians tormented by the lives they could not save.

"We should reach the first of the islands by nightfall," Begley remarked as he leaned heavily on the rail, favoring his wounded hip.

"Are there really a thousand islands?" the Duchess asked in a breathy, disbelieving tone.

"There are too many to count, Duchess, that's for sure," answered Cooper.

Hatter looked toward Clodword, "Clockwork, you'll need to use the tracker to help them navigate to the right one."

"We're still receiving a signal. I'll stay on deck with the helmsman to help with any course corrections."

Beside them Bore clapped his brother on the shoulder and spoke something in their native tongue. Alice was not certain her translation was completely correct, but she was fairly certain it was akin to *triumph or death*. She knew the very survival of their people depended upon the brothers earning the favor of the Red Queen, enough for her to relinquish their golden harp and allow them to return home. She was dubious of the Queen's willingness to do either, let alone both of those things. However, Alice had promised the brothers she would see the harp returned and she would fight, kill, and die before she broke that promise.

The lives of so many rested upon the success of this mission, not the least of which was Ava's. She thought of her sister, enslaved as a servant to the Red Queen and forced to endure hideous spider bites to abate the poison in her blood.

Alice looked at Lady Cheshire. The jaguar sat stoically on the deck, her yellow eyes fixed upon the islands ahead. The fate of her daughters, and Hatter's, Alice reminded herself, hung in the balance.

The Red Queen played the long game. She murdered the White Queen and spared Alice, Ava, Hatter, and Lady Cheshire the purge that followed; even Tinker was allowed to live just long enough to complete his devices for the journey. Holding Ava and the Cheshire girls hostage, even releasing the giants, was all part of a plan the Red Queen had mapped out in her mind well in advance. She wanted the Azure Queen dead and the Red King back. Now all her pieces were in play on the chessboard.

Like every game, chess had rules.

Alice never played by the rules.

She would make her own rules.

She would beat the Red Queen at her own game.

Alice doing Alice things.

About the Author

Jack Finn is a horror author and active Horror Writers Association member living in the wilds of the Pacific Northwest with his wife and two fiendishly clever dogs. He is a lifelong believer that the Tooth Fairy proves you can trade body parts for cold, hard cash. His books include: The Wolves of Kalinin werewolf duology: Prey Upon the Lambs (Anuci Press 2025) and The Desolation of Hunters (Anuci Press 2025); the horror collection They Come When You Sleep (Velox Books 2025), a re-envisioning of the Dracula mythos in the standalone novel The Seven Deaths of Prince Vlad (Anuci Press 2024), and the folk horror collection, Legend of the Deer Woman (Crow Street Press, 2023).

www.ingramcontent.com/pod-product-compliance
Lightning Source LLC
LaVergne TN
LVHW041107080826
845145LV00007B/1720
* 9 7 8 1 9 6 8 1 0 0 2 3 0 *